Chocolate, Chimpanzees & a Court Reporter at Chute Pond

A Continuation From The Story *Marry Christmas*

Linda Phillips

ISBN: 979-8-88653-211-1

Published by Satin Romance
An Imprint of Melange Books, LLC
White Bear Lake, MN 55110
www.satinromance.com

Published in the United States of America.

Cover Design by Caroline Andrus

It is an honest blessing to work with Melange Books and
Also dedicated to our
childhood memories.

Follow Brucie Clark down South Shore Drive, Oconto County,
Wisconsin, in this fictional story as she hides in the area of this
actual landmark on Chute Pond.

Onε

"IT'S A FUNNY THING." Words found in a transcript that sit on a kitchen table in the darkness of an empty room. Two pages of the transcript were wrinkled, as though they were read over and over. Grim. Sorrowful words.

One of the wrinkled pages had the words, "We pray for love; then we curse love."

The second wrinkled page near the end of the transcript had the words: 'It's a funny thing. Your life can change within seconds. You wake up one day and walk outside to the bluest sky you ever saw. Colorful butterflies floating in the air lifting your spirits. Clash! Thunder crashes to the ground and lightning strikes feet away. Life is like walking up to a fuzzy puppy, adding more sunshine and endless kisses. But then you walk next to a pile of leaves and STRIKE, a rattlesnake jumps out of it and bites you. Pain. Your life changes in that one lousy second. Rattlesnake bites. Not your fault. That's what life is really like.'

———

On her daily run, Brucie jolted to a complete stop. "What is that sound?" she whispered. *It sounds like something being dragged.*

1

That smell. What is it? I think it's from a cigar. She turned her head back and forth, searching, but it was barely dusk, causing thoughts of her mom telling her to run during daylight hours stinging her conscience. Just as she took off running, the loud cracking of a stick in the forest stopped her once again. Except this time there was a feeling. Goosebumps prickled up and down her body. Instead of running, she took off in a fast walk. Heart racing. Fingers beginning to tremble.

Then she saw a man standing in the shadows, resting his arm on a shotgun.

"Hhhh," she sighed. "You scared me," she said, patting her heart. "Guess you're out hunting. Ca...catch anything?"

Light filtering the sky made it easier now for her to see a man lying down on the ground, wearing a blue, multi-colored flannel shirt. "Looks like your friend is taking a nap," she said. She couldn't see the standing man's eyes, but there was an unfriendly vibe radiating around him. He was big and wore a vest outlined in fur.

———

"Well, I need to get ready for work. Have a great day." She took off running and she heard him make a gruff sound from his throat. Feeling his eyes on her, she glanced back to see he was still watching her, standing motionless. If there was ever a time to run faster than before, now was it. The way he stared at her creeped her out and she felt instant fear.

So he would not follow her to her cabin, she shot across the wooded landscape and ran to the back of her home. It sat on the shoreline of Chute Pond with a view of natural beauty and serenity. With trembling fingers, she unlocked the back door and closed it quietly behind her, then relocked it. She leaned against it until her shaking legs would move once again. Her breaths were heavy, but now balanced as she calmed down.

Brucie ran to the front window and peeked out very slowly, her gaze sweeping the area. "He didn't follow me." She blew out a *Woosh* sound and ran for the shower.

The man, dragging his kill, whom she thought was a friend of his napping, walked through the forest to the shoreline of Chute Pond, close to Brucie's cabin.

When Brucie finished showering and was dressed, she tore into the kitchen, grabbed the transcript sitting on the table and stuffed it in a briefcase, but then she pulled it back out and shuffled through it to find the two wrinkled pages. She read, while remembering the witness during the court deposition she worked on months ago, staring into her eyes while she typed—the woman speaking directly to her. *You think your life is stable. Really good. In an instant, it becomes bad. Unstable. It wasn't even your fault. Being in the wrong place at the wrong time. Nothing you could have done about it and nothing you did to deserve the outcome.*

"It's a funny thing; isn't it? The woman's eyes, Brucie recalled, were lifeless. Hopeless. Tragic. Completely unfair.

Why can't I strike these words from my mind, like they strike testimony from the record? She stuffed it in the briefcase, collected the coffee mug and work supplies, then walked outside to the bluest sky you ever saw, butterflies flitting from flower to flower.

———

The trial began with an intensity in the air. Never had there been a murder in this small, rural area of Wisconsin. As spectators waited in the hallway to get into the courtroom, two very burly men walked through the middle of them. The heavy stomp of each footstep intimidated the people. The rudeness of these men was uncommon in these quiet, friendly towns.

With sneers, the men literally used their upper shoulders to push through the crowd of people. The officer at the doors halted their entrance. Like the officer was light as a feather, the bigger of the two shook his head, eyes glaring, and with both hands pushed him out of the way.

Feeling somewhat embarrassed, with steam invisibly coming out of his head, the officer addressed their rudeness, but the bailiff yelled out to him that spectators were allowed in now. Officer Carter looked them over and pushed his top lip upward, then turned around and invited the rest of the spectators inside.

A courtroom packed with enthusiastic spectators waited impatiently for the trial to begin, as though they were part of an episode of some weekly crime television program. They chattered endlessly.

There was a mixture of reasons people in the area attended the trial. For some, nothing better to do; for others, a fear of crime in the neighborhood and they wanted to see justice prevail. And then there were those crime busters using it as a form of entertainment.

After all the opening statements and preliminaries, the first witness was called to the stand.

Brucie Clark sat at her station, ready to begin court reporting the testimonies during the deposition.

Conversations and speculation between spectators grew annoyingly loud. Finally, the judge pounded his gavel for complete silence. Then Judge Sloan warned the spectators to keep quiet or they would be escorted out of the courtroom, and testimony began.

MS. PENDLETON: "Please state your name for the record."

WITNESS 1: "****** *******"

COURT REPORTER: "Your Honor, a moment, please. Did he say his name was Mickey Mouse or Mmmm Mmmm? It sort of sounded that way."

Brucie mushed her words together and held her hands up looking at the judge.

THE COURT: "No. He said his name is Donald Duck. Couldn't you understand that?" He produced a one-sided grin at Brucie, then looked at the witness. "Sir, please open your mouth as you speak, and speak clearly and very slowly. Actually, spell your first and last name...very slowly."

The mouth puckered tightly as the witness snarled.

WITNESS 1: "H-a-f-s-a V-a-k-i-l-o-v."

The judge cocked his head and whispered to Brucie. "That doesn't sound at all like Mickey Mouse."
Brucie chuckled under her breath. Her court reporting teacher would have scolded her for laughing, she couldn't help but think.

MS. PENDLETON "What country are you from, sir?"

WITNESS 1: "Azarbaijan."

Judge Sloan and Brucie stared at each other.
The defense attorney noticed and walked up, then handed them both the witness's personal information.

THE COURT: "Ms. Pendleton, do you happen to know where it is located?"

MS. PENDLETON: "Your Honor, he says—from the best I can understand—the boundary of Eastern Europe and Western Asia." She typed something into her phone and held it up for him to see.

THE COURT: "Thank you, Ms. Pendleton. Now, please proceed and make certain he speaks very slowly."

MS. PENDLETON: "Yes, Your Honor. Now, Mr. Vakilov, what is your connection to the defendant, Mr. Azar Rzayev? Sorry if I mispronounce either of your names."

WITNESS 1: "We are cousins."

MS. PENDLETON: "What brings you to the United States, particularly Chute Pond, Wisconsin?"

WITNESS 1: "Work."

MS. PENDLETON: "What type of work do you do, sir?"

WITNESS 1: "Ranch work."

MS. PENDLETON: "What type of livestock do you care for?"

WITNESS 1: "Livestock?"

MS. PENDLETON: "Animals. Cows, horses, pigs?"

WITNESS 1: "Yeah."

MS. PENDLETON: "Yeah, what? Cows, horses or pigs?"

WITNESS 1: "Yeah."

She shook her head.

MS. PENDLETON: "Let's try this: Do you care for animals on this ranch? Sorry to say, but I have never heard of any ranch on Chute Pond."

WITNESS 1: "Yeah, animals."

She shook her head again.

MR. SCHULTZ: "Your Honor, I would be happy to get to the bottom of this quickly, if you would like," Prosecuting attorney, Richard Shultz offered as he pushed himself up from the chair.

MS. PENDLETON: "Objection! It's not my fault the witness doesn't understand our language. Have some patience."

Her glare didn't intimidate Mr. Schultz.

THE COURT: "Ms. Pendleton, please have Donald Duck get to the point. I'm getting rather impatient myself."

Brucie and the audience chuckled.

MS. PENDLETON: "Yes, Your Honor." Her pupils were like bullets firing at the prosecution.

Brucie looked around the courtroom and stopped suddenly, because something caught her attention. A man was wearing a baseball cap and sunglasses, no doubt in disguise in her mind. Her forehead wrinkled as she stared. *How is it he is being allowed to wear a cap and sunglasses? It is prohibited in a courtroom.*
Her eyes moved around the audience, and she spotted another man, big and burly, hat resting on his knee, wearing a vest of exotic fur that caused her a second glance.

MS. PENDLETON: "I'm sorry, Your Honor, but would you give me just a few minutes to go over my notes and try to help Mr. Vakilov understand my questions?"

MR. SCHULTZ: "Your Honor—"

THE COURT: "Ms. Pendleton, I understand your dilemma, but please make it snappy and make sure Mr. Duck understands and cooperates more fully than he has been thus far."

Brucie and the audience let out another chuckle. This judge always had a way of entertaining the court.

She glanced around again and stopped her eyes on that big, burly man once more. He stepped out, went to the back of the courtroom and pulled out his cellphone. She couldn't quit staring and then realized why. Not even realizing she started typing on her stenograph.

```
"T        E            L
PW R     EU                    T
EU
TP   O U       PB     D
T
 PW A                  D
 P H     E        PB
 WH O
 P R
 P H AO E         PB
T   O
 P H R           FPLT
 P H    E U    BG
 PW RAO EU              D
FPLT
  T H  E
   R
  W R            G
  KP  O          T
     EU    BG
  TP   U R
S R  ^E                  S
S
   A         PB          D
  PW AO                  TS
                      FPLT
        EU
S R
T  O
K  A  U       L
  H  E R
   RAO EU                T
  A EU
  W A EU              FPLT
```

The air conditioner kicked on and she shivered, squeezing her arms as she crossed them over her chest, or was she scared for some reason? Her eyes darted back and forth to the three men.

In real time the shorthand she'd typed came up on the screen for the attorneys and judge to see in normal words: "Tell Brit I found the bad men who were mean to Mr. McBride. They are wearing exotic fur vests and boots. I have to call her right away."

The judge cleared his throat. Brucie looked up at him.

"Ms. Clark, would you mind approaching the bench? First, turn the screen off, please."

"Yes, Your Honor." She faced him and he bent over and whispered, "What is the meaning of the words you just wrote for *All* to see? We are in a brief recess, so nothing should be written in the record."

She slapped a hand over her mouth. "I am sorry, Your Honor. I wasn't thinking—I mean, I was thinking, but didn't realize I was typing my thoughts. Sir, we—meaning Sheriff Andersand and others—have been looking for the witness and that big, burly man sitting in the audience, along with the defendant, for almost a year. They aren't good men. They almost hurt Mr. McBride at the winter festival. I will strike my thoughts from the record."

"Thank you, Ms. Clark. We'll discuss this further at lunch. Are we still on for the Cornerstone Nutrition restaurant?"

"Of course, Your Honor."

She walked back to her seat and deleted the words. Her eyes glanced around the room again and two of the rotten men were staring right at her. In her mind, they were rotten for how they'd behaved at the festival. Goosebumps traveled up her arms. Then she noticed that the guy wearing the baseball cap was watching her also. When their eyes locked, he jumped up and almost ran out of the courtroom.

MS. PENDLETON: "We're ready, Your Honor, and thank you for the break."

THE COURT: "You're welcome. Now, let's get on with it."

MS. PENDLETON: "Ms. Clark, would you mind reading the last words before the break?"

Silence.

MS. PENDLETON: "Ms. Clark?"

Brucie's eyes were glancing back and forth at the three men, oblivious to anything else going on.

THE COURT: "Ms. Clark, are you all right?"

Her mouth was open, and she looked at the judge still lost in thought.

THE COURT: "Ms. Clark!"

COURT REPORTER: "Yes, Your Honor."

THE COURT: "Would you indulge the court with your shorthand craft before my bedtime?"

COURT REPORTER: Her eyes squinted together. "Sure, Your Honor."

Court proceedings began again. Brucie was having a difficult time focusing, but managed. Some people get tongue-tied, but she was having a severe case of being finger-tied. She prayed silently that she wasn't making a gobbledygook mess on the screen. Now came the good part and she sat up straight, very interested.

MS. PENDLETON: "Mr. Vakilov, do you know the deceased, a Mr. Campbell?"

WITNESS 1: "No ma'am."

MS. PENDLETON: "It has been pointed out that your finger-prints have been found at the crime scene. Please explain."

Brucie typed fiercely, glued to the questions and answers, but still having a hard time understanding his accent. She had to ask him to repeat several times. While the defense was gathering their notes, she glanced over to the defendant and the big, burly man puckered his lips and narrowed his eyes staring straight at her. Goosebumps grew rapidly over her skin. Her eyes went directly to baseball-cap guy who was watching her with intensity too.

MS. PENDLETON: "I have no more questions for the witness, Your Honor."

THE COURT: "Mr. Schultz, do you wish to cross-examine this witness?"

MR. SCHULTZ: "Yes, Your Honor."

MR. SCHULTZ: "Good morning Mr. Vakilov."

The witness glared and said nothing.

MR. SCHULTZ: "Well then, let's get right to it. Did you kill Mr. Campbell?"

MS. PENDLETON: "Objection, Your Honor. Leading, specula-tion, take your pick."

THE COURT: "Overruled."

MR. SCHULTZ: "Please answer the question, Mr. Vakilov."

WITNESS 1: "No." His eyes were shooting invisible bullets.

MR. SCHULTZ: "May I approach the bench?"

THE COURT "Yes."

MR. SCHULTZ: "I present this evidence to the court."

He handed the bailiff two bullets and a Ruger GP100 revolver into an evidence bag. One had been found in a wooded area and the other near the body.

THE COURT: "The exhibit is accepted into evidence."

MR. SCHULTZ: "Mr. Vakilov, is this your weapon?"

WITNESS 1: "No."

MR. SCHULTZ: "You're not very talkative, are you? Moving on. Will you tell the court how your fingerprints came to be on this revolver?"

A: "No."

The questioning went on for a couple of hours and the witness would not elaborate. The judge and prosecution were very frustrated. The judge pounded his gavel and announced they would stop for the day.

Having to stay focused, Brucie couldn't ponder what else it was about these men; the one man in particular sitting in the spectator's section. Gathering her notes and stenograph, she looked over as the man in the baseball cap walked out, and he was glancing back at her. Goosebumps were a permanent fixture to her skin this day, and she rubbed her arms. When she looked for the big, burly man, he walked out, shooting hate from his eyes at her. This time, baseball-size goosebumps ran up and down her body and didn't disappear until the defendant walked through the door with officers on each side, but not before squinting his eyes and tightening his lips, deliberately staring at her.

Am I imagining this? They look like they want to kill me, but why? What have I ever done to them? Maybe they recognize me from the winter festival last year. She crossed her arms and hugged herself. *I'm getting creeped out.*

Two

STILL ON EDGE from the trial, Brucie pulled into the driveway at her cottage home on Chute Pond.

She opened the trunk of her 2020 MX-5 Miata Grand Touring sports car painted gray with red interior and pulled out grocery bags. She headed for the door, but something hit her in the head. Another clunking noise hit the driveway. Her head faced up to see what was going on. Just as she did, she sustained a direct hit to her head. An acorn fell to the ground. Then, one after the other were hitting her.

A hoot and soft panting sound like laughter grew loud. There! She spotted the culprits. Her face went white. *This is no jungle.* She attempted to scratch her head but forgot her hands were holding grocery bags. Then the chimpanzees broke out in more ruckus and bombed her with one acorn after the other.

"Ow! Stop it! OUCH." By this time, she had dropped the grocery bags, and the contents were rolling down the driveway, so she ran for cover. The chimpanzees were enjoying the game, and their hooting became louder while jumping up and down in the tree. They gathered some more acorns and started firing.

Brucie was confused and boy did they have accurate aim. Frustration, she could feel the flush of a red face taking the place of her olive-colored skin. Then she yelled with hands covering her head: "Stop it! Stop it right now!"

All the hooting, hollering and bombing of acorns kept her preoccupied as a shiny, black Ford Ranger drove up. A man jumped out of the truck and ran to the tree. "Bogie! Bacall! Get down here right now," he scolded them.

The chimpanzees held up their acorns, and it looked as if they were trying to debate in their minds to throw or drop them. "Bogie, drop it." Bacall dropped hers and Bogie threw his at Brucie making direct contact to her head.

"Ouch! I've had just about enough of this," she said, rubbing her head. Bogie jumped up and down in excitement.

"Come here right now you two monsters."

They crawled down, hooting and hollering. He pulled them into his arms. "That was not very nice. You apologize to this lady. Go on!"

The chimpanzees jumped down and walked up to Brucie. She backed up, pushing herself sideways against the door.

"They won't hurt you."

Her lips turned down, and she replied, "Oh, really? Tell that to my aching head." She rubbed the bumps.

The chimps held out their hands. She very carefully shook both of them, and darn if she couldn't help but smile. The man walked up at that moment, and she let out a quiet gasp.

"You were in the courtroom today. Why were you watching me?"

"Why yes, I was in the courtroom. Sometimes I like to sit in and observe, especially when a murder is involved. I wasn't watching you, though."

"Oh yes, you were. And no one is allowed to wear hats or sunglasses in the courtroom. How did you manage to get away with that?"

"I have no answer to that."

"And this is not a climate for chimpanzees, so I'm assuming

you have brought them here illegally. And to let them roam around and cause chaos, why I should sue you."

"Look, I'm really sorry for their actions, but they meant no harm. Do you need me to take you to a doctor? Could I check your head for injuries?"

"Don't you touch me." She wrapped her arms around her chest with shrugged shoulders while leaning back.

He threw his hands up. "Okay. Don't have a cow."

Her whole face wrinkled. "I haven't heard that slang in, like... forever. I don't know anything about you. You could be working with those murderers."

His hand covered a chuckle. The chimpanzees heard him laugh and they did their version of a laugh. Brucie couldn't resist and laughed right along with all of them.

"Come on you two, let's help pick up Ms.—"

"Brucie Clark."

"Ms. Clark's groceries."

He bent down and the chimpanzees joined him picking up her groceries. Bogie stuffed a piece of chocolate into his mouth and baseball-cap guy saw. He held onto Bogie and pulled the chocolate out of his mouth, throwing it so far, they heard it splash in the lake. "You know better than that. Chocolate is not good for your diet."

Bogie screeched his disappointment.

"Wow. Are you a professional baseball player?"

"Nope.

"And wow back. So your dinner consists of chocolate, choco-late and more chocolate?"

She grabbed the chocolate candies and gave him a smirk. Putting her items back into the grocery bags, she answered, "Not that it's any of your business, but I happen to like chocolate."

Something that sounded like "kkkhh" escaped his lips. "You probably bathe in it with the amount of chocolate in your purchase alone. I don't see much of anything nutritional."

While bending down to pick up her groceries, just her head

looked up at him. Lips puckered tightly. "Like I said, none of your business."

"No offense intended."

The two chimpanzees spotted some bananas in one of the bags and let their voices be heard.

"Oh, look at that. You do have something nutritional." He looked down, knowing she was firing invisible bullets. "Sorry to say, but these two aren't going to allow you to move until you give them one."

"Okay, you two little monsters. If you weren't so darn cute, I'd be mad at you." They hooted softly like they understood, mouths opened with a silly grin. "Here you go. Come here Bogie. Come on Bacall. You have a cute little bow there." They grinned and took the bananas.

"Now then, don't you think it appropriate to tell me your name and just where do you live? I know almost everyone on this road. When did you move in?"

"First things first. I moved in a month ago and have a small cabin way down that dirt road," he said, pointing. "My name is Riggins Malarkie."

She slapped a hand over her mouth and escaped a laugh. "For real?"

"Yes, it is. My dad was a huge fan—as am I—of John Riggins, fullback for the then-called Washington Redskins. He was so amazing as a fullback. He reminded me of a bull snorting and pushing his way through the other team. We used to watch videos of him all the time together."

"No kidding. I know who he is. I always loved football, but believe it or not, I was a Joe Montana fan. I sort of lost interest after he quit the game. Besides, I was a little girl when he was with the 49ers."

"Well, I need to get these guys home. I'm taking care of them for a friend, and you're right, this is not the right climate for them, but they will only be here for about a month. I hate to ask this, but

I need you to keep this quiet, so I don't get in trouble caring for them."

"That depends. Tell me why you were in that courtroom and in disguise?"

"Just an observer. Is that a crime?"

"Crime is just what I'm wondering about. Do you work with those murderers?"

"Like I would divulge that information if it were true. Yeah, I'm one of the murderers."

He threw his hands up and frowned with a slight shake of the head. "Will you drop this nonsense?"

"It's not nonsense, and if you think you can use subterfuge on me that easily, well, you're just full of…your last name." Thinking she was witty, she couldn't control the laughter.

"Yeah, like I never heard that one before. Suit yourself, but if you tell anyone about these two innocent victims, you will have to live with the tragedy of what will happen to them."

She frowned.

"Sorry about the bumps on your head." He pulled the chimpanzees into his arms, turned around and walked to the truck. She leaned against the door with her arms crossed. He turned back around after seat belting Bogie and Bacall, and made a comment.

"Chocolate, chimpanzees and a court reporter at Chute Pond. Who knew?" He shrugged his shoulders and gravel and dirt scattered through the air as he sped out of her driveway.

She watched with curiosity as his truck disappeared down the driveway. She couldn't help but snicker at his comment because it was so true and yet just so absurd, although she wasn't about to let him see her amusement. He seemed so sure of himself; so arrogant.

Three

SATURDAY MORNING ROLLED AROUND. Turning the percolator on and jumping back into bed, the smell and gurgle hypnotically pulled Brucie back into the kitchen. She poured a delightful, churned creamer into the coffee and clinked the spoon against the cup as she stirred.

Facing the lake, it looked so peaceful and inviting, sunrays flickering through the window, so she sat out on the deck to face it. The air was crisp and refreshing, causing her lips to curve up and nose lifted to inhale the fresh air. Sunrays sparkled on the water. Her eyes squinted, trying to adjust to the bright morning sunshine. Lips touching the scolding coffee, she blew air into the cup, but something caught her attention before taking a sip. A man was fishing in a boat not too far from her. It looked like he just pulled in a largemouth bass. It was flexing its body back and forth. To her surprise he took a selfie and threw the fish back into the lake.

She squinted her eyes more to try and see who the guy was. He wore a baseball cap, sunglasses and no shirt.

She jumped up so fast that coffee spilled from her cup, but she set it down and ran into the cottage. And she zipped back out like *the Flash* holding binoculars. Her eyes pushed against the binoculars and looked for the man. Uh-huh, it was Riggins.

"Ooh-la-la. Who knew he looked like that underneath his shirt? Mamma Mia!"

To her horrid surprise he waved at her. She lowered the binoculars and slid down in the chair.

Could he see her pink cheeks? She turned her head every way but toward him.

Riggins pulled out his binoculars and returned the favor.

Brucie heard a noise that sounded faintly familiar. It got louder. She ran in and grabbed a bike helmet and fastened it before going out. Just as she thought. Acorns hit the helmet.

"Bogie! Bacall! Come down from that tree right now." She shook her finger as she yelled.

They crawled down the tree and ran up to Brucie with their arms out. She smiled and pulled them into her arms. Then she walked out onto the pier and yelled to Riggins. He threw his hands up and shook his head.

"I'll be there in a few minutes to pick them up." He zoomed the boat in the direction of his home, threw on a t-shirt and sped away in his truck. Ring, ring, ring went the doorbell.

"Come in. How is it these guys are escaping? You must not be taking very good care of them. What would happen if they went to a different house or took off through the woods?"

"I deserve that. There has to be some form of a lock they can't figure out. Nice hairstyle, by the way. I'm guessing that's why you wore a bike helmet." Her fingers just got stuck in a clump of hair.

"Look smarty pants, it's Saturday and I haven't felt like brushing my hair yet."

"Or teeth!" His mouth turned down.

"Well, I didn't expect company so soon. For my safety I wore a helmet so these cute, little monsters"—she smiled at them but frowned at him— "wouldn't injure my head." She wrinkled up her nose. "You don't smell so good yourself."

He was sweating from rushing around. "Okay. I get it. I offended you and nothing I say will change your grouchy disposition. Man, you can't take kidding around. How exhausting."

"Oh yeah." Her face was burning up. "It's probably a good idea for you to leave, and I happen to enjoy kidding around, but you just aren't that funny. Looks like you're the one with the problem."

"You don't have a boyfriend, do you? I mean, who would want to walk on eggshells around you all day? I pity such a fool."

"I happen to go out on a lot of dates."

"Pbbbbbt," he rolled off his lips. "You need a personality makeover."

"Well...YOU should order some brain performance supplements and double the daily dose. Oh! And you're full of your last name."

He grabbed the chimpanzees, and they kept looking back and forth at him and Brucie like they were wondering why they were upset. Bacall was hooting and reaching for Brucie.

"Come on, Bacall. She'll suck the fun right out of you if you hang around ole Bruce too long," he remarked, walking out to the truck.

Before he placed them in the truck seat, she froze, and imaginary steam blew out of her head as though she just realized what he called her. Her expression was easy to analyze, and those long breaths sounded like a steam engine. "What did you call me?"

"Bruce. Bruce. Bruce. Catch you later, Bruce."

"Don't you EVER call me that again. My name is Brucie and if you ever step foot on my property again, I'll shoot you. Oh, yeah, I'm a good shot. Accurate. And I have a bullet with your name on it, Malarkey." She repeated his version of "Pbbbbbt" but spit came out of her mouth and sprayed in his face. The chimpanzees were wiping their faces.

How and why, she yelled, "You...you brussel sprout!" he didn't know.

He turned around and she saw the quizzical expression on his face. Then he put the chimpanzees in seat belts before he walked around to the driver's side. "Catch you later, Bruce." He stormed off, leaving skid marks.

Brucie was so mad her face was hot, and she knew her face had turned different shades of red. Feeling her cheeks, she said to herself, "Do I have a fever, or did he just burn my butt? I hate you, Malarkie." She kicked a book lying on the floor and yelled while holding her toe hopping around on one foot.

———

"Hey Gene, how's it going? It's Riggins."

"Well, going well. I heard you were back in town. What's going on?"

"International wildlife poachers. Murder. The norm. You're not going to believe it, so I thought we could get together and talk about it."

"Yeah, sure. But this is certainly not the 'norm' for our county. Where are you staying?"

"Off of South Shore Drive."

"What a coincidence. Britanica and I are visiting a friend for lunch on your street."

"No kidding. I don't know many people except this one displeasing woman I had the unfortunate pleasure of meeting. Her name is Brucie Clark. What a piece of work."

"You're going to think this is funny, so guess who we're having lunch with?"

Riggins wiped his hand over his forehead and through his hair. "Seriously! Look, she suspects something. I rescued two chimpanzees and they somehow escaped from my cottage and found her home. Let's just say it wasn't a very welcomed beginning. When she arrived home and started to walk up to her cabin carrying groceries, they bombed her with acorns."

Gene busted out in laughter. "Man, I would have paid to see her expression."

"She's not very friendly and acts like she has a chip on her shoulder. Does she hate men, or just me?"

"She is nothing like what you're describing. Look, I know you and I know that cocky attitude you get at times. Are you sure you didn't instigate her reaction?"

"Maybe a little, but she was more than ready to play the victim AND she makes fun of my last name, so I called her 'Bruce'."

"Yikes! Bad move. Last time someone called her that, she coldcocked them. She's pretty touchy about that."

"So I noticed. I won't deny it gave me great pleasure to see her seething with anger. She started it.

"You know what she called me?" he mentioned puzzled.

"What?"

"She called me a brussel sprout." He lifted a hand while saying it.

"Oh, that's bad."

"Huh?"

"She hates brussel sprouts. The smell and taste will make her vomit."

"Oh, I guess she really hates me."

"Doesn't look good, sorry to say.

"You're not going to believe this either, but Brit and I were planning on setting you two up on a blind date when I found out you were back in town."

"I thought we were friends. Obviously not."

"Do you know how many times I wanted to make fun of your last name? Especially when you told me that *Mission Impossible* story. I wanted to tell you that you were full of your last name then." Gene's giggle was muffled but Riggins heard it.

"I get it. It was the way she presented it that bothered me. Enough of that. She thinks I'm working with those murderers, because I was hanging out in the background of the courtroom. I noticed these guys watching her. Fear was in her face when she saw them glaring at her. They are looking for the two chimpanzees I rescued. You need to talk some sense into her. She is starting to dig around and could end up at the morgue if she's not careful. These are some bad dudes. Do NOT let her know we are friends.

Act like you don't know me. It's for her protection, as exasperating as she is."

"You got it. I'll drop Britanica off at Brucie's house and come over around lunch. Text me your address. Hey, you're still standing up for me in the wedding; right?"

"Why would you even ask? Of course. See you at lunch."

Four

BRUCIE AND BRITANICA HUGGED. "Hey, where's Gene going?" He waved as he drove off.

"He'll be back soon. Business."

They walked arm in arm into the house. Britanica lifted her nose and breathed in the delicious aromas. "You do know I'm watching my weight for the wedding; right?"

"As am I. I made honey-grilled chicken with a citrus salad."

"Shooie. I can't wait. But tell me about those rotten men while we finish making lunch. Now that murder is a part of the picture, my curiosity is shooting in all directions."

"Brit, I'm not kidding one bit. They were watching me and the look on their faces was of pure, one hundred percent hate. It scares me. It's the same men from the winter festival. Why would they look at me like that? They don't know me."

"The only thing I can think of is that they recognized you from the festival. What else could it be?"

"I don't know." She threw her arms up.

"You can relax. I told Gene and he is having undercover officers keep an eye out. They will be watching your place, and you need to keep out of sight until this case is over with."

"Shouldn't I know who will be watching out for me, so I don't freak out thinking they're one of the bad guys? I'm not kidding about the evil stares." A shiver just ran through her body. It almost looked like convulsions.

"No, silly girl. Undercover! They need to be inconspicuous and not act like they know you. Have you seen anyone around that looks suspicious?"

"Now that you mention it, yes. There is this obnoxious guy named Riggins Malarkie. Can you believe his last name?" She snickered.

Gene had explained to Britanica to act as if she didn't know him, basically for safety and security measures and to not compromise his identity. She cleared her throat. "No, I never heard of him." She cleared her throat again. "That pesky frog is back."

"Yeah, okay. Well, let's keep this chicken warm until Gene comes back and gets to the wedding arrangements." She squeezed Brit's wrists and smiled.

"Great idea. Your table setup should be photographed and placed in one of those cottage magazines. So beautiful."

As they sat on the couch, Britanica grabbed Brucie's hand and smiled excitedly. "I think we found our wedding song. We're going with the Troggs."

One side of Brucie's upper lip and nose pushed up. "Is that some type of reptilian?"

She shook her head. "Goof, that's the name of the group. Then she began to sing it. "'I feel it in my fingers, I feel it in my toes. Well, love is all around me and so the feeling grows.' Do you know it now?"

"I love that song. It's perfect for you both. You always comment how you get the 'tingles' every time Gene touches you, and Emmy heard Gene tell Webster that he feels it, too."

It was a family affair in this town. Britanica and Webster were twins, and Emmy, Brit's childhood best friend, married Webster. Gene and Webster also grew up as best friends. During college years, Brucie just fit in like family.

"But what kind of a name is 'Troggs'?" Brucie asked.

"I looked that up and it originated from Troglodytes. And guess what: They are the group who sang our theme song, which now includes Emmy: 'Wild Thing'."

"No kidding! Well, you know the saying: 'You learn something new every day'. By the way, does Emmy know you chose this for our theme song because of how wild I was in my beginning year of college?"

"There is truth in that, and yes, she knows."

"The song you picked is great, but not really a wedding song."

"Don't you know that I don't follow those stupid rules by now? We want a song that suits us personally. Not every wedding couple in the world. This song is specifically for us."

"Since you put it that way, I get it."

"Oh! I meant to tell you that I got Becky from the Mane Attraction hair salon to do our hair and makeup for the wedding."

"Marvelous! I need to make an appointment with her, but traveling to Marinette from Mountain takes time and planning. After the wedding, I'll schedule an appointment."

Lunch was great, wedding plans were great, conversation was great, and everyone went about their business for the rest of the day.

Now bored, Brucie threw on some running clothes and sneakers and went for a run. For being Wisconsin, it was a little muggy out, and she had beads of sweat on her forehead and part of her shirt. No breeze today. She ran all the way down S. Shore Drive but stopped dead in her tracks when she saw something.

Her eyes were glued to the apparition. She rubbed her eyes; it was still there but far off.

Was it a reflection? No! It moved. It looked like a ghost, but of a moose. She scratched her head. It disappeared. A truck was heading out of a dirt road, rather, one that didn't appear to be a road, just smashed down vegetation. Not just a truck, but it was one of the rotten men staring at her in court driving. Her body twitched and her eyes grew wide. She turned and tried to act like she didn't notice and purposely took on the best jogger's form she could come up with. The man driving started to turn the other way then stopped and drove in her direction, really slow.

"Don't hyperventilate. Breathe, just breathe." Heart racing, heavy inhales and exhales, she trembled. Good thing she had her hair up in a ponytail and sunglasses on, a good enough disguise. He drove past her like a snail, eyes glued on her face, expression blank, but yet causing fear. She waved, and turned her head around and ran faster and faster.

He noticed, so he kept following her.

"I can't let him know where I live. What should I do?" She pulled out her phone and answered it as though someone had just called her. Could he see her shaking hand? When he turned the corner, she ran through the woods and hid out of sight, peeking out from a boulder to watch him. This time, she had Gene on the line.

The scary man came back, driving slowly, looking in all directions for her. He stopped, rolled down his window, and looked around. Then he got out of the truck and walked into the wooded area looking for her. Her breathing was rapidly developing.

"Calm down before you hyperventilate. Don't let him see or hear you," Gene ordered.

She held the phone tight, peeked back out, and saw the man looking in her direction. Her head ducked down quickly, and she tried to relax those jittery nerves to listen for his footsteps. Debris crunching was audible, but thankfully it was in a different direction. The truck door slammed. She pushed her head out just far enough to see him drive off. That was nerve wracking, so she ended the call with Gene, ran home and locked the doors. She pulled all the window shades down. Almost lifeless, her body plopped down on the soft, oh so soft couch, arms dangling, head resting against the back tilted up, and eyes closed.

Brucie tapped the index finger against her forehead when she came up with a plan. Scrolling through the Internet, her fingers dialed the telephone number.

"Hello. I'm in need of a security system ASAP! I heard your company has easy to install systems."

After giving all the necessary information, the shipment was on the way. She breathed a sigh of relief, turned on a movie, and fell asleep on the couch. But outside, a truck was driving around the neighborhood slowly, stopping and starting. Tires hitting gravel alerted Brucie's senses, and she woke up in a fog feeling on the eerie side. Stumbling around, body not fully functioning, she ran to the window and spied through the shade. It was dark now and all she could see were the red brake lights from a vehicle braking and starting, braking and starting. Hands rubbed her body up and down from the chill in the air—or the fear. She glanced at the clock.

"Oh, my goodness, I slept three hours. I'll just have a bowl of cereal for dinner."

That night, she watched television, read a book and searched the Internet to occupy her mind. Still feeling uncertain and fearful, she propped chairs up against each exterior door and climbed into bed. All the anxiety caused her to feel sleepy and she passed out in no time.

Outside her house, the crunching of sticks and debris caused a stir in her sleep. She jumped up in bed as the motion light came on outside and swore she heard the door handle turning. First, her body went limp. Slowly getting out of bed, her foot got stuck on the blanket and she tripped to the floor. "Frickin-frackin-Frickin-frackin."

She peeked slowly out of the shade and didn't see anyone. Pillow and blanket in hand, she plopped on the couch and turned the television on low for noise. Sensibility had gone out the door and there would be no more sleep tonight. It was 3:00 a.m.

Five

BAGS UNDER HER EYES, Brucie's feet shuffled into church. Pastor Beard shook her hand.

"Good morning, Brucie. You feeling all right? You're beautiful as always, but there's tension and a tiredness in your face."

"I'm just tired, Pastor Mustache, that's all."

"That Britanica started this. Visitors don't know if my name is Pastor Mustache, Pastor Goatee and even—get this: Pastor Mutton Chops Beard."

"Ah, gee, sorry. It's just so much fun. You know what? You should grow a beard and mustache and shave it to look like each one of these styles at different times. That would be a hoot."

She sat behind Britanica and Emmy. Just before the service began, she asked, "Which one of you gave Pastor Beard the nickname Pastor Mutton Chops Beard?"

Emmy slowly, with a pinkish tint to her face, raised her arm.

"You're such a dork, Em."

"Yeah, like it's worse than Pastor Mustache or Goatee."

Brucie and Britanica locked eyes and nodded their heads in agreement, that yes, it was far worse than their nicknames.

Pastor Beard took the stage and introduced himself. "We welcome you visitors today. My name is Pastor Beard. Not Pastor

Mustache, Goatee or Mutton Chops Beard." He stared at all the three women who caused the uncertainty.

The congregation busted out in laughter.

After church services, the gang went out to lunch and laughed the whole way through the meal.

"Any news on those wretched men?" Brucie asked.

"No, nothing new. How's the trial going?" Gene asked.

"The same frustrating way. They can't seem to find enough evidence to incriminate them.

There has to be something they're missing. Something." Brucie thought about her statement.

"You be careful out there. Call me day or night," Gene offered.

"That goes for me as well," Webster added.

"Thanks, and I just may do that."

———

Brucie hung around her cabin home, called her parents, worked on transcripts and kicked back for a little while. Chocolate everything lied on the coffee table. She had a craving and tried everything she had in the form of chocolate to appease the god of cravings. Sadly, none of it worked, although she loved every bite of chocolate she took. *They say, 'all we need is love' but I say all we need is chocolate.* She rested against the back of the couch and crossed her legs on the coffee table.

It felt like she was a prisoner, not able to go for a run or have any fun. She jumped when she heard a loud noise.

"Was that a gunshot I just heard?"

She ran to each window, bending down and poking her head up just enough to look around.

Then she heard the sputtering of a boat motor. There. Riggins was running up and down the shoreline. She squinted her eyes and pushed her face against the window to see clearer. *Is he holding a gun? I can't tell.*

Not able to hold herself back, she ran out the back door, yelling, "Riggins! RIGGINS, what's going on?"

His face tense, eyes worried, he yelled back, "Nothing. Just go back inside."

"No, I won't. It's a free country, buster."

"I lost my phone, but I'll find it. You don't have to watch me." He let out a sigh. He had noticed Brucie peeking out the window just before she came outside.

"You sure you didn't lose Bogie and Bacall?"

With a strained voice, he inserted, "No, I didn't."

She waved his rude demeanor off with her hand and went back inside to peek out the window.

"Don't peek out the window like you've been doing!" he shouted.

"Hhhh! Well, I never…" She huffed her way into the cabin, forgetting she had on big, fuzzy slippers and fuzzy, cozy pajamas. She didn't notice him looking at her with an appreciative sweep of his eyes.

Digging in the refrigerator for more chocolate, she thought, *Something's going on around here and I'm going to get to the bottom of it. I will carry a handgun with me for protection, thanks to good buddy, Sheriff Gene, and do a little digging around myself.*

Around 8:00 p.m., she glanced out the windows, but it had gotten too dark to see anything. She watched some television, propped chairs up against the door and finally went to bed eagerly awaiting her alarm system to arrive.

Sleeping soundly, she didn't hear the rustling of leaves and branches snap, nor could she see anyone trying to peek in the windows.

A yawn three times the size of her mouth, it felt, covered Brucie's face as she stretched her arms. Percolator turned on, she jumped into the shower, dressed and sat down for a much needed cup of that wonderful smelling coffee. "How can any one person NOT start their day with a cup of coffee? It's virtually impossible." She held the cup with two hands and breathed in the aroma, feeling the warmth in her hand. Cellphone in hand, she sat out on the porch to drink coffee and read texts before work.

Brucie wasn't paying attention to anything else but decided to sit back in silence and stare at the peaceful lake. Except for one very disturbing thing: "Is that a body in the water?" She slapped a hand over her mouth and stood up. She slowly walked toward the body, praying in earnest it was her imagination.

As she got closer, heavy stomping was coming toward the body from a different direction. She ran back up by the cabin and hid out of sight, watching. Riggins ran up with a big gun in his hand as he bent over the body. It looked like he was checking for a pulse. He put his head down and shook it slowly back and forth.

Brucie let out a silent scream, grasping her mouth shut with her hands. Eyes as wide as a golf ball. *I knew he was no good. He's a murderer. I have to call Gene.*

She ran into the cabin, but very quietly. Good thing she had a key hidden in the front yard, somewhere no one would think to look. It would be bad news if Riggins saw her. She grabbed the phone, sat on the kitchen floor, and dialed Gene's number.

In a frantic tone, she said, "Gene, a guy named Riggins killed someone." She kept babbling at a mile per second.

"Brucie, slow down so I can understand you."

Gene said, "Go to work and leave this to me. It's too dangerous for you to get involved."

Brucie ran back to the window and looked out where the body was lying. It was gone.

Riggins was gone. She could hear it now: "No body; no crime." So being Brucie, she ran out and turned her head East to West, North to South looking for Riggins. But he was nowhere in sight. She ran to the shore to find some type of evidence. It was all cleaned up. No blood. No nothing. On her tiptoes, standing up straight she looked around for the killer. No one was around. All done so fast. "A world gone mad," she said out loud to herself.

Later, as she drove to work, she called Gene. "Gene, I went

back to the shore, but the body wasn't there anymore. Riggins was gone, too.

Just then, Riggins' truck sped past her. He didn't even acknowledge her. "What is going on around here, Gene?"

"I'll take care of everything. I have an incoming call. I'll call you later."

Did that bring her relief? On the contrary, she now was petrified.

Six

MR. SCHULTZ: "Mr. Flagstone, do you run an illegal hunting business? And by that, I mean, do you poach extinct and exotic animals from around the world and then bring in hunters from around the world to hunt them down and kill them for sport? An appalling thought, it is."

Gene sat in the audience, shaking his head. *Sure, he's just going to admit to all of it, idiot.*

The witness, Mr. Flagstone, rolled his eyes before answering.

WITNESS 2: "No, sir. I employ staff to take care of my livestock: cattle and horses."

MR. SCHULTZ: "On Chute Pond?"

WITNESS 2: "Yes, sir."

MR. SCHULTZ: "There is no legal description in Oconto County of any such operation."

WITNESS 2: "Really? Well, then the county must have incompetent employees. They must have misplaced my deed."

MR. SCHULTZ: "Certainly. Now then, please don't try to move any livestock, exotic or not, out anytime soon. I'm getting a warrant to search the premises. Officers will be standing watch until then."

Mr. Flagstone squirmed in his seat but kept his expression blank.

WITNESS 2: "Yes, sir."

MR. SCHULTZ: "Now, do you know the defendant? Does he work for you?"

WITNESS 2: "Yes sir to both."

MR. SCHULTZ: "Did you meet here in Chute Pond or where?"

WITNESS 2: "We met in his country when I was there on business. He needed work and I hired him."

MR. SCHULTZ: "We can't seem to find his legal documentation. Any idea why?"

WITNESS 2: "No, sir. I helped him fill out all legal documentation. It's a mystery to me."

MR. SCHULTZ: "I'm sure it is. A real mystery." His voice was satirical.

Brucie glanced over and Mr. Flagstone's eyes stared into hers without blinking. It felt freaky. While the attorney reviewed his notes, Mr. Flagstone mouthed something to her.

He formed his words very slowly. Brucie's eyes grew really big.

Without thinking, her fingers typed:

```
     STK            E
     S KWR   * U                S
     S   A  EU
     E               S
      TKPW  O                          G
      T   O
        K        EU            L
         P H AO E
     ST P H
```

On the screen it read: "Did he just say he is going to kill me?"

```
      KWR
       P H  AO E
       A                    PB          D
      KWR
     S          E
     S    O
      PW   EU       G
        A          PB        D
       H A                   S
     S          U  F P
      PW   EU       G
       H A    PB      D
       S
     A         PB      D
       P  R O B
       HR AO E
      PW     EU    G
     TKPW    U PB   S
     ST PH
```

It read: "Why me and why is he so big and has such big hands and probably big guns?"

THE COURT: "Ms. Clark, please turn off your screen and approach the bench."

She looked at the judge with a lost expression for a minute and then replied as she jumped up. "Yes, Your Honor."

"Care to explain?" the judge whispered.

"Explain what, Your Honor?"

"What you just typed on the screen?" He was twiddling his fingers.

"Not again?" Brucie gasped.

The judge nodded his head yes.

She rubbed her head before speaking. Then she whispered, "Sir, the witness just mouthed to me that he was going to kill me."

"Ms. Clark, come on."

"It's true, Your Honor. I wouldn't lie to you. We've worked together many times. I've always conducted myself professionally. This case has me fearful, I have to admit."

"That's true that we have worked together many times and you have always been professional. Even when I try to get a rise out of you, you manage to put your head down to keep from laughing. But think about it. Why would the witness risk someone seeing him mouth that to you? If you read those words, don't you think someone else could have also?"

"Of course, Your Honor." She turned her palms up. "I don't know what to say to convince you that I'm not imagining any of this."

"It's a good thing no one else was paying attention to what you typed. Now, delete that from the record and get your wits about you. Don't tell anyone." He leaned over and added, "But you're my favorite court reporter to work with. I have asked your agency to send you over many times. I'd like to keep it that way."

"Me too." She smiled affectionately and sat back down and focused, keeping her head down so the witness couldn't intimidate her.

Brucie plopped her stenograph and notes on the floor as she walked to her cabin. A package sitting near the front door encouraged a smile and she brought it in and opened it with relief written all over her face. Her long, black, silky hair and an olive skin tone sparkled as sunrays shined on her. With striking features, it was very obvious that native American traits were a part of her heritage. When she smiled, it lit up the whole place. Everywhere. Every time.

After a grueling day, she fell onto the couch and just rested her head and closed her eyes. A picture of safety and security right at her fingertips.

Scratch, scratch, and a soft pounding hit the door. She sat up and listened. Her head peeked around the curtain, and she saw she had company. She smiled.

"Welcome to my home," she said, opening the door. At first, they came in by knuckle-walking and then stood upright. Bacall raised her arms for Brucie to scoop her up. Who could resist that? She sat down in her swivel recliner and called Bogie. "Come on, Bogie. Sit with us just for a minute."

They were enjoying swiveling around and back and forth. Brucie, however, was feeling a little dizzy. "Okay, that's enough. Enough, I said, you two adorable monsters. Escape again?" she asked, nodding her head. They nodded back. "Let me search the Internet to see what snacks I may have for you. I better stock up for the next visit, huh?" They nodded.

"Oh, here we go. I have nuts, fruit and seeds and boiled eggs. Would you like some?" she asked, nodding her head again. They nodded back and gave a full-mouth smile.

"I may dislike your caretaker, and a lot, but I'm becoming quite fond of you two. Here, sit in these chairs while I fix your snack."

They sat in the kitchen chairs wiggling like ants were in their pants. They wore diapers and shorts. Bacall had a top that matched, and Bogie wore a t-shirt. She set bowls on the table, and they dug in. At first, they ate with manners until Bogie reached into Bacall's dish trying to steal her food. Bacall screeched like she was in pain. Food started flying. And landing in Brucie's hair.

"Hey, hey, HEY, enough. Bogie, keep your hands in your dish." She moved him further away from Bacall.

Knock, knock, knock, she heard. Brucie peeked out the curtain. Riggins was in a frantic state, looking around earnestly, bending his upper body back to look around, searching the top of trees, and just a basket of nerves.

Brucie had a witty idea. She grabbed a basket and opened the door. "Drop them in the basket," she said, straightforward.

His eyes squinted and his head pushed back.

"Drop your nerves into this basket. Get it? A basket of nerves?"

He still looked at her, lost in space. She waved a hand down and said, "Forget it. They're in the kitchen."

A huge sigh blew out of his mouth like a balloon was deflating. "Please save the lecture. I feel bad enough already."

"For your information, I did not plan on giving you a lecture. Today." She smiled and led him into the kitchen.

Plastic bowls on top of their heads, they started hooting and hollering at his presence. They jumped down and ran into his arms.

"What am I going to do with you two?" He kissed both of them on their cheeks. Brucie smiled at his affection for them.

"I'd like to tell you this won't happen again, but I know better. They could have shown Houdini a thing or two."

She chuckled.

"Now I understand why you choose to wear a helmet around them. Looks like they got you again."

Her fingers felt her hair and waved his statement off with the other hand. "These two are growing on me. I actually enjoy their company."

"The way they have taken to you, looks like you will be a good mother someday." Bacall was reaching for her and Brucie pulled her in her arms and kissed that adorable, but hairy, cheek.

"Thank you. That's actually a nice thing you said," looking a little puzzled. "By the way, what type of work do you do?"

"Handyman stuff. I'm pretty good at repairing, gluing, building, fixing anything."

"You don't say. Any chance you know how to put this security system up?" She pointed to the package.

"Oh, yeah. That's a really easy system to install. After all, I think I owe you that much."

"No, no. I'll pay you. You see, I have an expedited transcript that needs completion for tomorrow, and I would just feel safe having it in place." She couldn't help but replay the memory of him holding a gun over a dead body. *What am I saying? What a ding-dong.*

"I'll set it up for you in no time and you just go ahead and work on your transcript. Do you mind if these two sit at the table with you? Any chance you have puzzles or toys?" His upper lip curled as he threw his hands up. "That was a dumb thing to ask since you don't have children."

She lifted the chimpanzees and smiled down at them. "I think I have just what they need to occupy themselves, for a few minutes, anyway."

Her focus changed, and she listened intently, then walked to the curtain. "That one big man from the trial keeps driving really slow down the street. It's a good thing I can hide my car in the garage. He actually followed me one day while I was running. When he drove around the corner, I ran and hid behind some boulders. He actually got out of his truck and walked into the woods to look for me. I was terrified."

"I don't blame you. I think I know who you're talking about. He testified one day, and he looks like one mean, dirty-rotten guy."

"Oh no, you don't think he recognizes your truck, do you?"

"No-no-no. Don't worry. He has never seen my truck. He doesn't know me."

"Good, well, this security system will calm my nerves. She sat the chimpanzees down on a chair and got some crayons and drawing paper. "Now, you two draw me something pretty; okay?" She looked down at both of them and they smiled. Riggins watched and felt better about her soft side. Then he got right to it. She typed away and he installed. They were both done within the hour.

Brucie looked at their drawings. "Could I keep these?" She was bending over to speak to them. Riggins couldn't help but inspect her toned and fit physique. It was still too early to feel at ease around her, though. They had gotten off to a bad start.

They handed her their pictures. For some odd reason, maybe because of all the stress and tension, she teared up. She gave the chimps each a big hug, and they squirmed. Then she stuck the pictures on the refrigerator. They hooted and hollered and clapped their hands.

Riggins watched. Not wanting to embarrass her, he pretended to walk up at that moment with all plastic and paper left over placed in the box. "All done. Now, all you have to do is call to activate your alarm. Do you need me to hang around while you do that?"

"Oh, no, that's fine. Thank you. Thank you so much."

He smiled, pulled his shirt up to wipe sweat from his brow, and repaid her with his sincere gratitude. She stood there, speechless, then gulped, thinking about how great he looked. His hair was far too short for her, but he definitely had handsome features.

"I always say things that you misinterpret, but I just have to say that you have great hair, but have you ever considered growing it out? A little?"

His face was a puzzle. "Why?"

"It's just my silly preferences. I meant no criticism. You have great hair." She held her hands out hoping he didn't misinterpret her statement.

"Thank you?" Face still a puzzle. "You have great hair, too."

She smiled.

"Look, I need to get these two home, unless you need me to do anything else."

"No, you did plenty." She walked up close to him, bent down and kissed their cheeks.

It was his turn to gulp. The way she had walked straight up to him face to face before bending down, for a split second, gave him a thought that she was going to kiss him. His face flushed. He took the hand of each chimp and walked toward the door to leave. "Thanks again and call and activate when I leave. Wave goodbye to Ms. Brucie." They did.

She activated the alarm and went to bed that night feeling safe, and for some strange reason, memories of Riggins pulling up his shirt popped into her mind. Did she actually fall asleep with a smile? She would never know the answer to that.

Later that night, she didn't even wake up to the motion light turning on, nor was she aware of someone trying to peek into her windows and were only able to make out a flashing blue light and a security sign attached to the railing of her porch.

Seven

FORGETTING about the security system the following day, Brucie walked out the door. "An Eeeah, Eeeah, Eeeah sound blasted, and lights flashed. She ran in and called the service before a sheriff was sent out.

"Whooo," she sighed when it finally stopped. She looked around before backing out of the garage and all was safe, except for her slanted mailbox. A piece of red plastic from a vehicle's brake lights lay on the ground. Car in park, she jumped out, picked up the plastic, looking down the road, wondering. "Frickin-frackin. Frickin-frackin," she yelled. Then it hit her that maybe Riggins could fix the mailbox. "I'm sure those two will escape and he'll have to come looking for them, then I'll bribe him." She gave her head a good shake and drove to work.

She had had enough. Instead of these horrid men trying to instill fear in her at the courthouse, Brucie glared into their eyes. All three of them. As hard as they tried to intimidate her, she didn't budge. She pushed her top lip up on one side and narrowed her eyes. And she didn't look away. It was like a blanket of courage covered her body and she sat up straight, perfect posture and felt confident.

MR. SCHULTZ: "Mr. Flagstone, why is it we can never gain access into your estate? No one answers the intercom, and no one is anywhere around? By the way, we certainly don't want to ruin any of our days by getting electrocuted touching your gate. I know how voltage is used on farms, growing up around them, and that amount of voltage is to keep *King Kong* himself from escaping."

WITNESS 2: "My apologies. I have no explanation. But I will send out for technical assistance. Perhaps there is a short in the wiring."

"Oops." Brucie jumped a little in her chair and deleted the words on the screen: "Like anyone believes that."

The judge looked over and puckered his mouth off to one side. Then he relaxed.

It was another frustrating day in court. The prosecution wasn't getting any further along than day one. Nobody discussed the case, but in somewhat of a defeat they walked out of the courtroom without speaking. Except, those dirty-rotten scoundrels jabbed each other and laughed as they walked out.

Brucie diddled around her cabin. To distract her thoughts, she searched the internet and found artwork of a warrior angel, some adorable woodland animals, and some beautiful fairy artwork. Cha-Ching went her bank account. It was about time she decorated the cabin. Next, she found soft, luxurious throws, pillows and towels. Her log cabin needed some softening up. Cha-Ching her bank account went again.

The scent of something appetizing went right up her nostrils. The microwave sounded its buzzer. Her frozen dinner was ready. She set it down on the coffee table, turned on a comedy, and ate. Unfortunately, all the chocolate candy pieces lying on her coffee table brought it to her attention that she wasn't that hungry now. "Just one more bite of that devil's food cake with fudge frosting. You can do it, Brucie. One bite."

She forced the bite in her mouth. As full as she was, a smile broke out. All she could do now was lie back and relax. Wearing a one-piece fuzzy bunny pajamas, decked out with rabbit ears, whiskers and nose on each foot, she lied on the couch and began to watch some television. Not able to fight it, her eyes closed, and she immediately flew off into dreamland. But some outside noise woke her. She jolted to a sitting position and rubbed both eyes, completing it with a yawn. It was 2:30 a.m. She remained still and listened intently. To what? The outside motion light flickered in the mirror. Her body wilted.

Her legs dangled over the couch, frozen in time, but she eventually got them to move and walk to the window. A red light snuck through the bottom of her window shade. She pulled the shade out enough to see. Enough was enough. House key in hand, she deactivated the alarm and slowly cracked the door open. "Oops, I forgot something." Her handgun went into a pocket and a flashlight in her hand. She snuck out the door and ran quietly to the road. A little shaky, she looked around for signs of someone hiding. Feeling certain she was alone, she took off down the road looking for the red lights of the truck. It turned down the driveway of smashed down vegetation.

She jogged slowly, holding the flashlight down so it wouldn't be spotted. A shiver ran up and down her body. Again, was she cold or was she scared? Her hands reached for the hood decked out with bunny ears, pulling it over her head and tied it around the neck. Her nose lifted up. *What am I smelling?* The brake lights flashed not too far from her. *Burning oil. It figures that he doesn't take care of his vehicle.*

Standing perfectly still, she listened for any sound whatsoever. Nothing. She began to jog again, but the fluffy fabric on her feet didn't stop the sharp pain of the stones puncturing her feet. "Ouch! Oooch! Ow!" she whispered her outbursts of pain.

The crunching of leaves and sticks from someone walking caused her to jump behind a bush, barely able to make out the silhouette of a man up ahead. Then the footsteps became less and less audible as the person turned around and walked back. A tap-tap-tapping sound clicked, and then the sound of a gate opening made sense. Brucie ran up quietly, trying to see. By the time she got to the gate, it was abandoned but there was a distinct loud, buzzing sound.

She flashed her light around and saw just woods, rows and rows of trees. What in Sam Hill was that horrifying sound? No, no way. There is no way I just heard the roar of a lion." Her body shimmied. The roar got a little closer.

That was enough to prompt her to turn her around and run off as if she took over the role of the *Flash*.

Finally, back on pavement, she felt relieved but didn't slow down, constantly looking behind her.

Almost home, but as she looked behind to make certain a man-eating lion wasn't about to devour her, she slammed right into a man under the light pole by her cabin. They tumbled to the ground.

Sitting up for a second, she jumped up and started punching the man, then she delivered a karate kick.

Taking a stance before administering a final blow, the man threw out his arm while covering one of his eyes. "Stop! It's Riggins. Just stop."

"What are you doing hiding on my property? Are you stalking me?"

"What? Give me a break. No, I certainly was not stalking you." He removed his hand from his eye and squinted it as it watered. "You have some pretty powerful defense moves. I bet you took defense classes." He squinted his eye again as it watered more.

"Why yes, I did. My friend, Britanica, and I took classes. Good thing; huh?"

"Oh, yeah. Can't wait to tell the guys a girl gave me this black eye."

She giggled. "Well, what were you doing here?"

"Couldn't sleep, so I took a walk. What are you wearing? Is that some type of "Playboy" costume? Or Halloween costume?"

She snickered. "Pretty sure this costume covers up way too much for it to be a 'Playboy' bunny."

"Yeah, well, there's truth to that." He looked her up and down and it just hit him how funny she looked, so he broke out in hysterical laughter.

"Okay, 'full of Malarkie', I deserve that, but this is so comfortable, and the fabric is so soft.

This must be how rabbits feel."

He shook his head. "So what were you doing?"

"You're not going to believe this. I followed that truck down a path through the woods and it went through a gate with high voltage, which made it impossible to go any further. And then I heard a roar. Not just any roar, mind you, it was a lion's roar. I listened to make sure I wasn't making that up in my mind, but it was a real roar, so I ran like the dickens and that's where you came in.

"Now that I think about it, it's really strange that you are right outside of my cabin. Don't tell me it's a coincidence or I'll tell you you're full of your last name."

"That never gets old, Bruce."

Her hands formed a fist on her hips and those lips puckered tightly.

"Before you go all *Hulk* on me, I think you should get inside and lock up. I'll walk down there and see what I can see and hear what I can hear. Maybe I'll stop by tomorrow and let you know what I find. Maybe."

"Oh, how nice of you to 'maybe' let me know what's going on. Don't bother. Someone has to get to the bottom of what's going on around here, and it looks like I'm the only one willing and the only one getting somewhere."

"No! You need to leave this alone. Otherwise, I will inform the authorities that you are interfering with their investigation."

"Oh really?" She bent her upper body toward him, kept her fists on her hips and her mouth stretched open. "For your information, Malarkie, I have friends in high places: judges, prosecutors, sheriffs, etc., etc., and etc."

"Wow! Well, I have friends in even higher positions. I'm talking as high as you can go."

"Once again, you're full of your last name."

"Whatever you say, Bruce."

She inhaled deeply, holding her breath before exhaling. She shot him a dirty look, went into the cabin, slamming the door so loud sleeping birds fluttered out of the trees.

As hard as he tried, the look of her wearing what looked like child pajamas made him laugh hard for several minutes, then he walked off.

Steaming mad, she walked back out, stomping to where he stood on the road to give him another piece of her mind. But as she reached the road, Mr. Kinnard was walking past with his dog.

"Brucie, is that you?" he asked, squinting and blinking his eyes.

"Oh, hello. What brings you out this time of the night?"

"I should ask you the same thing. Are you hiding Easter eggs? Easter isn't for many months."

She realized how silly she must look, and her hand felt the bunny ears attached to the hood.

She gave him an embarrassed expression. "It's really soft and comfortable," she said and cast her eyes down. "Well, I'll talk to you soon. Bye Wylie." She patted his head and ran into the cabin with a red face, not from the cold but from embarrassment.

Eight

THE TRIAL SEEMED to go on and on and on. Brucie looked around for the glaring eyes she was expecting and Riggins' smug look, but he wasn't in the courtroom today. Instead, there was a really good-looking guy staring at her. When her eyes met his, he smiled. It made her nervous but mystified. Much better than looking at Riggins' face of arrogance that she would just love to punch right off his face. Ooh, he made her angry, just thinking about him.

It was lunch break. As Brucie walked out the door, that good-looking guy walked up to her.

"Hi there. My name is Sam." He extended his hand.

"Hello. My name is Brucie." She smiled while shaking his hand.

"I'm going to grab a bite and wondered if you'd like to accompany me. I'm new in town."

"As nice as it sounds, I don't know you and I'm not comfortable going anywhere with a guy I just met."

"How about this? Since we're both obviously going to that diner across the street, maybe we could walk together, and maybe if it is crowded, we could share a table."

"Wow, you work fast. But I guess it won't hurt, so sure, let's try that."

They looked around and the diner was crowded, so they sat at a table together. He offered to pay for her lunch, but she refused. Brucie found he was easy to talk to.

"So why are you observing the court proceeding?"

"I was meeting a friend here, but he hasn't shown up."

"Who might that be?"

"A guy named Riggins—"

"—Malarkie."

"Oh, so you do know him."

Her eyes rolled slightly, and her lips curved down a little. "Unfortunately, I do."

"Ouch! I take it you don't care for him."

"You take it right. He is full of himself, just like his last name."

"I'm sorry to hear that."

"So, are you interested in the outcome of this case as well? Why does it interest Riggins and now you so much?"

"I'm here to meet Riggins, and yes, he is very interested in this case for reasons I'm not at liberty to discuss."

Her eyes widened at that remark.

"Wait, you're the person who—as he describes you—is going to get killed or get someone else killed by interfering."

"You know, I'm a little bit tired of his interference. He has no right in accusing me of such codswallop since he is just as interested. At first, I thought he was one of them and possibly a murderer—the jury is still out on that one—but the way he treats animals, and a little sliver of a gentler side causes me to think he is just obnoxious and maybe involved unintentionally like me. I don't know yet. He just irritates me so much."

"Don't get mad at me, but I have to agree with him in a way—wait, wait, wait—" He held his hands up to stop the angry bull from attacking. "By that I mean, I would hate to see that pretty face of yours injured by this group of nogoodniks. It's pretty obvious they are not good people."

She glanced at the time on her cellphone. "I need to get back.

It's nice meeting you." She smiled reluctantly, not knowing him well enough to judge or misjudge his observation.

"Wait. Any chance we could go out for dinner or a drink later?"

"Not yet. I just don't know you." She turned and walked off.

Later that day, Brucie arrived home from work. As she pulled into her detached garage, Sam was getting out of his black SUV heading into the neighborhood bar just across the street from her place. He looked over at the same time as she did, and his face lit up and he waved. She squinted her eyes in wonder and barely waved back.

Of course, he ran across the street to speak to her.

"Are you following me?"

"No. I didn't know you lived here. You do live here?"

She slanted her head and couldn't help but crack a smile. "Yes, I do."

"I'm meeting Riggins at the bar. Hey, why don't you join us?"

"And allow that jerk to put me in a bad mood?"

"Oh, come on. We can sit by ourselves. Come on. Please?"

Sam had that *NCIS* Anthony DiNozzo charm. "I don't know," she said, shaking her head mildly.

"Please? Just for a few minutes?"

"Just a few, and I mean that. I'm going to throw my things on the porch, and I'll be right there."

He kept smiling at her as they walked into the bar. She said hello to Chris, the bartender, and neighbors as they walked up to Riggins.

Frowning, she said, "Full of Malarkie."

"Bruce," he replied.

She let out a sigh and went and found a seat. Sam stayed behind for a few minutes and spoke to Riggins.

"So what will it be?" Sam asked Brucie.

"I'll have a lemon-lime soda."

"Are you sure? A glass of wine could help you relax."

"No. I don't drink alcohol anymore because of my friend

Britanica. She pestered me so much, I quit. Not only that, I used to swear like a sailor, but she bugged me so much that I stopped that, too. Anytime I think about swearing or drinking alcohol, I see her face. It's a powerful face. She would get you to stop. I'd put money on her any day of the week."

"Really? She carries that much influence?"

"She sure does. I'm living proof."

He shook his head and snickered. Then he went to the bar. Brucie looked around and two women were hanging onto each one of Riggins' shoulders, laughing and carrying on. He was enjoying every bit of it, not to mention their cute figures wearing Daisy Duke skimpy shorts. Even Sam couldn't take his eyes off of them, to the point of leaning his head around to try and see under those shorts. She shook her head and frowned. Sam looked over at her with a wide smile. Realizing it was from watching the two women, his smile reduced to a mild, quivering smile at Brucie.

"Here we go." He kept his eyes on her as he gave her the soda.

"You know, it wouldn't offend me in the least if you want to go hang out with Riggins and those women. Actually, I have work to complete, so I think I'll just head home."

He quickly grabbed her wrist. "No, please don't go. My attention is solely on you. I promise."

"Maybe for just a few minutes." She took a good swig of the soda to help the time to move faster.

He put the beer bottle up to his mouth and chugged it down. Then he licked his lips. "So, you dating anyone?"

"Not many single men around, plus work keeps me quite busy, so no to your question."

"Good. Because I'm single myself."

"That's nice. So how long will you be hanging around here and where are you from originally?"

"For a couple of weeks and I live in DC."

Just then, a hoot and holler echoed through the bar. The women were getting tipsy and planting kisses on Riggins' cheeks. He was loving it. Brucie turned her head around to see Sam smiling wide, watching them, and staring really hard. She cleared her throat.

"Oh, sorry. That ruckus caught my attention."

"That's okay. I'm heading home to complete my work." The chair screeched as she hopped up fast, undoubtedly anxious to leave.

"Not already?"

"Sorry. Work calls. Besides, I think that scene over there with Riggins has your name written all over it."

"No, no. I'm really glad to spend time with you."

"Mmm-mmm. Maybe another time."

"Could I at least walk you home?"

"No, that's not necessary. I'll see you later." She took off so fast, he didn't have a chance to get out of his chair. Riggins' eyes followed her out the door before looking for Sam.

"What's all the fun I'm hearing over here?" Sam asked.

"What did I tell you?" Riggins jumped off the barstool and ran out the front door, causing the two women to portray shocked faces.

"What's that all about?" one of them asked.

"It's nothing. Now, where were we?"

They jumped into let's-have-fun mode and Sam dived in headfirst.

Riggins stood in the dark, watching Brucie walk home. When the door closed, he walked back inside the bar. He grabbed Sam by the shirt and pulled him to the side.

"This is warning one. Three strikes and you're out. I brought you out here for one reason and one reason only. If you don't keep track of her every move AND if you don't keep her safe—well, I'll just leave it right there. You can fill in the blanks on your own." He walked off, pushing Sam's body out of the way with his body. He left the bar. The two tipsy women watched puzzled, but Sam got them laughing in no time.

Nine

JUDGE SLOAN CALLED the attorneys into his chambers. "Look, this case is stagnant." He looked at the prosecution. "You need to come up with more evidence, or I will have to send the jury out to deliberate. I'm sorry, Mr. Schultz, but I have no choice. I give you until Friday."

"But Your Honor—"

He clanked his gavel and said, "Dismissed."

Ms. Pendleton shot her nose up at Mr. Schultz and smiled arrogantly.

Friday came and went. The trial was over with a big, fat "not guilty" causing much tension.

Brucie walked out of the courtroom in disgust. Sam was about a block away on his cellphone. She saw him hold the phone out from his ear as though someone was screaming in his ear. He shook his head and powered off the phone. He looked over at her just as she placed her stenograph in the trunk.

"Brucie." He waved and jogged toward her.

She wasn't in the mood, but waited, anyway. "Hi, Sam," she forced out in a solemn tone.

"Want to grab a bite?"

"Sorry, I'm just not in the mood. I'm going home, throwing on some pj's and watching my DVDs of *Sanditon*. If anything can make me feel better, Theo James has superpowers. You know what?" She looked up in thought. "Riggins reminds me of him. You hate him and then you love him. You hate him more and then you love him more. But I'll give Theo this: He actually looks good with short hair, but Riggins…nah, he needs to grow it out."

Sam leaned his head back and wrinkled his face. "You love Riggins?"

"No—heck no! He's the kind of guy you hate and love, but mostly hate." She laughed at her remark. Sam wasn't sure how he perceived it.

"Well, I'm coming over in the morning and taking you hiking. I won't take no for an answer."

"Wow! I like that take-charge attitude, mister. I'll be ready."

He gave her a nod, bent down and kissed her cheek, and closed the car door for her.

The next morning, Brucie sat up in bed wondering if she was too comfortable to get up and lay back down, all snuggly under the warm blanket, but then she remembered Sam was coming over in the morning. She turned on the percolator, jumped in the shower and dressed in hiking clothes, hair up in a cute ponytail. Like every morning, she grabbed a cup of coffee, flavoring it with a cinnamon-crème flavored coffee creamer. When she swallowed, her lips formed a satisfying smile.

Sitting outside on the back porch and checking text and email, she couldn't help but notice the crispness in the air. She laid the phone down and, with her head back as she sat looking out over the lake in her rocking chair, she enjoyed the peace, fragrant, crisp air and songbirds singing away. She hadn't had time to enjoy life's simple pleasures with the trial going on. It just felt good, and she sighed with gratefulness.

I haven't seen my adorable furry friends lately. I hope they're okay. After a minute or two, she swore she could hear a hooting and hollering, but it was wishful thinking. She kept looking around the lake, and coming from around the curve Riggins' boat floated into the open and the chimpanzees were jumping up and down excitedly at a fish he caught. They wore life jackets. It was adorable.

"Not again." There he was, shirtless, that very lean, muscular and toned body shouting at her, "Look at me. Look at me." And she couldn't stop looking.

———

Sam rang the doorbell, but there was no answer, so he walked around to the back and saw Brucie's eyes glued to Riggins while she sat on her back porch. *Is she smiling?* Even her hand made a cover over her eyes from the sun glare that shined onto the back porch, so she could see him better. She had no idea Sam was standing there.

He cleared his throat. "Hello there."

Her hand went to her heart. After a deep exhale, she answered back. "Hello to you, too. Man, you scared me." She laid the cup down on a side table and walked out the porch door to the side of the backyard where Sam stood. And she wasn't expecting him to do what he did. He pulled her in close, bent down and kissed her so satisfyingly perfectly.

The chimpanzees noticed her and began jumping up and down, hooting and hollering loudly.

She pushed away and looked over at them. Riggins was staring, but not smiling at all. She waved and yelled hello to the chimpanzees.

"Bogie, Bacall, I miss you terribly. Is your mean caretaker keeping you under lock and key?"

He just sat there with a disgruntled expression. She waved goodbye to the chimps and she and Sam walked off hand in hand. She didn't hear it, but Riggins used some not so nice words as they left.

Brucie brought Sam to Britanica's favorite spot on Chute Pond. They slid down the waterfall that ended in a small pond. After about twenty minutes, they hiked back, wet and chaffing. Brucie enjoyed every minute of her time with Sam, and he seemed genuinely happy spending time with her. When they got back to her cabin, he tried everything he could think of to get her to invite him in. She didn't budge. He pulled her into his arms and kissed her passionately, and they kissed for minutes. She pushed away with a really big smile and went into the cabin.

Sam, on the other hand, wasn't satisfied with the outcome and changed his clothes right outside of the open door to his truck across the street at the bar. Riggins was watching from the bushes, disgusted with what he saw. *I'd like to beat that jerk to a pulp.* He was using words he hadn't used in a while. Boy, would he get the lecture if Britanica was around, so he managed his speech for her sake. He loved her like a sister, one he never had and one he wished would have been her. Now calm, he began to walk over to the bar but stopped and watched Sam and one of the Daisy Duke girls get in his truck and speed off. She was almost sitting in his lap.

"What's the use of keeping him around? It's not like he's keeping watch on Brucie. She is most certainly not out of danger."

Once again disgusted, he turned around and went home. Bogie and Bacall were excited to see him. "I have an idea, guys. How about tomorrow I let you go visit Brucie? We'll make it look like you escaped. How about it?" His head looked back and forth, waiting for a reaction.

They both started nodding their heads up and down hollering their approval. He pulled them into his arms and kissed their cheeks. Then he pulled his head back and said, "P.U. You guys need a bath. Well, we'll get to that soon. Let's go see what we have for dinner."

They bounced their heads up and down and gave their addictive chimp smiles.

After a shower, Brucie sat on the couch and read some texts. "Let's meet tomorrow at LaVerne and Gail's diner, to go over wedding arrangements. I'm craving their omelets. Aren't they the best you've ever eaten?" Britanica asked.

Both Emmy and Brucie replied that they would love to.

That night, while Brucie slept soundly, a few men were walking around the houses on S. Shore Drive, trying to look into the windows and unsuccessfully at Brucie's cabin. She kept the shades pulled down in the evenings. These men were intent on finding someone. Something. Motion lights were popping on up and down the street.

A shot exploded through the air. Then shouting. Brucie jumped up in bed. Riggins jumped up in his bed. The sound of the gunshot was loud, and many lights went on in the homes on the street.

Brucie ran to the front window and peeked out. There was still shouting. She threw on slippers and a robe without tying it closed and ran outside. Her feet scuffled to the road. She looked down the street both ways and saw a figure standing on the road. Realizing she forgot something, she ran back inside and got her gun and ran down to the figure of a man, shaking inside not knowing what she would find.

As she arrived beside the man, so did Riggins.

"What happened?" Riggins asked Mr. Kinnard. Wylie, his dog was circling around him, agitated, nervous.

"Wylie, calm down. It's okay, boy. Good boy." Mr. Kinnard patted his head. "Found a man sneaking around my house. I fired a shot into that tree over there to scare him off. He'll think twice before coming back to my house."

"It was probably too dark to provide a description of the man; right?" Riggins stared into Brucie's eyes while waiting for an answer. It made her uncomfortable and she started darting her eyes around and swaying mildly. Her baby doll gown was revealed since she forgot to tie the bathrobe. When she glanced down, her gasp was heard by both men.

"Sorry. I ran out of my cabin without thinking clearly and forgot to tie my robe."

"If Mr. Kinnard was one of those criminals, you could have

been killed. Why do you risk your life unnecessarily? You should have stayed inside," Riggins snapped.

Her mouth puckered tightly, but she refused to give him the satisfaction of replying. She turned toward Mr. Kinnard. "So, did you see the man?'

A softened smile appeared on his face, and he answered. "No, it was too dark. I saw him scatter through the trees across the street, but that's all I got."

"Mr. Kinnard, I will stop over tomorrow and give you my cell number. Next time, for your safety, call me before stepping outside of your house. It is far too dangerous and you're lucky to be alive. These aren't good men. They have and will kill again if any of us gets in their way."

"First off, Mr. Kinnard, I agree with Mr. Malarkie. And secondly, who do you think you are throwing orders around, Agent Malarkie, emphasis on full of Malarkie? And what do you mean by saying they have killed somebody? How would you know that?"

Mr. Kinnard stood between them, holding his arms out. "Okay, you two, we're on the same side here. This grumbling isn't going to help any of us. Now, shake hands and let's work together, not against each other."

"You're right, Mr. Kinnard. I apologize." Brucie stood tall with a blank expression and extended her hand toward Riggins. "Truce."

Riggins copied her moves and agreed. "Truce."

He left before answering Brucie's questions. They all walked back to their homes and went back to sleep.

Riggins stopped before going down his dirt road and listened, looked around and thought to himself, *Gosh, she looked ravishing in that nightgown. Why does she irritate me so? So, so much. I wonder if she knows just how cute those fuzzy slippers look on her.* He smiled with affection.

Ten

THERE WAS much laughter as Brucie, Britanica and Emmy walked into LaVerne and Gail's diner. "Hi Mr. Kopaetz. Hello Ms. Hoffmander. Sharon, good to see you. How's the grandchildren?" They all stopped and addressed the people as they went to a table.

"Hot chocolate coming your way," Gail yelled out with a hand-held up to her mouth. They always ordered hot chocolate every time they came for breakfast.

"You guys, I didn't eat dinner last night in anticipation of my omelet this morning." Grrrr went her stomach. She patted it and said, "You behave. I'm working on it," Britanica said.

Emmy and Brucie giggled.

"So, how's the wedding arrangements going?"

"Done."

"Done?" Brucie asked Britanica.

"Yes. All we need to do is go for our last fittings and everything else is arranged. Mom and her friends have had a ball making arrangements, but now Mom's in full winter festival mode. Get ready, she's coming for you both."

They laughed. "I don't mind. It sure was fun last year, and I've been caught up on all my classwork. Webster is already bracing himself for the call. He's been so busy with both jobs," Emmy informed her.

"I just love my brother," Britanica said with an affectionate smile.

"Yeah, well, he loves you too." She rubbed Britanica's forearm.

"Hey, when are your parents coming back?" Britanica asked Brucie.

"I don't know. They're traveling and haven't even been to their home in Florida."

"That stinks. I bet you miss them terribly."

"I do, but I also understand. They deserve to travel. I hope when I have children, they don't try to guilt me when my retirement comes, and I do the same."

"Children? So how are things going with Sam?" Emmy asked curiously.

"Going well. I have a lot of fun with him. And isn't he just spectacular to look at?"

Sitting behind her, Riggins was reading the paper that covered his whole upper body and face. His eyes snapped closed for a second and he cringed at hearing her speak about Sam.

But at the same time, Brucie couldn't dispute the look Britanica and Emmy gave each other.

"Let's hear it. We are best friends and should not be talking about one another behind one of our backs."

"Geesh, Brucie, you're right. Truth serum time." "I'm ashamed that Emmy and I discussed it between ourselves, instead of bringing it to your attention. That won't happen again." They extended their arms as though they held swords and made the "clanking" sound with their tongues.

"I don't know the circumstances of your relationship, if you're going "steady" or what, but we have seen him around town with some really knockout girls. They look more like girls than women. They looked pretty cozy." Britanica's eyes drifted down as she made that statement."

"Really?" Brucie sat in thought before answering. "Well, truth is that we are not 'going steady.' What's the adult version of going steady, anyways?" Emmy and Britanica shrugged their shoulders.

"Look, I'm having fun, and if that is all it leads to, I'm good with that. He is a flirt, but if I plan to make it more, that would definitely have to change."

"He is quite handsome. I heard that Riggins guy is also very handsome."

Brucie's hands went around her neck, and she made the choking sound. "He is so arrogant, and he needs to grow his hair out before I would put him in the 'handsome' category."

"Well, I beg to differ," Britanica threw in her two cents. "What I mean is, I saw him down the street the other day."

"Beg all you want, sista. I know what I like in a man and he ain't that."

It was Britanica's turn to pretend to be choking. "You do remember I'm an English professor. That poor grammar hurt like sticking a knife in my stomach."

"First off, you're not a professor any longer and secondly, yeah, your overdramatizing is back. I missed that other character inside of you. Where's she been?'

"I think she possessed you, the new miss drama queen."

Emmy nodded in agreement, and then their food came.

"Okay, my truth serum time," Brucie said as she gobbled a huge piece of the omelet. "Sometimes I think I hate Riggins and other times I could fall in love with that jerk. I can't explain it or even try to. And he is very attractive, except for that full-of-himself, arrogant personality. But have you ever seen him with a shirt off?"

Emmy choked on her big mouthful and started coughing. After swallowing, she said, "No, I haven't, but how did you see him?"

"He was fishing just out from my pier. Oh-my-gosh, he looks gorgeous, but if you ever meet him, don't tell him that. His head is already the size of Big Ben. And if you get a chance, observe his proportioned-just-right Sitzfleish."

Britanica and Emmy gave each other a look. It was killing them to hide their friendship with Riggins, but it was for Brucie's safety.

"Can't believe you used a word I'm unfamiliar with. Just what is Sitzfleish?" Britanica couldn't wait to find out.

"It's a German term for buttocks."

"Ahh, yes. I have noticed. Don't breathe a word of that to Gene."

"And he has a jaw of granite, features that look like they were chiseled by Michelangelo himself. Jerk, he knows it, too."

"From what I heard, Brucie, he is nothing like a jerk," Britanica couldn't help but dispute.

Brucie waved her hand. "Yeah, yeah. Oh, and guess what?"

Britanica and Emmy raised their hands.

"When he touched me, did I tell you what I felt?"

"Butterflies," Emmy said with a wide smile.

"Nope. I felt those murder hornets."

Britanica slapped her arm. "You lie. You meanie."

"I just made that up."

"No kidding," Emmy interjected sarcastically.

Emmy rubbed her hands together. "But back to you, Britanica. I got you now. I won't mention how you observed Riggins' Sitzfleish." Emmy busted up laughing. "And when the time is right, I'll collect on my bribery." Britanica swirled her fist around and laughed.

Riggins couldn't help but smile at the conversation. *Should I grow my hair out?*

"Truthfully, I find it hard to believe any guy could look as good as Webster," Emmy interjected proudly.

"And Gene," Britanica added.

"Well, you're both right, but I think Riggins could give them a run for their money, or at least equally compare. And add Sam to that list. Who knew our little towns had the most gorgeous men in the world?" Brucie answered, meditating on her words.

Just then Riggins threw money on the table, laid down the

paper and screeched his chair as he strode out of the diner, telling Gail goodbye and a few of the customers on his way out. But first he yelled, "Ladies," as though he was tipping his hat.

Brucie's face turned shades of red, pink, purple and repeated. Her hands covered her warm cheeks, and she felt the changing temperature. "That jerk was listening this whole time!" Egg sprayed out of her mouth. Emmy and Britanica cringed as they wiped their faces. They broke out in a big laughing fit, and all Brucie could do was follow.

"Hey, how about you come to my house for lunch after church tomorrow and let the guys do guy things?" Brucie asked.

"That sounds like a plan," Britanica replied.

"I don't know why, but I get so tired after church and end up taking a nap when I get home. But it sounds like too much fun to pass up. I'm in," Emmy added happily.

"Are you feeling all right, Em, or are you bored with church?"

"Oh, no. Nothing like that. I'm just literally tired. Nothing to worry about." She yawned.

They both looked suspiciously at her but kept silent.

Around 7 p.m., a loud commotion was right outside Brucie's back porch. She grabbed the gun and looked around before opening the door. She spotted what was making all the noise.

"Bogie! Bacall! You quit tormenting that cute chipmunk. Get in here." She opened her door, and they used their knuckles to walk, looking into Brucie's eyes, as though they were trying to figure out if they were in trouble. "You okay, Alvin?" she said to the chipmunk. It stopped and looked around, then scattered into some rocks.

Brucie closed the door and stared down at them. She placed hands on the hips and spouted, "You know what this means, don't you?"

They both made low sounds of whimpering.

"It means your horrible caretaker will have to come and pick you up. And do you know what that means? That means I have to stand there, embarrassed, after what I said at the café, and he had the nerve to hide behind that stupid paper and listen. Do you know how exasperating he is?"

They whimpered again not knowing what to do.

"Enough of that. Can you two have a popsicle?" They made a mild screech and clapped their hands.

"Wait." She pulled out her phone and searched for answers. "Looks like you can." She bent down and tickled their necks, and they giggled in chimpanzee language. Then they sat at the table and licked their popsicles. They kept pulling it down and looking at it, smiling big, wide grins.

A knock at the door sounded.

"Ugh. Here we go. Come on. Oh, wipe your hands." She rubbed their hands with a paper towel.

They stood to attention. Still embarrassed by what she said at the diner, she opened the door, moved out of the way looking down at the floor, and signaled with her hand where they were.

"I figured they'd be here. Come here, you little pains in my butt." He smiled. Then he examined their faces and their red tongues. "What happened here? What did they get into?"

"They just had a popsicle."

"Are they allowed to have popsicles?"

"Do you really think I would let them have something that would be bad for them? Besides, they are organic and pure juice." She crossed her arms and leaned against the door waiting for him to leave.

He looked at her face and pressed his lips together snorting a laugh.

"What?"

Riggins pointed to her face. She reached up and wrinkled her brows. "What? Do I have something on my face?"

He touched the spot on her face gently. It made her shiver; she didn't know why.

"It's chilly," she said, avoiding her thoughts. She wiped the juice off that spot, but the red tongue was a lost cause.

He glanced around and saw chocolate pudding, cake and candy

from the kitchen to the living room. Even pieces of candy had fallen around the coffee table. His eyes grew big. "You didn't let them eat chocolate, did you?"

She re-crossed her arms and tapped her foot without realizing it. "Leave. Just leave." Her arm swung out and her finger pointed out of the door.

"Okay, Bruce."

Her face was bright red in an instant. She maneuvered her foot under his leg, and he fell. She crossed her arms and gave a smug look.

He jumped up, and as fast as lightning lifted her and threw her on the couch. He started to walk away, and she somehow pulled him back on the couch. Next thing she knew, she rolled over on top of him. They wrestled, and funnily enough, he wrapped his legs around her head, and she wrapped her legs around his head. Neither giving up nor knowing how they got into this position. Everything happened so fast. Her face was squished together, and she was getting madder and madder. Words burst from his mouth. "Truce?"

She, still steaming but realizing she was stuck, huffed out the word, "truce."

They both hesitantly eased their legs. When she jumped off the couch, she pushed him back down and moved out of the way. All he could do was laugh. Best efforts to resist the urge, a spitting laugh broke out of her as well.

"Get out of here, would ya?"

With a pleased smile, he grabbed the chimps' hands and walked away.

"Hold on, there. Give me a kiss you two." She bent down on her knees, and they ran to her.

After kisses on the cheek, she pushed them forward, waving as they walked away. They kept looking back at her. She avoided eye contact with Riggins.

His smile was rather odd. He appeared to look with fondness at Brucie. Adjusting his uncomfortable stance, he formed a blank expression. *Never let them see your thoughts*, pounded in his brain from countless hours of training.

———

The following weeks, things seemed to quiet down a little. She and Sam had been going out a lot. He kept pushing her to let him get closer in every way. She didn't trust him in any way, but she was having a good time. They drove to Green Bay to watch the Packers. They had a blast, except Sam got plastered, so she drove them home. His arm was around her shoulder as he stumbled. Her head dropped and breathing was heavier. A scorned expression lingered. Once she got him to the truck, he fell over and passed out. Strike one in her eyes.

When she arrived at the cabin, he was out cold. Her head dropped and she rested her forehead against the steering wheel. Now what was she supposed to do? She hopped out, looking around for answers. Riggins was sitting on his truck bed, talking to another guy. *Do I really want to ask for his help? Oh, brother.*

Her hands waved him down. He lifted his head in her direction and then looked around.

Certainly, she couldn't be trying to get his attention. Nobody else was around, so he mouthed the word "me" and pointed to himself. She nodded her head yes and almost cracked up at his response.

Will wonders never cease? he thought to himself.

"Um, I'm in a little bit of a predicament. Sam is out cold. He drank too much." She shook her head in disgust and pushed her lips to one side. "Any chance you would drive him home?"

"Sure. I'll leave my truck in your driveway until I get him in my house. Is that okay?"

"That's fine, but you're welcome to leave it here overnight and pick it up in the morning. I leave for work around eight."

"Yeah, that sounds like a plan. Thanks."

He moved Sam's truck out of the way, then pulled his into the driveway. Brucie waved her hand in a gesture to say thanks.

———

For some reason, Gene had a call just down the road from Brucie's house early in the morning. He passed her cabin and saw Riggins' truck. "What in the world?" he mumbled. His phone went to his ear. "Hey, Riggins' truck is sitting in Brucie's driveway, like it's been there all night."

"What!" Britanica snapped back. "I will have a talk with my friend."

"Oh no, you won't. Don't you dare. Maybe it is for protection."

"Yeah, maybe. I mean, she talks like she hates his guts. Must be."

"Brit, you can't say anything. It could be obstruction of justice."

"Hold on there. First of all, I hate lying to my friend. I would be hurt if they withheld information from me. Friends don't do that. And, secondly, the trial has ended, so there is *no* obstruction of justice."

"Okay. You have a point. I will talk with Riggins. Just wait until I talk to him. Okay?"

"Okay, you, you, wonderful husband to be." She made the words come out as aggravation at the beginning of her statement to trick him.

He smiled with affection. His love for Britanica was so deep that waiting for their wedding has taken way too long. Last year, he would have taken her to the justice of the peace, but everyone protested. Well, it's only a few months away, now, so he'll hang in there happily ever after. A loving smile formed on his lips.

Eleven

ON THE WAY TO WORK, Brucie waved out the window as she passed Sam, driving Riggins to pick up his truck from her cabin. Sam looked over at Riggins, who kept his eyes forward. "She didn't even smile. Looks like I'm in the doghouse."

"You can be a jerk; you know it?" He still stared straight ahead.

"Like you never get drunk?"

"Not when I'm with a lady. Is it that difficult for you to tell the difference between an easy target or a lady?"

Sam was in no mood to argue. His stomach was in no mood to live. He stopped the truck and ran to a bush to relieve his mistreated stomach. And now his head was protesting. He pressed a hand to his head while driving.

"I bet you would love to take a sick day? Sorry, Charlie, not today."

"The name's Sam." Hand still pressing tight against his forehead.

Riggins looked over for a brief minute, with a shake of his head.

They drove back to Riggins' cabin and made plans for the day.

Riggins threw on a camouflaged overall decked out with leaves and branches and a hat to match. Next, he threw binoculars on the chair. "Get changed and we'll work our way up to Flagstone's electric gate. We'll need to carry our weapons. You can get on one side, and I'll get on the other side of that road. I have a device that will detect any bombs planted around, and we need to look for motion cameras. He looked down at the two chimpanzees in his arms. "If these two hadn't escaped, they'd be hanging on someone's wall by now."

"You know, with this type of person who has no regard for life, I would love to hunt them in sport and hang them on a wall. What kind of person thinks hunting for sport is an actual sport? I mean facing them in hand to paw battle would make it more even. Weapons don't give these animals a fighting chance."

"What's the big deal? They're not killing humans. They're just animals."

Sam cowered in his chair. He was in no condition for hand-to-hand combat because the dilated nostrils and icy stare from Riggins was causing him a great deal of anxiety. Riggins threw the pair of binoculars at his face. Sam caught them just before they hit him. He dropped his mouth, then gritted his teeth, exposing almost all of them, but he was no dummy. Riggins' reputation was nothing to fool around with.

The more Sam brewed, he foolishly reacted to his own thoughts. "I thought you and Brucie hated each other's guts. Why do you worry so much for her safety? The trial is over." Sam was standing up straight with his chin held high, hands resting on his hips.

Riggins turned around slowly, head facing down toward the floor. His expression was blank. He walked up to Sam and stood over him about an inch from his face. He looked down into Sam's eyes and, in a normal voice, said, "It's absolutely none of your business whose guts she or I hate. The only reason you're on my assignment is because there was no one else available. You're here to watch over her and nothing more. Nowhere in your contract does it say to be intimate with her. What are you trying to prove? She's way out of your league.

"Let's just say you would like to remain an agent. So far, your performance does not meet up to the standards. If I were you, I'd focus more on that aspect of the job than your other hobby. Are we clear on that?" Spit sprayed out of his mouth, but he didn't raise his voice.

Sam stood his ground, but inside he was shaking. "Crystal clear, sir."

Sam thought about what Riggins had said while hiding in the bushes. Riggins was known for being a womanizer and excessive drinker when out with the guys, but he never let his guard down while on duty. Never touched alcohol, never fooled around with women on the job. Maybe Riggins made some good points. If he wanted to be a good agent, then changes in his attitude and work ethics needed to be made. But could he make those changes? Oh, how he loved women: morning, noon and night. How would he ever get himself to ignore such delight while on the job? This was looking like the impossible dream.

Sure enough, as they sat there, both of their heads popped up. A lion roared. They crawled around the fence without touching it because it was set up to shock the animals so they wouldn't escape. Riggins pulled out his phone. Sam answered his.

"Look over to your right about 800 feet. Use binoculars. It's a lion and it's leucistic."

"Excuse me?"

"That means it has a recessive gene mutation—which means it looks white," Riggins added, knowing Sam would not understand the meaning. He had taken many courses to fully understand why these rare animals were so valuable to sport hunters. He could never understand why Bogie and Bacall were of value to the hunters. They weren't rare. It didn't add up.

Brucie had told Sam that she saw a ghost of a moose. Riggins had thought about it when Sam mentioned it to him, and now it made sense. Exotic hunters. He could feel his face steaming like it would in treating his allergy problem. Sometimes steam helped to clear his sinus cavities. But taking the life of these beautiful creatures just to hang on their wall and brag, caused his blood to boil.

"Oh, wow," Sam spoke, quietly amazed.

"Somehow, they are managing to haul these animals here without anyone seeing. How are they doing that?"

"That's a good question. How are we going to get in there and find out? I sure don't want to tangle with a lion, not to mention what else they have in there," Sam replied.

"We need to take turns and watch around the clock. You go first and I'll take the night shift. I'll drop by and bring you lunch."

"But what about Brucie? I'm supposed to be guarding her, plus, we have a date tonight."

Riggins remained silent. He could have sworn he heard Sam gulp. It made him chuckle. "I'll check on Brucie and inform her that you won't be able to make the date. When you're done here, you need to stay with the chimps."

Sam's eyes rolled as he tilted his head up.

Riggins couldn't stop laughing, holding his hand over the mouthpiece. He cleared his throat. "Keep me informed of any updates and I'll see you at lunch. Do *not* fall asleep."

Sam's eyes twirled in the sockets. He needed to step up to the plate and show Riggins he could be a good agent, but the roar of the lion getting closer caused shivers to run, not walk, down his back.

An hour later, Sam heard voices. He peeked out of his hiding spot very slowly. Two of the Azarbaijan's were walking around as security guards holding rifles. Good thing they didn't have dogs because he would be spotted. As they walked back, he crawled low among the bushes and trees to follow them. They were at the gate. He pushed the binoculars to his eyes and tried to see what numbers they pushed for the code.

"Seriously! 1, 2, 3, 4, 5 is what they chose?" he whispered. He couldn't wait to tell Riggins when he brought lunch.

Not that he could eat a thing. There was no way his stomach would hold anything. His hands pressed hard into his temple, rubbing back and forth. "Oh, the pain."

He pushed his body up quickly and stood perfectly still. There it was. A shadow moved in the trees about 800 feet away. Binoculars to his eyes, all he could make out was movement and a whitish reflection. No sound, except a branch or two breaking upon impact. His body slowly slid down, and he looked in all directions.

———

Riggins walked up to Brucie's door in his usual attire. He rang the doorbell. She looked through the curtain. Her mouth dropped open and her tongue dangled. "Frickin-frackin." She opened the door wearing a spaghetti strapped undergarment and a slightly tight skirt. She couldn't help but wonder what he was doing here. A thought hit her, then, and her eyes popped open. Riggins stared at her, concerned.

"Oh no. You lost them?" Her face looked worried, and her eyes became blurry.

He reached over and gently grabbed her wrist. "No, no. They're fine. Really."

She blew out a heavy sigh. "Well, then, why are you here?"

"I just needed to let you know that Sam won't be able to make your date tonight."

Her lips pressed together, and she chewed on a small part of her mouth. "Is he that bored with me?"

"No, I don't think so." *You idiot, Riggins, be nice*, he scolded himself. "Just kidding. He had something important come up."

"Something too important to tell me?" She propped an arm against the door and tipped her head slightly.

"Look, it's not my place to say anything, but I can tell you it's completely legit." A half smile formed, and he added, "Nothing to do with girls."

She tried to act like it wouldn't bother her in the least, but he noticed her stance relaxed. He didn't mean to let his guard down, but his eyes drifted to her shirt and skirt and how they fit nice and snug. She kept herself in good shape.

Feeling uncomfortable, she cleared her throat.

His eyes blinked a few times and he commented, "I'll see you later," and he ran to his truck.

She continued to lean against the cabin door in wonder. Then she looked at her reflection in the window, wondering what caused his nervousness. *Huh*, she thought. *It sure looked like he was giving me the once over.* She walked to the road and followed his truck with her eyes as it disappeared down the long dirt driveway. Dirt was flying sky high, making it difficult to see the truck. When he was out of view, she walked back into the cabin.

———

"Take good care of these guys," Riggins told Sam. "Just imagine how they must have been treated. Bogie here," patting the top of his head, "had a cut on his head, blood splattering when I found him." Riggins turned his head because his eyes started tearing up and quickly his thoughts turned to anger. "I'm going in the gate. Keep your cellphone charged and nearby."

As Riggins left, disguised in camouflaged overalls, including a hat, he called Gene. He decided it best to bring in backup because Sam wasn't reliable. Not yet anyways, but he could see the change in Sam's expression after he tore into him earlier. There was a hint of hope that he started taking the work seriously.

"Give me fifteen minutes. I need to leave quickly before Britanica pulls it out of me. See you soon."

Riggins looked in through the window to see Sam holding the chimps. That made him feel better. He grabbed the other camouflage suit and waited for Gene to park in front of his driveway.

Gene and Riggins ran through the fence as it opened. Before proceeding, Riggins went over a detailed summary of what to look for, what could happen, and as much briefing as time spared. They moved slowly. It must have been two miles they walked before spotting lights ahead. Gene jumped back.

"What's wrong?" Riggins asked him as quietly as possible.

"I just saw a shadow of something along the fence line over there." He pointed and they both walked up slowly. Riggins placed his night goggles over his eyes and scanned the area in question. He saw it.

"Magnificent."

"What? What do you see?"

Riggins handed the night goggles to Gene. He pushed his eyes quickly against it and scanned the same area.

"I can't believe my eyes."

"An albino moose. It has a recessive gene that causes its fur to grow white with specks of brown in it, more commonly referred to as piebald."

Gene stared at him with a wrinkled forehead.

"Don't worry. I'm not as smart as I sound. I did an extensive study of rare animal breeds. It has helped me to understand the severity of the situation and urgency. They're pretty rare, as is most types of albino animals. You can look it up on the Internet and find the same info. This seems to be this jerk's specialty, specifically albino animals. How do you not feel guilty taking these beautiful creatures' lives? It irks every ounce of my being."

"I just wonder what else they keep in here."

"The reason these animals are rare is because they can't camouflage themselves against poachers and even predators. Poachers get good money for their skins.

"We need to fly over in the daytime. That's the only way to find out," Riggins added.

"That could be potentially dangerous. You know they carry weaponry that will be used to shoot down any type of aircraft. How do you plan to do this without getting shot down?"

"And then there's that. The truth is, like most missions we have to take the chance. I have to find out how they're getting these animals in here and just what kind of animals they poached before they bring in hunters."

"I hear you. We should probably leave before they send dogs out to patrol the area. It's weird that they aren't roaming around right now. Maybe Flagstone's guard is down since the trial has been dismissed."

"That's exactly what I was thinking and hoping."

———

Since Brucie's plans for the evening had changed, she decided to drive to the market in Lakewood and pick up some dinner. She drove slowly past Gene's sheriff car, wondering why it was parked outside of Riggins' dirt drive. The cellphone automatically went to her ear.

"Hey girl. What's up?" Britanica asked.

"Why is Gene's car parked outside of Riggins' driveway?"

"Oh, I have no idea. He just said he had to run out for a little while but would stop back over at my parent's house when he was done."

"I'm just being nosey. It really doesn't matter. He probably had to stop a fight or something, knowing Riggins."

"Being nosey seems to be your new profession. Just kidding. Don't get mad. Well, I doubt that he had to stop a fight. Riggins is very controlled and a really good man."

"Yeah, sure he is. Okay. Heading to the market. I'll speak with ya later, gator."

"After a while, crocodile."

They both snickered and hung up the phone.

Gene drove home and Riggins spent hours on the phone setting up a flyover.

———

Early the next morning, Riggins left a note for Sam explaining his plans. Sam dropped his head and swung it back and forth at the chimps. "Looks like I'm babysitting you two again."

They made some chimp noises and walked into the kitchen. Sam knew they were hungry.

"Here we go. Instructions for your breakfast." He plopped them at the table, put bibs around their necks and handed them their breakfast. He sat down across from them, leaning his head on his hand. It felt heavier than usual. Chimp sitting was not his idea of being an agent, but if he ever wanted to get better jobs, he needed to step up to the plate. "Think he'll ever see me as an agent —not just in name only but in action?"

He looked over at the chimps and they whimpered while eating. They were so cute. They took a bite, looked at his eyes, and whimpered again. Then repeated that action over and over.

Sam suddenly thought about Daisy Duke girls. "Man, I wish I were hanging out with them."

His face turned white. There it was. The one thing keeping his mind off of his work: women. He couldn't keep them out of his mind. But being on the job, his training should help him focus on the danger around them instead of having a good time. "Man, I do have a ways to go." He shook his head hard and sighed loudly. The chimps stopped eating and looked over at him.

"Keep eating guys. I'm fine. Go ahead," he urged them.

———

"Agent Malarkie, this is Agent Banginci."

Riggins held his phone in front of his face and stared. "Who?"

"It's me, buddy, Dan."

"Dan! What are you doing here?"

"Got a call that this is a serious assignment. Dangerous. Just my style. And that I would be working with you, Commander."

"That is so great. Can't wait to see you. Where are you now?"

He could hear the humming of helicopter blades in the background.

"I'm coming up on a town called...Lakewood? Just passed a Super Value store."

"Ahh, yes. Keep going east. You'll pass a boulder painted white outlined in the state of Wisconsin. A red heart indicates you are in Mountain. Keep following the road for a minute or two. I'll shoot a flare in the sky to direct you to the landing area."

"You got it. See you shortly."

Riggins pulled into a clear spot, awaiting the helicopter. He could hear the humming in the distance. It was still somewhat dark out, but that should keep them safe with these goons having their guard down because of the not guilty trial. The blades spun louder, and the rotation was plain to hear. His eyes turned to view the sky from all directions. "There it is. Who could miss that muscle mass flying in it?"

When it landed and the pilot turned the engine off, he jumped down and headed toward Riggins. Riggins' face lit up, and he opened his mouth with a wide smile.

"Oh, man, I would have never guessed it would be you coming." They hugged. It was one of his best friends on the police force back in Michigan before they both turned into agents. "Dan Banginci, you really are a sight for sore eyes."

"Good to see you, Riggins. I can't tell you how surprised I was to find out I would be involved in a mission with you again. Talk about old times."

"I know; right? Hey, guess who else has helped out? The sheriff here."

Dan looked puzzled and shrugged his shoulders.

"Gene Andersand."

"You got to be kidding. We were the three musketeers. This is so cool."

"Yeah, and I'm one of the guys standing up for him in his wedding this December."

He patted Riggins' shoulder. "No kidding. Man, I wish I would have stayed in contact with you guys. My bad. What do you think about his fiancée?"

"Britanica? She's great. Beautiful, charming, angelic qualities and super intelligent."

"No kidding! I'm happy for him. I hope to get to see him before I leave."

"Well, we'll just have to make that a priority. I know how. He texted me a message that the bridal team is gathering at Mulligan's Bar & Grill tomorrow evening. Can you stay that long?"

"Oh, yeah. I passed it on the way here. I'll just have to figure out a way. Don't tell him. I want to surprise him."

"You got it. You can stay with me. Sam Peters is helping out with the case and staying at my place."

Dan's head leaned back, and he made this weird frown. "He's still an agent? I can't believe that. I would never trust him with my life."

"I'd like to say he's changed, but that would be a lie. It seems being a womanizer is his true goal in life. He can't seem to break away from his obsession with women. Anyway, we should get going before these knuckleheads wake up."

"Ahh, yes, you're right. By the way, you growing your hair out? It's a lot longer than I've ever seen."

Brucie's statement about how he needed to grow his hair out came to his mind. He shook her out of his memory and shrugged his shoulders. They were up in the air in no time.

The chopper flew as low as possible over the areas that were further out, not wanting to get too close to quarters until they had to. How often did anyone ever hear a helicopter go over this area? Seems never. The pilot followed the fence line, that seemed to have no end. It was sectioned off in areas. Riggins' mouth dropped and kept dropping. He was speechless at the variety of albino animals he counted.

What was odd was that there was a huge area of boulders, really high boulders, piled on top of one another. A driveway went up to the beginning of the boulders and came back out at the end. It actually looked like there should be a road that cut through the boulders. Now that they had inspected most of the area, the chopper went up to a higher altitude as they flew over the housing area. There were three manufactured homes. And as they suspected, men came flying out the doors, no shirt, rifles in hand. Some of the men fired off rounds at them.

The pilot flew them away quickly. "Well, now that we have been shot at, looks like we have legal cause to enter their premises without a court order. Let's get to my place and call in backup."

The chopper was on the ground in no time. They jumped in Riggins' truck and sped to his cabin. Dan and Riggins walked in laughing like old times, not even noticing Sam standing near the sink. They grabbed something to drink out of the refrigerator and started writing their federal raid plans in a notebook. Both were on and off their cells for hours. Finally, Sam cleared his throat. The chimps were napping.

"Oh, hi Sam. Didn't see you standing there."

"I've been standing right here since you came in. Am I not a part of this team or just a babysitter?"

"I presume you know Dan?"

Dan tipped his head in Sam's direction while in conversation on the phone.

"Have a seat, Sam, and I'll fill you in."

Sam slowly pulled the chair out and sat down very disinterested. He crossed his arms and leaned back in the chair.

"These brutes are planning a huge hunting expedition, right here in Chute Pond. Must be hundreds of acres they own. They have so many varieties of albino animals. It looks like they are set up for the big hunt any day now. We are going to raid the place this evening. They started shooting at us, so now we have probable cause to break in there. I'm starting to wonder if some of these local judges are in on this scheme. Why haven't they shown more interest in getting us in there?"

"Because there wasn't enough evidence to give them cause. Not guilty trial, remember?" Sam pointed out.

"That may be true, but if we could have raided the area sooner, we would have evidence. Something isn't adding up."

"Do I have a part in the raid, or am I just going to babysit?" He frowned.

"We're working it all out. When we get things set, I'll fill you in. If you want, you have a couple hours. Why don't you go visit Brucie?" He looked up at the clock on the wall. "She could be home by now. You deserve a break."

With a forced smile, he said, "Ah, gee, thanks." But he was gone in a split second.

Just before Sam pulled into Brucie's driveway, the two Daisy Duke girls were sitting outside at the bar. They smiled big and waved him over.

"What the heck." He pulled into the bar parking lot. They jumped up and ran to him, embracing him and kissing his face. Their touch was feeling really good to him.

"Where have you been? We missed you," one of the girls proclaimed.

He grabbed them both and pulled them into his arms and squeezed. "Not as much as I missed you."

They headed into the bar. "What'll it be?" Chris asked.

"Just a soda for me, Chris. I have to work later. But please get my girls something. What would you like?"

They puckered their mouths with kissy face and ordered a beer. Between all the kissing, snuggling and laughing, Sam's phone rang. He didn't hear it. There was loud talking, the cue ball clanking against object balls and loud music.

Riggins slammed his phone down. "Go figure. I have an idea: Let's take these two guys over to a friend of Gene's just down the road from me. They seem to enjoy her company. Then we can meet up with the teams."

"Absolutely. Let's get with it."

Brucie had just stuffed a big piece of chocolate cake into her mouth when someone pounded on the door. Glancing out the window, her head dropped. She couldn't say "Frickin-frackin" because of the huge bite of cake in her mouth. She opened it with her mouth puffed out trying to hide the mouthful.

"Hello Brucie. I was wondering if I could ask you a favor."

She couldn't speak without cake dropping out of her mouth, so she tried mumbling. Riggins cocked his head and slanted an eye. "Huh?"

A finger tapped her mouth as she mumbled. He glanced at the coffee table and smiled sarcastically. "Ahh, dinner?"

She followed his gaze and placed her hands on her hips and scrunched her mouth together.

Dan had had enough and pushed himself in front of Riggins. "How do you do? My name is Dan." She shook his hand, and a smile formed.

"Move over, lover boy," Riggins expressed in a hurried tone. "I don't guess Sam is here?"

She took a huge swallow and moved her neck around like she was trying to force the food to go down. Finally, she spoke. "Didn't you notice his truck across the street?"

"I should've guessed. No, I was preoccupied. Well, he won't be much good to us now. So...I was wondering if there is anyway these two could hang out with you for a while."

Bacall was reaching for her. "Forgive me, you two cutie pies. I didn't mean to ignore you.

Of course you can stay with me." They tried pushing Riggins' arms away to get to her. Then they ran so she could lift them in her arms.

"I owe you big time."

"Yes, you do." Her sarcasm was well received.

"Not sure how long we'll be, but I hope not too long."

"Okay. I enjoy their company. And I enjoy the fact that you owe me. Ta-ta."

She closed the door and Dan's face was in shock. "Who...who is that knockout?"

"Brucie Clark. She's been going out with Sam."

Dan's expression was priceless. "Say it isn't so."

"It's so."

He shook his head in a confused state. Both men turned into full-gear agent mode.

Twelve

AFTER THE MEETING, Riggins ran to the market to pick up a bouquet of flowers to show his gratitude to Brucie for taking care of the chimps. Dan hung out at Riggins' cabin, and Sam was still at the bar.

Coloring with the chimps, blue mouths and tongues from blue raspberry popsicles, a knock softly pounded on the door. Brucie jumped, forgetting that Riggins was coming back. "Stay here," she ordered the chimps in a very loving, with adoration tone of voice. They shook their heads as though they understood.

As the door opened, a bouquet of flowers was in front of his face. "Why thank you, Sam."

He moved his head around the flowers enough for her to see his face. He raised his eyebrows up a couple of times and held a silly grin.

"Hate to disappoint you, but it's just me."

Her cheeks puffed out with puckered lips. "Sorry, I just never put you and holding a bouquet of beautiful flowers together. A beehive would be more your style."

He tilted his head and frowned slightly as he handed them to her. It was a full moon, and he could see its reflection in her eyes, a glow sheathing her. It was an enchanting scene.

"Thanks. They are beautiful. But I hope you don't think this covers the 'I-owe-you-bigtime statement you made earlier." She cracked a smile. "Come on in."

His wide eyes and slightly dropped mouth made Brucie giggle.

"Blue raspberry popsicles, all natural," she told him before he had a chance to throw out accusatory remarks, as if she would do anything to hurt these two treasures.

His eyes looked down at her hands and back at her face to see a blue tongue as she spoke. It was all he could do but break out in a laugh. "If I didn't know better, I would think you were eight years old." He noticed her pupils constricting and waved his hands fast. "But I think that is an adorable quality."

Her head leaned back and bobbed up and down for a second. She wasn't buying it. Nope, not at all. "Okay, full of Malarkie, get your children and get out before World War III strikes."

His features were completely innocent and sincere. "No, I really meant that."

"Oh, well, thanks." Her smile showed confusion. *What's he up to? He's never this nice.*

Flowers?

———

Back at Riggins' cabin Sam walked in. He looked around for Riggins and ignored Dan's presence. "Where's Malarkie?"

"He went to pick up the chimps from Brucie. Since you were at the bar, he needed someone who would focus and keep them safe. You didn't fit that description and he expected you back hours ago."

Sam dropped his head and sucked in his lower lip to bite on it. He did it again. Women before his assignment. No conversation needed. He walked out the back door, shuffling his feet.

Hooting and hollering, the chimps ran into Riggins' cabin. They climbed all over Dan, and snorts and guffaws rang through the air.

"I love these guys," Dan expressed, still laughing. "What are you going to do with them when this is all over? No way could they live in this cold climate," he said, trying to talk and laugh, at the same time wrestling Bogie.

"Yeah, I know. I don't want them put in a zoo. They would hate that. They like the one-on-one attention. I don't know what to do," Riggins answered.

"Thankfully, you have me for a friend." Dan pointed to himself and continued making his case. "I would keep them. You know I live in Florida. I would build them a big play area outside and take perfect care of them. Paula and the girls would love them. I've actually been contemplating taking less dangerous jobs and maybe even a permanent position in an agency in Florida. These guys would get the best care and attention."

"That actually sounds perfect, except I've grown really fond of them, too," Riggins admitted. "To be honest, I've been considering moving here permanently. I have had a few offers myself. As far as one of us keeping them, we would have to go through all the channels and paperwork and apply for custody. Who knows how long that would take? They couldn't survive in this climate permanently, but I'll miss them so much," Riggins said sorrowfully.

Dan pushed himself up from the couch with a serious face. "You would give up working for the agency? Who's the woman? Come on, man, give it up," Dan asked.

Riggins shook his head back and forth. "There is no woman. Sheesh, man. Can't a guy just settle down because he likes the area?"

Dan's lips curved up slowly. "Sure, that's it. So, how long have you been in love with Brucie?"

Riggins' eyes widened, and his lips began to pucker. "Don't be ridiculous. She hates my guts and I'm not thrilled with hers either. Where do you come up with this stuff?"

"Maybe it's that twinkle in your eyes when you look at her, that's where," Dan said with a smirk.

"Is it just me," Riggins thought out loud, "or is she the most beautiful girl you've ever seen? Her dark, shiny hair is perfection, even when it's a mess. Those deep, dark eyes are hypnotizing, and the perfectly shaped mouth, I mean wow. And then there's that toned, lean shape of hers. How does she keep it with all the junk she eats?" His hand was holding his head up, leaning his elbow on the couch arm. Totally lost in thought.

Dan patted his shoulder. "That's a confession if I ever heard one. You're guilty as charged."

Riggins sneered.

"Come on guys," Riggins said. "You want to go play on your playground?" They jumped up and down and screeched their approval.

Dan watched Riggins' face turn red. He heard Riggins mumbling as they walked out the door.

"I guess you're angry with me," Sam said as he walked up behind Riggins, who was watching the chimps on the playground.

He didn't even look up at Sam's face. Expressionless, he answered, "I don't know if keeping you around is beneficial to any of us. Why don't you pack up and get a flight out of here?"

"Look, I deserve that. I didn't drink a lick of alcohol, waiting on your call. I guess it was too loud in the bar to hear my phone ring. I'm really sorry. If you give me one last chance, I promise to stay out of the bar and stay nearby until you need me. So far, it's only been one strike. You gave me permission to go out for a while, so you can't count this as strike two."

"I'm a man of my word, so be grateful for that. For your sake, you better follow orders to a "T.""

"Thank you so much. I won't let you down this time."

"I'll be in soon. I want to let these guys work off some energy for a while, then we'll go over the details of the raid tomorrow."

Sam's mouth dropped to his chin. His first real raid. The thought terrified him and excited him at the same time. He walked into the cabin and sat down across from Dan and tried to speak in a civilized tone to him instead of the jealous sarcasm he had done previously. He was finally going to be one of them. This time, Riggins will be proud of him.

Plans were being made. Dan and Riggins stayed on the phone, making the necessary arrangements. The raid would take place early morning before light to give the extra team time to get up here. They were coming from all over the country.

"Flagstone has to figure it was me flying over their property. My one-on-one with him after we found my dad murdered back then made it clear that I wasn't going to stop until he was behind bars. The man has no soul, so I didn't think a swelled face would affect him that day. Sometimes I wonder if he paid people to keep him out of jail. The fact they found chimpanzee saliva in his hand after they bit him, was pretty condemning evidence. Anyway, he's always known that my goal in life is to bring him down. I'm pretty sure he recognized me in court just that one time near the end of the trial. He stared at me that whole day. There is no way they could round up these animals by the morning and haul them out of there. But now they'll be waiting for us to make a move. We have no idea what weaponry they are carrying." Riggins spoke with frustration.

"I agree, but this isn't much different from any other mission we have worked on. But this is the first time we are dealing with animals, mainly predators, so that's a little concerning," Dan added.

"A team of specialists is flying in and will arrive tomorrow late afternoon. They'll handle taking care of and evacuating the animals. We have nothing to do with that part," Riggins added.

Bacall crawled up to Riggins and sat next to him, her hairy hand lying on his wrist. He smiled down at her. "I take that back. We will have everything to do with these two. Nothing scary or upsetting will happen to them." Bogie was wrestling with Dan, who could not for the life of him stop laughing.

Sam watched, feeling left out again, but as he sat expression-less, thoughts poured through his mind: *You haven't given these chimps the time of day. Actually, you have been annoyed with taking care of them, so suck it up and knock off the feeling sorry for yourself routine. Enough is enough*, he scolded himself.

"What are the plans with the chimps during the raid?" Sam asked, honestly concerned.

"Oh, yeah, what am I going to do with you two?" Riggins asked tickling Bacall. She was hooting and hollering.

"I would be glad to ask Brucie, if you'd like."

"Why not? I'm always making a pest out of myself. She seems to enjoy your company, so have at it."

Sam jumped up and took Riggins' truck over to Brucie's. He didn't even look over at the bar as he passed it. The bang of slamming the truck door caught Daisy Duke girls' attention and they started calling for him. He acted like he couldn't hear them and strolled up to the door and knocked gently. No answer. He banged louder. Still no answer, so he walked to the back, and she was sitting on the pier with her feet dangling and splashing in the water. Riggins would have noticed how adorable she looked.

"There you are," he said cheerfully.

She turned her head, no smile, nothing. "Hello," she said almost in a cold tone.

"I guess you're mad at me. I don't blame you. I'm sorry. Honest."

She looked into his eyes, just barely squinting hers. "Take your shoes off and roll up your pants so you can feel the refreshing, crisp water."

The amount of lines on his forehead expressed his thoughts, but he blew it, so it was best to follow instructions. His feet went in slowly and he sat up quickly with wide eyes and mouth. "This water is freezing. Aren't you cold?"

"I think it feels great. Just give it a minute."

She didn't see his eyes roll. "Not any better. I think I'll let them dry so I can put my socks and shoes back on."

Sissy, she couldn't help but think.

As he moved to grab a sock, it fell into the water. He cursed under his breath. Bending down to pick it up, a fish must have swum past at the moment and touched him. He felt it and the fast action of pulling his hand back caused him to lose balance. The splash was loud. His cursing was loud. His face was angry. He stood up straight shivering, not speaking, trying to think past the solid block of ice he felt like.

It was too much. Brucie covered her mouth and fell back on the pier, laughing, tried to stop laughing, hand constantly moving back and forth from her mouth. He stared at her, licking his lips over and over, face growing redder and redder, which only put fuel on the fire in Brucie's eyes. His expression was so hilarious that she had a few more rounds of outright laughter before she could catch her breath.

Stuttering, "I…I'm sorry for laughing. You…you just look so hilarious. Let's get you inside and I'll dry your clothes." She turned her head as she helped to pull him up with an occasional outbreak deflating from her mouth.

Brucie found a pair of her dad's lounging pants and a sweatshirt. It was too small and annoyingly tight on him, but it would have to do. He made it perfectly clear that he didn't want her to wash and dry the clothes because it would take too long. How many times did she have to turn her face away from him to hide the laugh. She handed him a nice cup of hot cocoa.

"Thanks. This is perfect."

Brucie sat down on the chair across from him, holding her cup in both hands while savoring the yummy cocoa. Slowly, her lips touched the lid of the cup. She pulled back and licked her lips. After a few good blows, she took a sip and sat back with a smile. As she watched him, he chugged his down like a glass of water.

"You're supposed to sip it and let the taste build up in your taste buds."

"Oh, I wasn't aware."

She noticed his lack of interest in being there, so she tried small talk until his clothes were dry enough.

Warm now, he remembered why he came here in the first place. "I meant to ask you if you would mind watching the chimps really early in the morning tomorrow. Something came up and I can't. Riggins can't either."

Her eyes stared at him like he wasn't even there. Then it hit her. "Just what do you have to do early in the morning? Aren't you on vacation?"

He meditated on what he would say before blurting something out that would make Riggins angry with him. "I'm actually helping him on a job, and we forgot about the chimps before agreeing to do the job."

Eyes staring hard into his, she said without moving a muscle, "That sounds rehearsed. But, if it wasn't for my affection for those two, I would tell you no in a second. Since I would do anything for *them*, I'll do it, but don't even think I'm doing this for you or Malarkie. Now, what time will you bring them over?"

"Five?"

Golf-ball eyes stared at him as she replied, "You're kidding; right?"

He just shook his head no.

After a long sigh, she said, "Why not?"

Thankfully, the buzzer on the dryer hummed loudly. She jumped up. "I'll get your clothes so you can change and get out of here. Since we have to get up so early, I think we both need sleep. Don't you?" she asked him with much sarcasm.

All he could do was nod. She had the floor, and he knew it.

Riggins drilled Sam when he walked in. "She seemed upset?" Riggins' face was of concern.

He didn't know it, but Dan was studying his reaction. He knew Riggins almost as well as he knew himself.

"Maybe perturbed. Five in the morning is a little early," Sam assured him.

"Man, you're right. How insensitive of me." He ran his fingers through his growing hair.

"She seems to love those chimps. She'll be fine," Sam added.

"Man, I hope so. That's it. I'm doing something really nice for her to make up for the kindness, even if it kills her. She always looks disappointed when she answers the door and sees me standing there. I'll ask Britanica at the get together tomorrow what I could do for her or buy her—or maybe pay her like a babysitter." He was pacing back and forth gently rubbing his head. Dan watched him with a growing smile.

Thirteen

HUMMERS, trucks, SUVs and helicopters met at a clearing down the road. Now all together, Riggins had the floor. He looked around the group with serious eyes, and a somber face. Taking control of a situation was one thing he was good at.

"This is a delicate operation. There are a lot of rare animals inside and a lot of them predators. Not one of those animals better be killed. These are some bad dudes. Killing people is just as easy as killing animals for them."

Sam listened intently. His eyes barely blinked. He rubbed his hands together in anticipation of the raid.

"Check your weapons, then follow me." Before leaving, he pulled Sam to the side. "Did it go okay when you left the chimps? Was Brucie mad at you?"

"I think she was too tired and forgot about it until she opened the door. She was wearing some fuzzy one-piece—looked like a bear pj's or something. Something an eight-year-old would wear." He scratched his head.

Riggins smiled to himself, picturing her in the pj's. *How does he not find that adorable?*

Back to the task at hand, he gave Sam his own personal instructions since this was his first raid. "I want you to jump out of the truck and hide near the housing. Walk up slowly in the bushes and check for any ambushes. Here, these are for you."

Sam took the night goggles and held them proudly. The teams jumped in the vehicles well-armed and followed Riggins. Sam jumped out and punched in the code to open the gate. Dirt, rocks flying up in the air, dusting and hitting him in the camouflage suit. And that, too, he wore proudly. As the vehicles sped off, he walked among the vegetation and trees, holding his rifle. He honed into his training over the years in preparation.

About 500 feet away, Riggins stopped the convoy, and everyone got out. They were all dressed in bulletproof uniforms. Riggins motioned with his hands for which way each team to go. He gave the nod and Dan busted through the front door. The rest of the team followed. It was dark, so they used flashlights. Blood pumping, heart racing, the game was on.

They walked into each room of each housing unit. Nobody was there. The men and women outside scouted the area surrounding the house. A man rushed in one housing unit looking for Riggins.

"Sir, the place has been abandoned. It seems as though they were aware of the raid and left beforehand."

"Yeah, that's what I thought might happen. When we flew over with the helicopter yesterday, they ran at us with weapons. Looks like we need to wait until it gets light so that we can assess how they hauled these animals in here in the first place. Please inform the team not to go into the fenced areas. There are many predators inside," Riggins instructed.

"Yes, sir."

Just as the agent left, a gunshot echoed through the housing unit. The agents ran out, using protection from bullets.

Sam yelled. "Over here!"

Riggins and Dan were the first to get to him. They both stood to attention. Speechless. "Are you okay?" Riggins asked.

"I'm fine, and so will this guy be. I purposely shot him in the arm so we could take him hostage and gain information."

Dan and Riggins' eyes met before he spoke. "You do know you have been shot in the arm, don't you?"

Blood was dripping down Sam's sleeve. "Of course I know. I just wanted to keep my weapon aimed on this guy until you got here."

Riggins walked up and patted his other shoulder. "Good job, agent."

Sam's face beamed with pride. "Thank you, sir."

"Somebody get Sam to a hospital. *Now*. I need another team to get the prisoner to the hospital, too, and keep watch over him. At least two guards around the clock. I'll get to the hospital after we're done here. Thanks everyone."

You wouldn't even know Sam was shot by the energy he felt at the moment. Dan and Riggins watched him climb into a truck, posture of G.I. Joe. They both gave a smirk.

Now that it was light out, they walked through the housing units searching for evidence, names, anything. What they found was filth and stench. Couldn't be humans who lived like this, but it was certain they were dealing with monsters, not people. They did an inch-by-inch search of the grounds to find clues to how they got the animals in without anyone seeing them.

A loud roar came from right behind one of the agents. He jumped sky high. His weapon aimed automatically. A lion stood just about five feet away in the brush. The agent's eyes didn't blink but froze in a shocked state.

"Don't get too close to those fences, agent," Dan said as he patted his shoulder.

"Over here. Over here," Riggins yelled. "The road leads right up to this huge pile of boulders, then stops. But something looks really off about the setting."

The boulders sat upon some tall, hilly areas that gave the impression of a mountain.

"There has to be an entrance somewhere. This is just strange the way it stops. It almost looks like fake rock right here," he said touching the area. Look around everyone. It's here somewhere."

In about thirty minutes, an agent yelled out, "I think I found something."

The rest of the team ran up. It was obvious there was an opening, but how? After about thirty more minutes, one of the agents figured it out. The door opened. It was wide enough for a semi-truck to drive through and constructed with fake material to look like rock. They held their weapons and placed night goggles on. It was dark inside. Cautiously, they walked around realizing the road was underground and must have gone on for miles. From the information Riggins found previously, they owned about five hundred acres.

"Good job, Agent Schnoopers, our very best snooper," Riggins said laughing. The agent always laughed at his nickname. "Let's take a few trucks to drive through. Keep your weapons out and be prepared for an ambush."

Riggins and Dan led the way in his truck. A hummer and another truck followed. They drove slowly, searching all around. They came to a dead end. Agents jumped out of the vehicles. Some of them stood guard while others searched the area to find an opening. Just like the doorway at the front, it opened the same way.

The agents gathered together and discussed how they got the animals in here. "Talk about a well-planned operation. Too bad they're on the wrong side of the law. Our agencies would be grateful for their ambition and creativity. Since they own all this property and only a dirt road takes them out of here, it was easy to sneak the animals in here. I can't get over how well their distorted scheme worked. This tunnel had to take years to complete. Pretty sure there is no documentation anywhere or permits for any of this. Dirty dogs."

———

Dan and Riggins visited Sam in the hospital just as he was released. His arm was in a sling.

"Mind if I hang with you and catch a ride home?"

"That's fine, Sam," Riggings answered.

They went into the captured man's room. He did not speak English. The guards stood watch.

Riggins pulled his cellphone out. "Director, we need an interpreter for this Azarbaijan prisoner." He continued speaking outside of the room. The prisoner lay in bed with a scowling face not facing any of them. Riggins spoke to the guards and got back on his cellphone.

"Agent Perez. How are you?"

"Special Agent Malarkie. I am well. It's been a pleasure to work with you again."

He always envisioned in his mind her beautiful brown eyes, eyelashes so long they probably needed to be combed. He couldn't dismiss the memories they shared in the past. "I have a huge favor. I'm running late and need you to pick up my chimps from a neighbor of mine and stay with them until after my dinner engagement. Pleaseeeee."

She chuckled. "You know I'd do anything in the world for you. Lucky for you, I've been informed about your mission. No one mentioned anything to me about taking care of those chimps, though. I have no idea how to take care of them. Shouldn't you get someone with experience to take care of them until you return?"

Riggins sighed. "Unfortunately, all animal caretakers are here specifically to round up all the animals within the fenced areas, mostly predators. I forgot to mention anything about the chimps since I have been caring for them. It will just be for a little while until I can wrap things up here. There are instructions on what to feed them lying on the counter in the kitchen."

"Well, this will be a first, but if I can handle men and women with weapons, I think I can handle a couple of chimps. Besides, when I met them a couple of months ago after you rescued them, they seemed to be comfortable with me. I remember how cute they were. Regardless, you will owe me, just know that."

"Thanks. I owe you. Please give Brucie my sincere apologies

and tell her I will make it up to her." He gave her addresses and pertinent information.

———

Brucie jumped off the couch when someone knocked on the door. She fell asleep with each chimp lying against each side of her. Hair in her eyes, a rat's nest building, she opened the door with a big yawn. "It's about time Malarkie."

She blinked her eyes at the beautiful woman. "I'm sorry. I was expecting someone else."

"It's perfectly fine. Actually, I'm here in place of Malarkie. I'm Deannie Perez and I came to get these two adorable monsters. Hello guys." She kneeled and held her arms out. They ran into them, screeching with joy. She kissed their cheeks. "I didn't think I would ever get to see you two again. Look how good you look." She pushed them out far enough so she could take a good look at them.

Brucie stared at this gorgeous woman with a strong, fit and toned body, beautiful black hair that went to her hips and a smile that should place her on a toothpaste commercial. "I don't feel right about letting you take them. Riggins didn't give me any warning. I'm sorry, but I can't let you take them until I hear from him."

Agent Perez pulled out her cellphone. "Riggs, Brucie won't let me take them until you give permission." She smiled at Brucie and made a comment. "Now, that's a person I would trust anytime. You chose the right caretaker. Okay. She's right here."

She handed the phone to Brucie. "Go ahead. He's on the line."

"Hello," she spoke quietly.

"Hey, sorry about that. I couldn't make it back and a—Deannie is helping me out. Thanks so much for your help. I will pay you back. I promise."

Clicking the phone off, she handed it back to Deannie. "Your name is Deannie?"

"Yes, but most people call me De Annie. I always have to say it rhymes with beanie, like beanie babies."

"How funny. My name is Brucie, and your name is Deannie. Does Riggins ever call you Dean?"

"Not since I slugged him."

She grabbed her stomach and fell over laughing. Her hand extended and she said, "It's been a pleasure meeting you, Deannie."

Deannie replied with a huge smile: "Likewise."

After hugs and kisses, the chimps left with Deannie. Brucie sat on the couch for a minute staring at the floor. "Could they be dating? She is gorgeous. Hmmm."

Her phone chimed to let her know she had a text. "Don't be late and dress up, just for the fun of it," Britanica sent. Emmy replied to the group text, and Brucie froze. "Oh, no. I forgot all about the get together. I better move it."

Fourteen

AFTER A QUICK SHOWER, she was dressed in no time. She threw on an attractive black, snug dress. Her heels were every bit of sexy. A dab of lipstick and she was out the door. I better send Sam a quick text to see if he's still coming. A ding sound verified it was sent.

A quick reply said, "I'll meet you there." She smiled.

The group arrived at the restaurant. They had a spot in the corner where they could talk and not be disturbed. If it was a contest for who looked the best, men and women alike, there would be no contest. They all looked great. While carrying on, Riggins and Sam walked in. Gene jumped up and hugged Riggins, then shook his hand.

"Glad you could make it. Come on and join us."

Sam walked over to Brucie. Her face stared at the scene in front of her, expression blank.

She looked at Gene and back at Riggins. Questions grew in her stare. Her eyes turned to Britanica and Emmy, not speaking but eyes pleading for them to tell her they have not betrayed their friendship to her. She was so puzzled she didn't even notice Sam's arm in a sling.

Britanica's hand flew to her mouth. She looked at Gene. "Oh my gosh, we totally forgot about Riggins."

He made the "yikes" expression.

"So you have known Riggins all along?" Brucie asked with fire burning in her eyes.

Flabbergasted, Britanica answered. "Yes, but we—"

"—pretended not to know him. You lied to me. All of you. Why? I don't understand."

All she could hear was mumble, mumble, and mumble as everyone tried to explain.

She bit her lip, then said, "Never mind. Real friends wouldn't make an idiot out of me." Out of the restaurant, she stormed. When she exited the building, she busted out crying. Britanica and Emmy ran up before she could get in the car.

"Brucie, we are so sorry. We didn't want to hide it from you. We were given strict orders to keep it secret for your safety. It seems those bad men had a grudge against you, and Riggins was scared for you. The less you knew, the safer you were. Please, it tore us up. I told Gene the other day that I was going to tell you. He asked me to wait until he could speak with Riggins. Then Riggins got tied up in—Aah, geesh, more secrets."

She stared at Britanica and Emmy, puzzled. Her hands went up. "What's going on?"

"Come back inside and we'll tell you. Please. We were so scared you would get killed.

That's the only reason we kept it from you." Emmy stood still just shaking her head in agreement.

They pulled her inside. She was hesitant. The guys were speechless, not knowing what to say. "Enough is enough. Tell her Gene. She deserves to know."

"Um, well…Riggins is the man for the job." He held his hand out to Riggins to take the floor. Riggins gave him a smirk.

"It was for your protection. I'm a federal agent assigned to a case of poachers, who have captured exotic and rare animals for sport hunting. I think you actually saw the white moose, yourself."

Her mouth dropped to the floor. At least that's how it felt as her fingers adjusted her jaw.

"They planned to hunt Bogie and Bacall. I rescued them. I just found out why. Now we are trying to rescue the rest of the animals. Zoologists from all around the world flew in this afternoon to prep and care for these animals and work on getting them back to a sanctuary habitat. Those guys in court were behind it but escaped before we could capture them.

"For some reason—and I don't know why—these guys are interested in you. They killed two of our agents a couple weeks ago."

"Hhhh," she gasped. "So I did see you bending over a dead body. That was one of your agents?"

His eyes blurred and he nodded his head.

"Did they know who you were?"

"Not sure, but I think they did, or do now."

"So, what are you doing here at this wedding group gathering?"

"He's one of my groomsmen," Gene responded.

Her eyes bulged and she couldn't speak. Just grunts came out.

"Please don't be mad at them. It was killing them, but I couldn't take a chance of those criminals knowing that you know me or any of these agents, except Sam. He is new to the scene. Keeping it from you may have saved your life," Riggins added to soften the blow.

"All I can say is 'Wow'!"

Sam rubbed her arms. She looked at him. "So you're pretending to date me so you can watch over me? And, what happened to your arm?"

"Yes, and no. It started out that way, but now I'm dating you because I just like you. I was shot, but I'm totally fine. Honest."

At first, she produced a sympathetic cast, then she didn't reply or move. Just trying to take it all in.

Webster looked out the window and saw Dan walk up. He nudged Riggins. Riggins looked.

"And I have a surprise for you, Gene."

Before Gene could turn around, he heard, "Hey, there, buddy." Gene snapped his head around, and the two men embraced.

"Dan! What…what are you doing here?"

"Working with Riggs. I couldn't leave without seeing you. Now, where's the bride?"

Gene turned his hand towards Britanica. "Dan, please meet Britanica."

She stood and shook his hand. He dropped his mouth and said, "She's your fiancée? Wait! Is this Peanut Brittle?"

He placed his arm around her and answered happily. "Yes, she is."

"Wow. You're just beautiful," Dan said, facing her.

Her cheeks turned a pink color. Gene kissed the top of her head.

Dan looked around. "Do all little towns have the most beautiful women?"

"And the most handsome men," Britanica added.

Brucie was glad the attention was off of her. She glanced over and saw that Riggins was staring at her. Feeling awkward, her hand brushed pieces of hair away from her face, and she started swaying nervously. He noticed and smiled. His eyes displayed a look of adoration as he watched her.

"I will be right back. Please order me a huge glass of—" she stared straight into Britanica's eyes before answering— "iced tea." She turned around and walked to the restroom, smiling with her back to them as she walked. Sam, Riggins and Dan watched her walk away.

"Who knew she could look like that? Wowwy!" Sam commented. Riggins glared at him, and Dan watched Riggins' expression. *He won't admit to having feelings for her, that stubborn head of his. But I know that guy. He likes her.*

The rest of the evening went well. The women sat at the table making small talk and the men stood in a circle talking in front of them. As the women took a few bites of wedding fare, Emmy looked over at Brucie and followed her eyes to Riggins. She was just staring. She nudged Britanica and motioned toward Brucie. Britanica turned back and shook Emmy's index finger with hers, smiling ear to ear.

"Man, that Riggins is a hunk of man," Britanica said matter-of-fact.

"Wha...What did you say?" Brucie asked.

Emmy kept her head turned to hide the giggle. "She said Riggins is a hunk of a man and boy do I agree," Emmy replied. "I mean, he looks like he just walked off the magazine of *GQ*, and actually, so do our men. That Dan is mmm-mmm yummy, too."

Britanica patted her heart. "How true is all that?"

"I'm the one who told Riggins to grow his hair out. So, you can thank me for that. That hair hanging over his eyes is quite sexy," Brucie added. She glanced over and saw Sam flirting with some waitresses. Her mouth formed a slight frown, and she brushed it off to *flirting again*.

"Listen, guys," Britanica said with excitement.

"It's our song. Come on. Belt it out," Brucie ordered.

"Wild Thing...You make my heart sing. You make everything groovy..."

They were cracking up as they sang. The guys stood, shaking their heads. Next, a saucy song played. Come on, you two. Let's Salsa," Brucie ordered again. Before they made it to the floor, Webster grabbed Emmy and Gene grabbed Britanica.

"If you're not going to grab her, I will," Dan said to Riggins.

"Paula will not like it."

"Nah, I'll call her after." He grabbed Brucie. They were having a blast. Riggins walked up and patted Dan's shoulder. "I know you hate my guts," Brucie tilted her head a bit and a smirky smile formed, "but this guy has nothing compared to my moves. Out of the way Banginci."

Dan let go of Brucie and Riggins moved in. The rest of the gang stopped and watched. Their movements were in perfect sync. "Now, that's a perfect match," Dan said. The gang agreed.

Brucie looked into his eyes and blushed. She didn't know how to react, but he twirled and dipped her enough to lose the tenseness her countenance revealed. Then they laughed and danced and danced some more. Sam walked up, standing like a statue. Brucie and Riggins glanced over, but neither was fazed. The whole restaurant watched them.

"Look out, *Dancing with the Stars*. Meet your new contestants," Britanica commented. When the dance ended, everyone in the establishment clapped. Riggins grabbed Brucie's hand, and they bowed, then laughed hysterically.

"Are you with me or him tonight?" Sam asked.

"I don't know. Are you with me or them tonight?" She looked in the direction of the waitresses.

"Well played," Sam answered dryly.

———

Gene jumped up and answered his phone as he moved to the exit door. It was too loud inside, and he couldn't hear anything. Britanica and Webster watched his facial muscles tense up. He was pacing back and forth with a heaviness. He came back to the door and yelled for Riggins and Dan. They walked out quickly as Gene clicked off.

"Flagstone was arrested for an illegal weapon in Madison a few days ago and released the same day. It was the same style gun that killed your father, Riggins. Forensics is pretty sure he's the one. Since he's had no prior arrests, it will take a day or so to check the prints. He is out on bail," Gene informed him.

"He'll run! He's not stupid enough to stick around. He'll be on a plane to who knows where," Riggins said as his face turned shades of red. He paced back and forth, staring at the ground. "I'm heading over there tonight," he said, running his fingers angrily through his hair.

"Riggs, he's not going to stick around there. Let's wait a day or two and find out. Gene can find out more," Dan suggested.

Riggins rubbed his forehead frantically. "I can't sit around and wait for him to escape." A tear dropped. He turned his head.

Inside the restaurant, the rest of the gang watched the scene outside.

"Wow, he's really upset. I think his eyes are watering," Brucie remarked.

"Oh my, he looks devastated. Maybe we should go out and try and comfort him," Britanica said.

"No. That will only embarrass him. Let Gene and Dan handle it," Webster instructed in a loving manner.

"Do you know what's going on?" Brucie asked Sam.

He shrugged his shoulders. "Not a clue."

Back outside, Riggins walked away fast as he walked toward his car. Tires squealed as he pulled out of the parking lot.

Gene and Dan walked back inside to bombarding questions. Gene's hands went up. "I just got a call from forensics. They arrested Flagstone on carrying an illegal weapon but didn't incarcerate him because it was his first arrest. He is out on bail. They are pretty certain this is the gun that killed Riggins' dad years ago. It was another poaching and murder investigation that Flagstone escaped without any convictions. Riggins is upset. Flagstone is probably on a plane to Mars right now. Riggins is going to check all flights leaving Madison and, well, looks like an all-nighter. We better get you gals home. What about you, Dan? Are you staying or going?"

He bent his head down and frowned. "What do you think? I have the chopper. The pilot had another mission and the department decided we may need to use it. Once we find out where Flagstone is heading, I'll fly him to that location. He has waited a long time to find this man."

The women were wiping tears from their faces. Brucie sat in thought why Flagstone and his men were after her and not Britanica. She jumped up from her chair and her face had frozen in fear.

"Bru, what's wrong?" Sam asked. Emmy and Britanica gave each other a smirk at his name for her.

I can't believe she lets him call her that. She won't even let us call her that, Britanica wondered.

Brucie bit her lip before speaking. "Don't ever call me that again," she said turning in his direction. Emmy and Britanica gave each other a high five with their eyes.

"I know why they're after me. One day I was jogging, and Mr. Flagstone came out of some bushes. He looked shocked. I didn't know it was him because he wore a big, floppy hat. But those eyes stared at me just like they did in court. Now that I think about it— Hhhh!" Her hands flew to her face and eyes of fear, big and bulging, stared blankly.

"What? What is it, Brucie?" Sam asked.

She dropped her hands and spoke without moving. "I think I remember seeing the same flannel shirt of the body that Riggins was leaning over. I didn't put it together then. In my mind, the man was sleeping. You know hunters stay out for hours. I naturally thought Flagstone was taking his turn to watch for deer while the other man napped. Plus, it was still dark outside.

"Why would I suspect anything? When I waved hello, he glared at me instead of a greeting. If I knew he just killed someone, would I be calm and wave to him? Surely, he has to know I didn't realize anything. So what changed?"

She thought for a minute. "I know now. Being the court reporter in the trial, he must have recognized me. He didn't have anything in his hands, so maybe he was hiding the weapon. I'm sure it's gone by now. But it did look like he was resting his arm on a shotgun. It was still too dark to know for sure."

"That's not the style of gun that killed Riggins' dad, though. Do you think you can remember where you saw him?" Sam asked.

"I certainly do. It was just down the road. I'd run a few miles and was heading home when he came out about a few feet in from that stump with the smiley face painted on it. Come on and I'll show you."

Everyone said their goodbyes and Brucie drove Sam to the location. It was dark, so they used flashlights but couldn't find anything. They would come back in the morning. Since everything was out in the open, Brucie drove Sam to Riggins' cabin. What a night. He kissed her with every ounce of passion he could muster up. She was hesitant but felt the need for intimacy at the moment. Insecurity was a little high and it just felt right. Now she would sit alone in her cabin and think about everything she just found out.

She walked inside, clicked the dead bolt in place and activated the alarm immediately. Her body felt shaky knowing those men may be after her too, and now she knew why. A thought hit her, and she ran into the bedroom, pulled a drawer open, and grabbed the revolver. The sound of the drawer slamming caused her to jump. *Maybe Sam would want to spend the night. I'm not in the mood to fight him off. Forget that idea.* She could feel her hand trembling.

The phone chimed. She ran out to the living room and read a text from Riggins.

RIGGINS

Don't worry. We're keeping watch out for you. You are safe.

She let out a sigh and dropped her head for a moment. Chime went her phone again. Twice.

BRITANICA

I love you, Brucie.

Brucie smiled.

EMMY

I love you, Brucie.

She giggled.

"I guess they did feel bad and were worried for my safety. How can I be mad at that?"

Changing into some soft, fuzzy pj's, she made hot cocoa and watched some television. What a night.

Just as she dozed off, the outdoor motion lights flickered on and off. Blue flashed from her alarm tower and through the crack at the bottom of the window. The squeak of turning a door handle stopped abruptly, probably because the person noticed the blue flashing light and ran off.

Fifteen

BRUCIE'S FINGERS typed to a new trial. In her mind, she focused on hopes Gene and Riggins would get the evidence needed to start a new trial on those rotten rascals. She stared at the person talking while typing, expression always blank. The bailiff approached the judge with a note, she couldn't help but notice.

"Excuse me, Counselor. I'm sorry to interrupt but I just received some news that requires we take a recess. I'll explain it to you in 15 minutes. Ms. Clark, please accompany me to my chambers."

She looked at his face to try and determine why he would need to speak with her, but the judge's face remained expressionless. When she walked into his chambers, the door clinked shut. She turned around and looked back.

"Brucie, there is no easy way to say this, so I'll hand you the note. Please sit," he motioned toward the chair.

Keeping her eyes on his, she felt for the chair handle and sat cautiously. Now hesitant, she peered into his eyes for relief. He nodded his head toward the note and leaned back on the desk.

She gasped and brought a hand to her mouth as tears trickled down her cheeks. Her head fell down, and she moved her hand to her forehead for support as she bawled. A tissue was handed to her automatically. She wiped her tears, but they just kept coming. The judge sat on the other chair handle and held his hand on top of her shoulder.

"I'm so sorry." That's all he could say and all he needed to say. "Do you need help packing up your equipment? There are plenty of preparations you need to make. I'm so sorry," he said as he choked up with blurry eyes.

"I think that's a good idea. If you have someone..." she coughed trying to complete her sentence..."who could move my equipment in a room, I'll have my office pick it up. I'll call them to see if they can send someone over now. Please send the bailiff to wait outside the door until I can make this call. I'll send a note with him. Thank you, Judge, for your kindness."

"Don't thank me. You know you're my favorite court reporter and a friend. Anything, anything at all I can do, you just holler. Please."

"Thank you. I will."

When he quietly walked out of his chambers, she called the office. "Hi Mindy. I need to speak with Clarice. It's urgent."

"Certainly. I'll get her right away."

"Brucie? Are you okay?"

She sniffled. "No, I can't say that I am. Can you send someone over to fill in for me? My stenograph is set up in one of the rooms. They would just have to ask the judge which room." Her words were a bit of a mess, but she held back the tears long enough to get the words out. Then, the dam broke.

"What happened, Brucie? What's wrong?"

"My...my dad just passed away from a freak accident in the woods. They couldn't revive him. The judge will make the call to stop the proceeding today if there is no one available. I just have to send him a note. The bailiff is waiting."

With a cracked voice, Clarice said, "You just go home and take care of everything and yourself. Just call the office and let us know how long you'll be gone. I'll finish the case for you. I'm so sorry, Brucie." By this time, Clarice was crying right along with her.

On the drive home, she called her mother. Finding it hard to speak for both of them, Brucie said, "I'm on my way home to make flight arrangements. I will get there as soon as I can, Mom. How did this happen? I don't understand."

"Nor do I. Nor do I."

After some texts to Emmy and Britanica, they showed up at her doorstep. She was too upset to call them and couldn't speak without sobbing. They knocked quietly. With red, swollen eyes the door opened. The three embraced and cried and cried and cried.

"We couldn't let you drive to Green Bay in your condition. You know we would do anything for you."

After sniffling in her tears, she answered, "I didn't want to impose on anyone like that. I thought about asking Sam but didn't think he would want to drive me that far away. So, I just figured I'd pay for long-term parking."

"Well, you were wrong as usual," Emmy added with a saddened, affectionate look on her face. Brucie nodded and turned her head down as a few tears dropped.

The plane took off. Their eyes were red from crying so much. When they walked into Emmy's house, Webster and Gene ran up with questions. "How is she? Is she going to be okay? How did it happen?"

"She's on the plane. As far as the other questions, I have no way of knowing. I forgot to call Donny. We three were best friends in college," Britanica said, overreacting.

Gene, feeling ashamed of himself at the thought of her calling Donny, became quiet. He knew there was nothing between them but friendship, but in college he remembered how she talked about Donny all the time. He was being silly, but the guy was quite handsome, had a great profession and they could talk for hours and still do. But he was getting pretty serious with Maria, so that comforted him.

Britanica ended the phone call and discussed plans to fly to Fort Myers, Florida. "Donny is checking for flights, and he was so upset. His voice kept cracking. I love that guy." Gene lowered his head again. Now is not the time to act like a schoolboy.

"Hey, you all right?" Britanica asked Gene. "You got awfully quiet."

Webster stood in the background, watching them both. He knew Gene and always wondered if he was jealous of Britanica's friendship with Donny.

"Nothing's wrong. Just not in a talkative mood. But I was thinking, she is our friend, too, so maybe the group should go to the funeral. Riggins, Dan and Sam can handle things. We should all be there for Brucie."

Britanica got emotional. "That is so sweet, Gene. She would appreciate that. I think she could use all the encouragement we could offer, not to mention her mother."

"Well then, it's settled. I'll get my sister to watch Tiny and Hercules and make arrangements. I'll be on the phone for a bit, so please get my ticket when you go online."

"Emmy, would you do the same for me?" Webster asked. "I have a few phone calls to make myself."

She smiled sympathetically at him and replied, "Of course I will." Britanica offered her brother an appreciative nod filled with blurry eyes.

The keyboard clicked with speed. The printer popped out the itinerary and texts began chiming on their cellphones.

"I need to call my parents and we need to call the principal," Britanica said, motioning to Emmy. She nodded.

———

"Awe, man. I feel so bad for her," Riggins offered. "If it weren't for the fact she hates my guts, I would come along, but it just wouldn't be appropriate to add more anxiety to her frame of mind. Forget about Sam. I guarantee he'll offer her no comfort. What does she see in him, anyway?" He was speaking with Gene on the phone.

"You may be right, but at least you three will be here to take care of things and keep an eye out for—well, you know," Gene added.

"Hey, give her my sincere condolences and tell her I will keep a lookout around her cabin."

"Thanks, man, she'll appreciate that," Gene said as he ended the phone call.

At Riggins' cabin, Sam strolled inside. Riggins was sitting quietly on the couch.

"Hey, is something wrong? You look like you lost your best friend."

Not even realizing Sam walked in, Riggins looked up. "Did you say something?"

"Yeah. Is something wrong?"

"Actually, yes. Brucie's dad passed away."

"Oh, no. What happened?"

"Gene didn't know. She's on a flight to Florida. The gang is heading there soon, so they need us to keep watch for them. I need you to make sure no one is snooping around Brucie's cabin. Do you think you can do that?"

Sam rolled his eyes and thankfully Riggins wasn't paying attention. Annoyed, he retorted, "Yeah, I think I can handle that. Actually, I'm going to head to the bar and sit out on my truck bed and keep an eye out for anyone lurking around her place."

Riggins looked up at him and frowned.

"I have no plans of drinking alcohol or fooling around." He squished his lips together and eyes slanted carefully, not wanting to get on Riggins' bad side.

Without speaking, Riggins nodded his head. Sam noticed the sadness in his eyes and wondered: *Why is he so sad? It's not like she's his girlfriend.* The screen door slammed shut on Sam's way out, but any sympathy for Brucie didn't register on Sam's face or in his mannerism.

The screen door slammed again, and Riggins looked up to see what Sam must have forgotten.

Dan sat down next to him and placed a hand on his shoulder. "What's wrong?"

"Oh, Brucie's dad passed away. I just feel really bad for her. If anyone knows what it feels like to lose a parent, it's me."

"There's a lot of truth in that, buddy." He patted Riggins' shoulder and lied back against the couch.

"I don't know if now is a bad time to bring this up, but I apologize beforehand."

Riggins stared into his face, wondering.

"You have real feelings for her. Why don't you talk to her?"

Fingers went through his hair as he looked down, trying to keep from exploding. "Seriously! I can't show compassion for her without you turning it into something ridiculous?"

"Like I said, apologies beforehand. It's just…it's just that I can tell you have feelings for her. Your responses, facial expressions and words, is an open book. But it is obviously the wrong time to bring it up."

"Besides the fact I feel bad for her, she really gets on my nerves, and she hates my guts.

"And you know it."

"Sure, buddy. I know."

Riggins stared at the television but wasn't watching it. For some reason, thoughts of Brucie came to his mind. Their wrestling match, the way her hair and eyes sparkle in the sunlight, and that darn cute temper, but yet a gentle and kind spirit. "She's different from most girls. I can't tell if I hate her guts or love them. She is so infuriating, but there are so many aspects to her personality. She's brave and gentle, touchy and confident, spontaneous and reliable, even if she irks my butt."

A gurgling snore came out of Dan's mouth, and he tucked his hands under his armpits and changed positions.

Riggins jumped up from the couch to check on Bacall and Bogie.

———

Over at the bar, Sam sat outside on his truck bed, facing Brucie's house. The Daisy Dukes girls joined him. Oh, how he tried to pay attention to his detail, but darn if those girls didn't keep his attention on them. They all laughed. The girls cuddled up to him, making it quite difficult to keep his eye on the place. He would try pushing them off of him, but they always ended up almost in his lap.

Sam was quite the good-looking guy. He had a real charm, and most women fell head over heels for him. He liked Brucie a lot, but he wasn't in love with her. It was too much fun not being committed, but if he ever felt the need, she would be the girl for him.

It was turning dark outside. Their laughter echoed through the air. Some men were sneaking around, trying to look into the windows of the cabins on South Shore Drive. When they tried looking in Brucie's windows, the blinds covered too well for them to see inside, and the garage didn't have windows. There would be no way to identify which house she lived in, except for the few houses they were able to see into and find out she didn't live there. That, at least, cut down the list, but now they questioned whether she even lived on this street.

Sam still laughing, didn't even see the shadows going by amongst the trees.

"Okay, you two. I need to take a walk, so you should head inside."

"Don't leave us."

"Go on, get in there," he said, giving them a gentle shove. They kept looking back with puckered lips. But a beautiful red truck pulled in beeping at them. They waved and chattered at the men in the truck, and soon enough, arm in arm, they all walked into the bar.

Sam walked quietly around Brucie's cabin. It was dark. He really did commit to a thorough search, just a little too late. All was good, so he drove back to Riggins' cabin.

Sixteen

"I SAW her running on South Shore Drive. She has to live in one of those cabins.

"What is so hard about locating her?" Mr. Flagstone asked Hafsa and Azar.

"We can't see into all the cabins. Some of them have blinds pulled down, making it impossible to see inside. Also, we still don't know what type of car she drives," Hafsa replied.

"You know I can't be seen, so there is no way for me to try and find out where she lives. She saw me stash the gun that day when she was running. Why else did she stare at me the way she did in court? She knows, and once they confiscate it, we're doomed."

"Sir, agents—or nosey neighbors—are hanging around and watching out for each other. That one man who walks his dog keeps walking up and down the street at night with his gun," Azar added.

"Yeah, boss, and that gal hasn't been at the courthouse in days. She might be gone or something," Hafsa mentioned.

"Okay, here's what we're going to do. Hafsa, you pretend to take walks every day up and down the road. If anyone questions you, tell them the doc said you need to lose weight and exercise. That's true, anyways. You're staying with a friend, a Mister Fern," he said, looking over at an area of ferns growing. "If they say they don't know anyone by that name, just shrug your shoulders and start moving. Just throw out something like, Sorry, I need to keep moving. Then you can hide in the woods and watch the people driving by to see which house she lives in.

"Now, Azar, you hang out by the courthouse. Wait until you see her, then hide out in the new truck and follow her home. That old truck of ours has been identified one too many times. Don't let her know you're following her.

"But wait. I have another idea. While waiting for her to come out of the courthouse, if she walks across the road, you run her over. You didn't even see her or know you did it." He belted out a huge, over-excited laugh. "The parking lot is behind the courthouse, so when she crosses it to get to her car, run her over." He let out another maniacal laugh. They laughed too.

"I have a question, boss." Mr. Flagstone sat still while he asked. "If she hasn't reported you and the whereabouts of the weapon, what makes you think she knows it's there? By now you should have been questioned about it," Hafsa asked casually.

"Good point. But there's something in the way she stares at me. I don't know what I think, but it rattles my nerves. She definitely doesn't trust us, and she is suspicious. We can't take the chance. I lost the weapon and can't find it. By her showing up that day, I had no choice but to abandon the weapon. Now I can't find it. Plus, I know she is part of the reason the agents found out what we were up to and destroyed the millions we could have made in a month or two."

Throwing his hands up in the air, "Now we have to begin all over. And it gets worse. The feds are working with all these countries, making it really difficult to capture any rare animals. For that reason alone, she deserves to die." He spit on the ground.

"Are we set, then?"

They shook their heads.

"Sir, do you think that local cop is involved?" Azar asked.

"He hasn't testified, but I'm beginning to wonder. Some guy in the audience kept watching the trial. He took off every day before it ended, so I can't identify him. There is a guy we have seen dating that Brucie girl. I sort of wonder about him, but he doesn't strike me as a threat yet. He must just be her boyfriend."

———

Sam and Riggins were taking turns watching Brucie's house. They hid different places each night to watch the activity. Each day, they scoured the wooded area where Brucie saw Mr. Flagstone coming out the first time she saw him on the day she was out running.

Riggins, Sam and Dan sat at the kitchen table, eating dinner. "Why can't we find that weapon? Maybe they went back and grabbed it. I asked for a detector to be sent here days ago. What's the holdup?" Riggins asked out loud contemplating his thoughts.

Dan patted his shoulder. "Don't give up just yet. I have a gut feeling it is still there. No word on Flagstone. I was told they think he is hiding around here somewhere. Why? No idea."

Sam hopped up with his plate and utensils, then washed them at the sink and stacked them on the drainer. "I'm going to head back near Brucie's house and walk around the lake next to the houses to see if I can see or hear anyone sneaking around. I'm going to use the night goggles and hearing gadget."

"That's a good idea, Sam," Riggins said in a meaningful voice.

When he left, Riggins and Dan hung around outside with the chimps. "Wonder why these guys have never checked around my cabin. Do you think they're onto me? If they do suspect me, there has been no attempt to harm me."

"All I can think of is that they don't realize you live here. Your alarm around the perimeter has never activated, nor do we have anything but deer on the motion cameras," Dan wondered out loud.

"He can't get away. We can't let Flagstone escape. Gosh, that man must have Houdini blood in him."

"I hear ya, Riggs. The helicopter will only tip them off that we're searching for them, so using that is out of the question."

After a long sigh, Riggins changed topics. "Hear anything about Brucie and her father's funeral?"

"Nah, man. I was just going to ask you."

"We can check with Sam when he comes back. That's if he even bothers to stay in touch with her. You know what bugs me?" Dan shrugged his shoulders as if to say *what*. "He never talks about her. She's going through some very agonizing emotions, and he doesn't seem to care or know how to care."

"To be fair to Sam, we don't know if he's been in touch with her. I get the feeling he is jealous of our friendship. You have to admit we don't include him in our discussions. Maybe we should include him more."

"Maybe you're right. I'm still not convinced he is agent material, but he did motivate himself to observe the area without me commanding him to do it. So, I'll give him that one."

———

Sam walked carefully along the bank of the lake, listening and searching. A noise caused him to halt. He lowered to the ground and listened, then scanned the surroundings with night goggles. He continued to listen for a while. All was quiet, so he walked closer to Brucie's house, still taking slow steps. By the time he heard a snapping of twigs and leaves rustling close to him, it was too late. A branch smashed his head and he fell unconscious.

Just before making the next fatal hit, someone called out Sam's name. The man who hit him took off.

"Sam! Sam! Are you out here? Speak up. We just saw someone take off running. Sam!" Riggins yelled.

"Here, use my goggles. I'll check out the bar and we'll meet back behind Brucie's house in ten," Dan suggested.

"Good idea. Ten minutes," Riggins agreed.

Riggins proceeded to walk along the bank. He heard a moan and then saw a heat source with his goggles. Since he couldn't identify what or who he would find, he snuck up as quietly as possible. As he approached, he found Sam lying on the ground. "Sam, you okay?" Riggins asked concerned bending over him.

Sam didn't answer but slowly opened his eyes. Rubbing the back of his head, he said: "What happened?"

"Hold on a minute," Riggins said. He texted Dan.

"We saw someone running away. The guy must have knocked you out."

"Yeah, now I remember. I saw a heat source from my goggles, just too late. Then the next thing I knew, I was opening my eyes while you walked up."

"Unfortunately, whoever it was escaped. We need to get you to a hospital to be checked out. Can you walk?"

"I'll try."

Sam stood up but started to fall. Everything was swirling around him. He kept blinking his eyes and sort of staggered. Thankfully, Dan walked up, and the two of them put an arm around his shoulders and helped him walk. The truck was at the bar. To any bystander, it would look like Sam had too much to drink. It was too dark to see the blood streak on the back of his head.

"Dan, you keep an eye out and get in touch with base. Watch my kids, a/k/a Bacall and Bogart, please," Riggins asked.

"You got it. And they will be my kids at the end of this nightmare." Noticing Riggins' questionable expression, Dan added, "They can't live in this climate, you know that."

Releasing a knowing sigh, Riggins answered, "Unfortunately, I do know that."

"Hey, take er easy there, Sam," Dan said as they were leaving.

Sam just shook his head as they stormed down the road in Riggins' truck.

Seventeen

THE DAY of the funeral arrived. Family and closest friends didn't wear the traditional funeral attire. Instead, they dressed in some of Brucie's dad's clothing, anything that would make them feel close to him. A lot of people wondered why they didn't dress up but kept it to themselves.

Riggins had staged a couple of agents at the funeral, but he only informed Gene. He didn't want to cause anymore anxiety to Brucie and her mother than was needed. Just a precautionary measure that he felt was needed.

At the luncheon, people walked up and hugged Brucie and her mom, not speaking too much, just saying something from the heart. Someone walked up and said, "He's in a better place, dear. Don't be sad."

Britanica and Emmy were standing on each side of Brucie. Her eyes grew big, and lips tightened together. Britanica and Emmy's eyes interlocked. They pulled her away.

"She needs a break. Thank you for the kind words," Britanica said.

Now in a different room, Brucie snapped, "Why did you do that?"

"Because you were about to go off on her. I was afraid you were going to strike her."

"Did you hear how unsympathetic she sounded?"

"We thought so, too, but some people don't know what to say or how to react. So they use a phrase that is probably in a book about funeral etiquette. I don't think she really meant to sound uncaring," Emmy offered.

"First off, I know he's in a better place. Don't be sad? How could a person not be sad knowing they will never see their dad again? How?"

Britanica rubbed her arm. "It's almost over. Let's just hang on for a few more minutes and we'll get you and your mom out of here. Okay?" Britanica said softly, leaning her head down to see into Brucie's eyes.

"Hey, everything okay in here?" Donny, a college friend of Brucie and Britanica, asked.

"Yes. I think it's time to get Brucie and her mother out of here," Britanica informed him.

"Leave it to me. I have a plan. Brit, you go lead Brucie's mother outside and Emmy, you take Brucie out this side door. I'll make an announcement. Being a physician, I know just what to say."

All three women kissed his cheek. The plan was in motion. Now that they were out of the building, Donny took the stage.

"Ladies and gentlemen. Thank you for showing your support today. I had to insist Brucie and Ms. Clark leave for their well-being. I'm a physician and close friend. I think they need to go home and rest, but they send their deepest gratitude for the love you all have shown them. Thank you."

When he stepped down, Gene and Webster ran up to him immediately.

"Hey, where"—Gene and Webster's cellphones clanged. They read the text from Britanica and Emmy.

"Never mind," Gene commented. The three men left the building and drove to Ms. Clark's home.

No talking, smiling or conversations were taking place at Ms. Clark's home. Everyone just stared mindlessly at whatever was on the television. It was too sad of a day and joking around would make things worse. So, now was as good of a time as any to talk about the list of tasks needing to be done. Ms. Clark just nodded. Brucie watched her. *She doesn't comprehend what we're saying. She's like in a twilight zone.* A tear slipped down her face.

"Brucie. If you need us to stay longer, please just tell us," Britanica offered.

"No, no. You should leave tomorrow. I'm going to hang around for a week or two and help my mother handle the exhaustive list of tasks to be done. I appreciate you guys so much, but I think it's better if you leave. You're the best group of friends a person could have." She teared up.

"Okay, but if—"

"I will call you. I'm going to help Mom get ready for bed. I'll see you shortly."

"Oh, I forgot to tell you that Riggins asked me to give you his most sincere sympathy. Losing his own dad, he understands what you're feeling and he's just really sad for you both," Gene said sympathetically.

"That's nice. Thank him for me."

———

Riggins was lying on the couch watching sports when Sam walked out of a bedroom. He held his bandaged head and squinted. His eyes kept squinting.

"Hey, you need anything?"

"No, the doc said it would hurt pretty badly for a few days. Look, I was being really quiet and listening for movement out there. The second I heard someone walk up behind me, I was attacked. I heard my name yelled just before losing consciousness. That probably saved my life. Thank you."

"Don't mention it. That same exact thing happened to me in Mozambique."

"Ahh, good."

Riggins looked at him, puzzled by his response.

"What I mean is that I was afraid you were thinking I wasn't taking it seriously and caused this to happen. I really was being quiet and searched that whole area."

Riggins jumped up and patted his shoulder. "I believe you. But… your performance is still under evaluation. It wasn't easy for me to get into the department either. I started out with a cocky attitude and paid for it."

"No kidding."

"No kidding. Hey, I'm getting something to drink. How about a bottle of water? You should stay hydrated."

"Sure," he responded and then sat carefully down on the chair, reclining it back.

Handing him the bottle of water, Riggins asked, "Have you spoken with Brucie since she left?"

"Once, but she was in a sulky mood, so we didn't speak very long."

"Sulky! She has every right to feel sulky. You didn't even take the opportunity to console her?"

Sam stuck his hand up. "Hold on. She's the one who ended the call. I tried asking her questions, but she told me she wasn't in a very good mood and needed some time to think. I tried." Both hands went out.

"Looks like you need a book that teaches you how to console someone. Especially someone you're supposed to care about."

"Hey, man. Why you getting so upset? It's not like you even like her."

"Any person with a heart would feel sympathy for her situation. Any person."

"She must be okay with me since she hasn't ended our relationship. Maybe you need to find your own girlfriend and leave mine out of the conversation," Sam said.

Sam's eyes widened watching Riggins' face turn red.

"Girlfriend? She's your girlfriend?" Riggins retorted.

"Okay. Maybe not 'girlfriend' but we do have fun together."

"Why don't you just try and treat her with respect at a time like this? What she's going through is very painful. Be gentle with her." He walked out of the cabin, and the door shattered loudly behind him.

Sam's brows arched and his mouth dropped. "I'm going back to bed. Gees, how about some sympathy for me?"

Eighteen

A GLOOMINESS CAST over Chute Pond. Brucie walked outside and sat on the deck facing the lake. Was it just gloomy outside or was she just depressed? Truthfully, she didn't care. Glancing at her phone, text message after text message stayed unread. The first line always asked when she would return. Was it wrong to let them think she was still in Florida? She just didn't feel like speaking with anyone. A text message chimed, so she glanced at the phone.

"Who is this?"

> I know every move you make. It won't be long before we meet up. By the way, your mother is next. Then it's your turn. Those pink pajamas are pretty cute.

The cellphone fell out of her hands. Brucie's mouth dropped, and her body immediately began to tremble. She looked all around but saw nobody. Viewing more texts as she entered the cabin, one from Sam lit up.

SAM

> Hey, Brucie, you okay? I'm worried about you.

She forced a grin. Then her trembling fingers dialed his number.

"There you are. I was so worried about you. Are you home yet?"

With a stutter to her words, she said, "Yes. Could you... Could you come over right away?"

He sensed the fear in her voice. "Sure. I'll be right there." He hung up the phone and ran out of the cabin. Riggins was cleaning up the yard when he saw him run to the truck.

"Where's the fire?"

"Sorry. I have to go." He zoomed off, tires squealing in the gravel.

Riggins stopped what he was doing and rested his chin on the rake, wondering what was really going on. Sam was gone before he could question him.

The door opened and Sam pulled Brucie into his arms. "What's wrong? I could tell by the tone of your voice you were upset." He let go of her and stood back.

"Come in. Quick. Close and lock the door."

His brows pushed up.

"Here, read this." Her hand was shaking as she held out her cell to him.

Sam read the text and looked toward the ceiling in thought. She nervously scratched her neck area.

"He killed my dad. It wasn't an accident. How did he get my number, and why would he be stupid enough to confess that knowing he is being investigated?"

"First things first. We don't know who sent this text. I'm going to stay with you. Wherever you go, I go. I won't take no for an answer. Your life is in real danger."

"I don't know about that. You don't look so well. Did something happen while I was gone?"

"Yes, but that's not important right now. I need to call Riggins."

Sam dialed Riggins' number. Brucie listened intently. The only movement was her hands twirling around and around.

"I'm perfectly capable of taking care of her."

"No way!" Riggins yelled. "You aren't released by the doctor to continue with the assignment. Have her pack a suitcase and she'll stay here. No one, and I mean *no one* will get to her here."

Sam ended the call and looked over at Brucie. "He"—

"I heard every word. Man, he has a big mouth. I'll pack my things. Should I drive over there myself?"

"Never. Wherever you need to go, I'll drive you."

"The last thing I wanted was to have to see or talk with anyone. Now I'm stuck with three men."

"Don't worry. You can have my room. There will be no need to talk if you don't feel up to it."

Her lips formed into a pretend smile, and she nodded without speaking. In minutes, she walked out of the room with luggage. Sam pulled his gun out, took a stance, and opened the door. He peeked around and waved her to follow. They ran to his truck. When they pulled up to Riggins' cottage, he ran out.

She climbed out slowly, scared and depressed.

"Let me help you with that luggage. We got it. I took the liberty of clearing out Sam's room and the bathroom for you."

For a second, that same uninterested look came back to her.

After leaving the luggage, Riggins walked up to her. With caution and concern, he spoke.

"We'll discuss the text in a moment. But first, I just want you to know how deeply sorry I am for your loss. I'm not going to even try to say something magical to make you feel better, because I know from experience, there are no magic words. Please know, I'm here for you should you need to talk."

For some reason, his genuine concern did help her feel better and she replied softly, "Thank you. I really do appreciate that." As she looked over at Sam, she couldn't help but review his reaction when he came to her cabin. He never consoled her once, and here this arrogant, ego maniac sincerely showed compassion. She bit her lip and turned back to Riggins.

"I understand you probably just want to be alone, but first, may I see your phone and take it to see if our technical team can figure out where the text came from?"

"Yeah, sure. Wait! What if my mom needs to call me or work?"

"Good question. Provide both contacts with Sam's number. He will be staying near you until we can figure this out."

"So, I'm more of a prisoner than before?"

"Yeah, I guess it does feel like being imprisoned. We'll work as fast as possible to get the information. I could never live with the fact you got killed or injured on my watch. Your mother is already in hiding with some women agents. We'll get them, Brucie. You have my word," Riggins replied.

"When did that happen with my mom?" Brucie asked.

"While you were packing your bags to move in here, I made the arrangements. Sam mentioned the context of your text over my phone conversation with him. Your mother is safe. I promise," he assured her.

In a very lethargic manner, she thanked him, grabbed Sam's phone and closed the door to his room.

"Sam, I'm going to make arrangements for different transportation for both of us. We can't take any chances, now more than ever. How low to kill her father, especially when she didn't even know he was a murderer. Obviously, Flagstone thought it over and realized she may be able to identify him when the agent's body was found. It's their stupidity that she figured it out. I want to kill him with my bare hands." Spit flew out of Riggins' mouth when he made the last remark and Sam saw something in his eyes. Something that scared even him.

––––––––

Brucie fell asleep for approximately two hours. The mental and emotional exhaustion took everything out of her. She sat up in bed and could hear voices in the living room. The door opened slowly, quietly, and she poked her head around. Riggins, Dan and Sam were discussing the case. Not able to focus or form a complete sentence, she walked out nervously. Sam jumped up and ran over to her, pulling her into his arms.

"You slept for a while. Do you feel better?"

She shrugged her shoulders and maneuvered out of his arms. Looking around, she found a vacant chair. Feeling all eyes on her, in order to avoid talking about the painful events, she glanced around the cabin. "Your cabin is really nice. I have to admit that, in my mind, I imagined it would be messy with odds and ends furniture. I'm pleasantly surprised."

"Why thank you. Actually, I'm kind of a neat freak. When Sam came, my blood pressure was rising to new heights. He's kind of a slob."

Sam's piercing eyes stared at Riggins.

Brucie looked around. "So, where are the chimps?"

"I was just getting ready to go out to their pen and get them. They would rather be outside. Would you like to come with me to get them?" Riggins asked.

"Fresh air and seeing them is just what the doctor ordered."

He held the door open, and Sam sat stewing.

"What's the big deal? It's not like he's stealing her from you. She's not even your girlfriend," Dan remarked.

"Didn't say she was. I have been thinking that maybe it's time to settle down. Brucie would be the right type of girl to do that with."

"Truth to that, except for one tiny detail. You're not the settle down type, and I'm pretty sure she is aware of that. Seriously, you have no idea how to comfort her. Man, can't you see the pain in her face?"

"No. She looks fine."

"Trust me, she's not," Dan replied with a shake of his head.

"Okay, okay. I'll help to cheer her up. I'm always getting her to laugh."

"Sure. Have at it, Don Juan. Care to place a wager that you have no idea how to do that? I'll give you two hours to work your magic. How about fifty dollars?"

Sam's nose wrinkled and he replied, "You're on." Out the door he went.

Dan watched him walk up to Brucie. She was playing with the chimps. Sam said something to her, and she acted like he was invisible.

"Brucie, did I tell you what funny thing happened to me?"

She shook her head. "No."

With arms flinging around, a face plastered with expression, jumping around like an ape, Brucie's face remained blank watching him. Dan saw her force a smile, and Sam's shoulders slumped.

That wasn't working, so on with the next attempt.

"Take a walk with me," Sam suggested.

Riggins' face grew concerned, and he began to rise.

"Just over there to the porch," Sam said. "We could sit on the porch swing?" He bent down and gave her a gentle, mildly pleading smile.

"Oh, why not?" As if cement blocks were holding her down, she arose. "I'll play with you soon," she remarked to the chimps. They started hooting and reaching for her. Riggins pulled them back.

"Okay, you two, time for a bath. They climbed into Riggins' arms.

Dan found the perfect spot to watch Sam and Brucie.

"What are you doing there?" Riggins asked him.

Dan shook his head fast, saying, "Nothing. Nothing at all," he said, trying his best to get Riggins to leave. He did.

"Brucie, are you doing okay? Do you need to talk? I'm concerned about you," Sam said.

"No, I don't need to talk, and I'm fine."

Without saying it, her face showed it. "Period." They sat in silence.

"What about your mother? Is she okay?"

"What do you think? She just lost her husband and just found out he was murdered, and she's stuck in confinement with agents she doesn't know, just wanting to be alone. So, what do you think?" Her face was serious, even annoyed.

"I just want to make you feel better. Talking things out could help you."

"How sweet," she said sarcastically. "Well, you're not going to make me feel better. Do you not get the concept of mourning? Obviously not. I don't want to feel better. " She jumped up so fast that his head was spinning. The slam of the door caused him to flinch.

Standing in the window was Dan. Sam looked at him and gritted his teeth. He mumbled to himself. "Fifty dollars down the drain." Expletives followed.

Dan felt remorse for being happy about winning the bet. Even to the point of tearing up at the heartbreak in Brucie's eyes. But it wasn't meant to hurt her feelings; it was meant to hurt Sam's, who has no feelings.

Sam rummaged through his sack and threw the money in Dan's lap. "Happy?"

"For Brucie's predicament, no. For watching you bomb out with that ego of yours; yes." The door slammed behind Sam as he strolled out the door.

Nineteen

THE SUN BLINKED through the windows. Brucie used a hand to cover her eyes. She glanced at the clock: six thirty am. Her body leaped out of bed. Cellphone in hand, she checked the alarm alert. "Frickin-frackin. I forgot to turn it on."

Peeking around a corner, she eyed the guys sitting outside drinking coffee. She jumped in the shower, threw on a small amount of makeup and dressed. With a coffee cup in hand, a case holding her stenograph and supplies, she stood in the doorway. The guys weren't talking but checking their text and email. With a clearing of the throat, they all turned toward her at once.

Riggins jumped up. "Hey there. You look like a person on the way to work?"

"Yeah. I called my office and told them I would be in today. It's a day of depositions. You don't need to worry about me driving. Those monsters don't scare me."

"Well, they scare me. Sam, take her."

Sam jumped up, resenting how Riggins ordered him around. "Sure, Brucie. Here. Let me carry that for you." He refused to look at Riggins.

"I'm fine. Really. Could we just go? I don't want to be late."

"Um, yeah. Just let me grab my keys."

Riggins pulled him to the side. "Every step and every move; okay?"

"Yes, sir." Sam's tone was on the annoying side.

Just before Sam closed the door, Riggins yelled, "Keep me updated every couple of hours. Find out what time she should be done and send me a text, please."

Why did it kill him to talk to Sam? It was like physical work for him. He and Dan could talk for hours about nothing. He couldn't even attempt to joke around with Sam. But why not? He couldn't put his finger on it."

———

Mr. Flagstone strolled into the living room. He held up a set of keys. "New plan, boys."

Both men's eyebrows smashed together.

"What is so special about that stupid court reporter at Chute Pond? It seems agents are with her constantly. I scared her good. You should have seen her face when she read my text. There was such terror in her face. I told her I killed her father, and mom was next...and then it was her turn." His inhumane laugh was disturbing.

The men laughed loudly, in spite of his creepy demeanor, but then Hafsa stopped and produced a serious face.

"What is that look for?" Mr. Flagstone asked.

"It's just... It's just that I don't think that was a wise decision; you know, saying you killed her father and all of that. With technology today, they can figure those things out. How'd you get her phone number? So I guess she does live in that log cabin?"

"Relax. She never knew I was watching her, nor did those pesky agents. There is no way they'll be able to figure it out. Never mind how I got her cell number. Now, let's get on with my plan. I assume she is working at the courthouse today. I saw her in one of the agent's trucks coming out of a long, dirt driveway. Remember, the one with detectors everywhere?" Their eyes lit up as they nodded their heads. "Then it hit me to execute the plan we discussed previously, so I bought a new truck, so we won't be identified. The license plate is stolen from an out-of-state car. One of you will hide in the parking lot and notify the other when she is walking out to the car. Then, whichever one of you is driving will run her down. Get out of there fast. Pretty good plan; isn't it?"

They both nodded their heads, no excitement in their faces, though.

"I thought you guys would like this plan."

"It could work, but there will always be a risk of being seen. Why can't we kill her at night?"

"Because I'm paying you. And because she is always being guarded."

"Oh, yeah. That's true."

Azar asked a question, while his forehead produced wrinkles. "Why do you want her dead?"

"Because she saw me with the body. Since you work for me and are involved, you will be arrested as accomplices. Okay?" he spat at the end of his reply.

Flagstone handed them both a wad of cash. Eyes grew wide while they sifted through the wad.

"Sure, we'll get it done," Azar replied, as his face lit up.

―――――

Brucie was glad her day was over. She didn't realize how much exhaustion emotional pain caused. Trying to speak to Sam, her hand covered the yawn for seconds before she could talk.

"Wow. Nap emergency?"

She yawned again. "Yup. I'm going to take the stenograph tripod off and gather my supplies. It will only take a few minutes. Why don't I meet you outside?"

"Okay. I'll be waiting for you."

Judge Sloan stopped Brucie before leaving. He just wanted to make sure she understood he was there for her if she should need to talk. His wife had asked him to relay that message. Brucie's eyes grew tender as she listened to the judge.

Sam looked through the glass doors and saw Brucie talking with the judge. He sent a text that they were leaving in ten minutes. Riggins was in the parking lot watching. A gut feeling urged him to be there.

As usual, some pretty woman walked by, and Sam greeted her. She stopped and they talked.

His arm was supported by the wall, and she was caught in his trap. Loving her predicament. Her eyelashes had a serious case of blinking.

Brucie walked out and saw Sam, but he didn't see her. She sighed and shook her head. Not in the mood to watch him flirt, she took off for his truck.

Riggins looked for anything suspicious. No time to think! He jumped out from his hiding spot and pulled her in between cars. Both of them falling onto the pavement as the tires screeched past, while the smell of burnt rubber floated up their nostrils. He jumped up quickly to identify the truck and license plate, but it was already gone.

"You guys okay?" Sam asked, panting.

Riggins grabbed his collar and, with spit flying, replied, "Strike two."

Sam cautiously pulled away from him, body tight. "She told me to wait outside for her."

"Did she tell you to take your focus off of her and put it on that woman?"

Sam rubbed his thighs and his head dropped slightly. There was nothing he could say, and he knew it.

Brucie was still sitting on the ground, rubbing her ankle. "You okay? I'm really sorry, but there wasn't time to think. If I didn't pull you when I did—well, you know."

"It's okay. Thank you for saving me."

"You okay? Gee, I'm sorry I wasn't here, but you were supposed to wait for me," Sam said, swallowing with guilt.

"You were preoccupied," she said with sarcasm.

"Any chance you got the license plate and model of the truck?" Riggins asked with gritted teeth.

"It happened so fast. It was a two-door silver truck is all I got for you."

Riggins puckered his lips. "Wait here, Brucie. I'll drive you to my cabin." Riggins grabbed her case and was back in a flash. Sam just leaned back on his truck and watched them pull away. One more strike and he would never work again for the agency.

———

Riggins helped Brucie to the couch. It was a mild sprain, but he didn't want to take any chances. "Get comfortable and I'll get some ice. Then I'll bandage it up."

She didn't mean to, but an annoyed sigh escaped from her. "Look Riggins, I'm fine. If it is sprained, it is mild. I can even walk on it. I'd rather go to the room and rest."

He knew she wasn't meaning to be ungrateful, because he'd been in her shoes. You just don't feel like talking or putting up a front. And add an attempt on a person's life, what would any sensible person expect?

"Okay. I'll help you to the room and bring ice there."

"Thank you."

Ice was secured around the ankle. Riggins left the room, advising her he'd be back in ten minutes to bandage it. He knocked on the door and entered slowly. Her foot was elevated, resting on a pillow. Music played softly from the television. She didn't speak. After wiping off the condensation, he treated the sprain and bandaged it. He looked warmly at her and responded with genuine concern. "If you need anything, just yell."

She nodded and he closed the door so quietly, the latch didn't make a sound as it clicked.

Not expecting it, the music was lifting her gloomy spirit. Her mouth couldn't help but form a smile. "I think I'll note these songs on my pad and let Brit and Em listen to them. These are really uplifting songs. Sorry for being angry with You, Lord. My father being murdered is something I couldn't accept. My thoughts rested on one word: Why? How many times a day do you hear that word? We blame You for everything. For everything. Please hug my father for me, Lord."

What Flagstone told her about murdering her dad was a lie. A lie to scare her, but she and everyone else had no reason at this point to suspect he was lying. In about thirty minutes, the doorbell rang. Riggins welcomed the guests inside.

Brucie broke out in happy tears after a talk with the Lord. It was so needed. She turned the volume down low because of a tapping noise. Her eyes squinted, wondering if someone was knocking on the door. "Is someone knocking on the door?"

"Yes, it's Riggins. I didn't want to wake you. Anyway, you have visitors. Are you up for visitors?"

"Yes. Give me a minute, please." Her fingers wiped the tears away from her eyes. She smoothed her hair and stood up carefully, limping to the door. As the knob turned, Riggins escorted her out to the living room. Being emotionally over-whelmed by her life, just seeing her friends brought her to tears. Britanica and Emmy ran up and embraced her. Sentimental themselves, they cried together. What their poor friend has been through.

"Hey, let's get Brucie comfortable. She sprained her ankle."

Brucie sneered at Riggins without speaking.

Dan and Riggins brought out a pot of coffee, condiments and some store-bought cookies.

"Wow, girl. Living it up, huh?" Britanica jested.

"Yeah, living it up," she replied sarcastically.

"Well, we certainly understand how probably nothing makes you feel better during this time, but I would take a moment to cherish three hunks waiting on you hand and foot," Emmy replied with eyebrows moving up and down.

Brucie giggled. It felt so good to giggle.

"Hey, why are you holding that pad and pen?" Britanica's curiosity couldn't help but ask.

"Gosh. I didn't even realize I was holding it. But since you asked, I'll tell you. I was listening to Christian music videos. Haven't done that in a long while. It was so uplifting that I decided to write down these names so you guys could look them up."

"Let's hear it," Britanica replied eagerly.

"This first choir made you want to jump around the room praising God. Let me see if I can find my notes." She shuffled through the pad and found what she was looking for. "You just have to find this video of 'More Abundantly Medley' by Ricky Dillard. If you don't move to the song, your joyful gage is stuck.

"Oh, and this video will bring you tears of joy: 'Talking to Jesus" off the album 'Old Church Basement' and Brandon Lake is the song artist. It's so sweet, humble and sincere. Then try Todd Dulaney, Jonathan Nelson and J.J. Hairston. What I loved about these videos is that it draws you right into the song. When they're singing, it doesn't appear they're performing for an audience, just for the Lord. There's a sincerity even in their expressions. I think we need to speak to Pastor Beard—"

"You mean Pastor Mustache?"

"Brit! Anyway, we need to liven up our song time. Let's find the songs and watch them."

Emmy had already found it on her phone and pushed play.

"You have to watch them sing and dance around; it's a must," Brucie requested.

The guys watched them through the window while on the deck. They wanted to give her some privacy. Not able to help it, they cracked up as the women bounced and wiggled, raising their hands up and down. Brucie looked at her friends and smiled. Another uplifting moment. Then the guys walked in with the chimps. Hooting and hollering, Riggins allowed the chimps to get down. Bacall and Bogie crawled right up Brucie's legs and into her arms. They had her laughing.

The pad and pen clinked on the floor as Brucie cuddled the

chimpanzees. Britanica picked them up and couldn't help but notice the topic on paper. "What's this all about?" Britanica asked, studying the page.

"I can't see. What does it say?"

"It looks like a court case dealing with solar panels."

"Oh. Don't look at that. It's confidential. I could get in big trouble if anyone knew you saw my notes."

"Well, I didn't see much. I would need *Superman* vision to read it that fast. Come on Brucie.

"Can't you tell us anything?"

"Since the article in the newspaper wrote about it, I can only tell you that part."

Britanica's hands waved back and forth with speed.

"Be patient, young lady. I'm getting to it. The case is about an employee who got poisoning from handling solar panels. Solar panels contain toxic minerals such as lead. When they get thrown in a landfill, it also causes major environmental issues. He's suing the company for both. That's all I can tell you. Whether true or not, let the jury decide."

"No kidding," Riggins remarked. "I thought solar panels were supposed to be good for the environment."

"I guess the news outlets prefer to leave out such important information," Dan replied.

"All I know is that solar thermal systems use hazardous fluids to transfer heat. So, leaks are obviously harmful to the environment," Brucie added. "Besides, I'm just giving you info from the news. I don't know if there is any truth to it or not."

"Well, get this," Emmy interjected. "I just read an article by the American Medical Association that said LED technology may impact human health. Supposedly, life-long exposure of the retina and lens to blue peaks from LEDs can increase the risk of cataracts and age-related macular degeneration."

"Get out of town," Britanica blurted.

"Just when you thought it was safe to go into the water—or turn your lights on," Riggins commented curiously.

Dan joined in by humming the *Jaws* theme.

"Why does everything seem to end up political? Just tell us the truth and let us make the decision for ourselves whether or not we use the products." Brucie said, ending the conversation.

"Only this group could start off laughing and switch gears so fast," Britanica added shaking her head.

"Anyway, we took up enough of your time. You get some rest," Britanica ordered.

The women hugged goodbye, not wanting to overstay their welcome. "You guys are the best. The best friend a girl could have," Brucie tearfully admitted.

As they walked out the door, Sam walked in. "Hello."

"Hello," Brucie replied, disinterested.

"You want to watch a movie?"

"No thanks. It's time to get some rest." *You jerk. How about a sincere apology? Something.*

"Okay. Need help getting to the room?"

"No, I don't. *Riggins wouldn't even ask. He'd insist on helping me, you jerk wad.*

She pulled herself up and hobbled towards the room. Riggins walked in at that moment. "Let me help you," he insisted, glaring at Sam. Sam raised his hands.

Told you, jerk wad.

Chimpanzees in their beds, all the rest of the lights went out. Exhaustion consumed all of them.

———

Outside the windows, eyes peered into the house. Through binoculars. Searching. Taking mental notes of the layout. Now realizing who lived in this cabin, Azar gave a thumb's up to his partner, and they scattered back to the boss, but not before the alarm sounded, not realizing one of them had entered an alarm zone. They ran fast, dirt flying behind them and then the sound of tires squealing as they sped off.

All three men ran out of their rooms, no shirt, weapon in hand, looking every direction. Dan ran to the road and saw the lights of a vehicle but couldn't even make out anything else about it.

"Looks like they still are determined to get to Brucie," Riggins admitted. "When are we going to catch them? This is so frustrating." His last words came out with an irate snort.

"Well, they're not going to make another attempt tonight, so let's get some sleep and work a new plan tomorrow," Dan said while patting Riggins' shoulder.

Twenty

THE NEXT MORNING, Riggins and Dan strolled into the kitchen. Coffee was percolating, sputtering and sending its aroma through the air. Riggins poured a cup for Dan and himself, and they proceeded to the living room. Just as Riggins opened the exterior door to fetch the newspaper, Brucie's door creaked open. Both men jumped. She walked slowly and put her hands up towards Riggins. "I don't need help. I'm good."

He went outside and grabbed the newspaper as Dan sat back down.

"Could I get you a cup of coffee?" Dan asked hesitantly, not wanting to provoke a snide remark from her.

"That would be lovely, thanks. Please add some of that delicious peppermint bark creamer."

"You got it." In minutes, Dan walked back into the living room and handed her the coffee.

She held the cup between her hands and sniffed it.

"Did you sleep okay?" Riggins asked wondering if she heard the alarm.

"I slept great. I needed that sleep. Where's Sam?" The sun streaked through the window, reflecting in her eyes with a sparkling diamond-like effect. Riggins was glued to them.

He bit his lip and started to respond, but Sam walked into the living room holding a big box of chocolate everything. He laid it next to her on the couch. Her eyes bulged and a smile developed. She let out a hoot and holler. It was the first time since her dad passed away that a smile was sincere. Sam breathed out a sigh of relief.

As she shuffled her fingers through the box, eyes full of delight, she spoke out loud to herself being in chocolate heaven. "I can't decide which to eat first." She closed her eyes and with a finger poked at each item, saying, "'Eenie, meenie, miney, mo…'" She unwrapped a Little Debbie Ho Ho and stuffed it into her mouth. Sam kissed her cheek and she smiled sincerely at him.

"Let's watch a comedy while we snack on this box of heaven."

"Sure, but I need to run out and grab my phone out of the truck. You find something and I'll be right back," Sam insisted.

"Let's see what you have in the recordings," Brucie said, strolling through the titles. "*The Singing Buckaroo* and *Git Along Little Dogie*?" she questioned Riggins, with one side of her mouth curling.

Cheeks flushing, he responded. "My dad would watch these old movies for hours. Every Friday evening growing up, we would sit together as a family and watch them. I like to watch them once in a while to bring that memory back." He looked away as his eyes teared up, and then to hide his sentimental mistake, he started questioning Sam's intentions.

He looked out the window and saw Sam talking away on the phone. "Are you that stupid to fall for this guy's scam techniques again?"

Her mouth dropped, and so did Dan's.

"How much longer are you going to let him trick you? He's not interested in a relationship. He's a womanizer. Can't you see that?" He threw a strand of lights on the floor and started to walk out of the room.

"Dan, grab the fire extinguisher and put out that fire. Where did that all come from, and I'm glad he isn't looking to settle down. Neither am I! You're as wound up as that tangled strand of lights. Dan, you take one side and I'll take the other and pull hard until he untangles," she spit out of her mouth in anger.

Dan extended both arms. "Okay, you two, that's enough. Riggs, how about fixing some bacon and eggs? I'll help."

With fists on her hips and a scowl on her face, Riggins turned away from her and mumbled, "Sure. Why not?"

"Make sure he doesn't poison my food," she added, crossing her arms.

Moving his arms around like the robot on *Lost in Space*, Riggins kept the fight going.

"'Danger, Will Robinson.' We have just encountered a disgruntled alien from the planet, Naiveturn." He looked at Dan and explained. "You know naïve plus Saturn equals Naiveturn."

Dan patted his shoulder saying, "Yeah, sure buddy."

Brucie shook her tightened fists, so Riggins opened his mouth and began making fun of her outrage.

"Oh, no! I'm caught in crossfire."

Dan leapt on to the recliner yelling, "Duck for cover. Duck!"

A chuckle escaped Riggins' scornful lips. Dan jumped off the recliner and spoke to Riggins while rubbing his bottom. "I think I have shrapnel embedded in my butt."

"Aren't you just clever?" Riggins commented with a playful punch to Dan's arm.

She sat down on the couch, scrolled for a comedy and clicked on *Frasier*. Sam came back in and plopped down on the couch, kissing her cheek several times. "Oh, good. I like *Frasier*." She handed the remote to Sam so she could devour more chocolate. He forwarded past the commercials and hit play.

"Go back! Go back!"

"Huh?" Sam uttered.

She stuffed a chocolate chip cookie in her mouth, grabbed the remote out of his hands, and reversed it. When she pushed play, it started at the beginning where the cityscape was being drawn. Riggins and Dan walked back into the room at that moment.

Sam's forehead wrinkled and he commented quizzically. "You want to watch the very beginning instead of going straight to the show itself?"

"How can you pass that part? Each episode, they add something different to the drawing. For instance, did you see the lightning flash?"

"I wasn't paying attention."

She reversed the recording so he could see it. "Now, watch the next episode and you'll see." On to the next episode, the drawing ended with a Christmas tree twinkling on the cityscape.

"I never knew it did that, and never really cared, to be honest," Sam said in a bored voice.

"That's why I always have to start the recording where the cityscape is sketched. It's silly, but I just have to know if it rains, snows, fireworks or what is going to happen."

"My favorite is the tower crane," Riggins added.

Mine is the train," Dan joined into the conversation.

"Train?" both Brucie and Riggins questioned together.

"That's the best one," Dan said.

"But seriously, I thought you'd go for the helicopter?" Riggins said. Brucie nodded in agreement.

"Helicopter? I didn't know there was one."

"You know what I think would have been fun? If they had a flying saucer and it beamed light right into Frasier's apartment," Brucie said with a giggle.

"Oh, yeah. Wouldn't it have been funny if they drew a cartoon character of Frasier as an alien, or if they had him being abducted?" Riggins asked enthusiastically.

The three of them laughed.

Sam held his hands up and turned his head to see each one of their faces with a serious look.

His hands dropped and he laid his head against the couch with a mild shaking.

"You know, Riggins, you move from hot to cold. You're as mad as a rattlesnake one minute and then completely opposite the next. You have to be bipolar or are in need of a protein emergency. Just sayin'," Brucie commented.

She and Sam just stared at him for a moment. He walked back to the kitchen and Dan followed. Brucie shrugged her shoulders and they continued to watch more episodes. They laughed through the episode, pointing out Martin's torn up recliner. Riggins walked in and heard the conversation.

"That's so funny. My dad was a lot like Martin. He used duct tape for everything. The front seat of his old truck was held together with it." He cracked a memorable smile. "I couldn't tell you how many times he yelled to me: 'Riggins, bring the duct tape.' Well, anyway, breakfast is served. Come and get it."

Brucie stared at him as he walked away, feeling sentimental about how she noticed a softer side to him. It was sweet and provoked a frustrating, likable image of him.

As they walked into the kitchen, Riggins was eating with the chimps at the table. They started hooting and hollering and reaching for Brucie.

She held up a finger and said, "I'll be right back." When she sat down at the table, Riggins' phone rang, so he gathered his dishes and jumped up. She still watched him like she was trying to analyze if he was a kind, soft, but brave man. Was she imagining this about him? Even though they bicker constantly, look at all he has done to protect and make her feel at home.

As they sat around the table eating, they couldn't help but notice Riggins pacing in the backyard, face serious, even tense. He ended the call and just stood still for a moment in thought. He walked back into the kitchen.

"I have a bit of interesting news. Not that this makes the situation any less sad, but your father was not murdered. They tracked Flagstone and his merry band of hoodlums to Canada during this time. He was trying to scare you, and you should be scared. They are back in the US. We just don't know where. They are being extra careful instead of making their usual sloppy mistakes."

"Actually, it does make me feel better that they didn't murder him. I felt such guilt that I was the cause of my dad's death. But you're right, it still hurts just as bad. I need to phone my mother." Her chair screeched as she quickly walked to the bedroom.

"I feel for her. You, of anyone, understands the pain," Dan said looking at Riggins.

"It seems to always hang out in my subconscious. The fact my dad was murdered and the fact he is gone. Some things just hang on, no matter how hard you try to move forward." He kicked the chimp's ball out of frustration. Dan patted his shoulder.

"We'll get him Riggs. I promise you."

Riggins bobbed his head.

The door to Brucie's bedroom flung open, causing the guys to look up.

"Ooof! Mmmmf!" She kept blowing out sounds relating to anger.

"I may be misinterpreting it, but is it possible you would like to talk about something?" Riggins asked carefully.

Tears of anger burned in her eyes. "Those are the most insensitive words in the English language."

"What words would those be?" Dan asked quite interested.

"Sorry. There's nothing we can do."

"Ahh, yeah. I agree," Riggins said.

"It's like customer service or a 'representative' pushes a button with that recording. I literally pulled the phone cord out of the wall after hearing it one too many times, and yes, it was costly to repair," Dan admitted.

"What's going on, Brucie?" Riggins asked sincerely.

"My poor mother. Not only is she having to deal with my father's death, but now the IRS.

You see, when Dad retired, he had to get insurance for both of them. A nurse at my mom's doctor's office gave her an agent's phone number to call. Since my dad's passing, she is okay with money and even managed to save some in case of an emergency.

"They got insurance with Florida Blue. My father had this insurance previously, and it was not the Affordable Healthcare Act

(AHCA). On the phone with both the Florida Blue and the Affordable Healthcare representative, the Florida Blue rep confirmed that they do offer personal insurance packages.

"So, they didn't think anything of it when Daniel, the insurance agent, signed them up for Florida Blue. There was one tiny problem. The agent didn't identify the insurance as the Affordable Healthcare Act. So now, she owes $14,000.00. That's right, and all the rep from the AHCA said was, 'Sorry, there's nothing we can do.' Mom said her voice was boring and lifeless. How is this affordable insurance? My mother won't even make it close to $50,000.00 this year. That $14,000.00 is her portion of the insurance.

"First of all, she is a widow and now without healthcare insurance. She canceled. The agent never told them they would owe their life or blood when taxes are done at the end of the year. She didn't even know. After hearing all the horror stories, they would have never gone with AHCA.

"Now she receives threatening letters after filing an appeal or something like that. Barb, the tax accountant, told her that she has dealt with other clients where they keep getting a letter from IRS that they need additional time to work on the case. We're talking a year or more of additional time. Then they start taking money from the person's social security. It's okay for the IRS to put people's cases off for years, penalizing them and threatening them and taking money from their accounts, but if a person doesn't respond to their threatening letters, they're in trouble.

"Barb was almost in tears, giving my mother the bad news. Mom tried to explain how she was scammed and had no idea the insurance was AHCA. Statements from Florida Blue came, but it has never been identified as AHCA. How evil. These insurance agents aren't human. They have to have the blood of demons."

"Could she hire an attorney?" Dan asked.

"Right. And have to pay attorney fees that will reach higher than the crazy amount from AHCA? IRS knows all of this. My mom only went to the doctor about three or four times the whole year. I'm sick, just sick," she said in her castigation.

"You would think the IRS agents would look at that unnatural amount owed and see the flaws. I tend to agree with you, they must be demons. We'll try and help you. There is no easy way to offer you hope, but we'll be here for you," Riggins offered with sensitivity.

"Thanks, but it's criminal what they get away with. And get this: My mother called the phone number they provided, and she keeps getting the recording that says, 'I'm sorry. Due to the high volume of calls, we cannot answer your call. Please try back tomorrow.' Over and over and over. It's reprehensible."

"Talk about a hopeless and cruel situation. We're so sorry," Dan said emotionally.

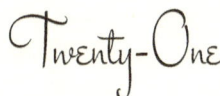

Twenty-One

THE DREARY MOOD LINGERED, so Riggins brought out Christmas decorations. "Anyone want to help?"

"Sure. My wife is probably upset that I'm not there to help her, but she totally understands the need for me to be here. She wants you to know that, Riggs," Dan said.

"How did you end up with her? She's way out of your league," he said, chuckling.

"I have been wondering that myself. She is special." Dan stopped for a moment to picture her face in his mind. "I know what will bring a smile to her face. When we put up the tree, let's take a picture of us decorating it."

"That's a plan. But after Gene and Britanica's wedding, you need to head home to be with your family for Christmas. We'll be fine."

"If you're sure, I will then."

"While you decorate, I'm going to take some time and drive to Green Bay to get some gifts for Brucie," Sam said. He walked out the door before Riggins could object.

"Do you think you'll ever be able to be civil to him?" Dan asked sincerely.

"I don't know, and it doesn't matter. Once this is over, I'll never have to work with him again. I'm going to go cut down a tree and I'll be right back."

They decorated the house and put the tree up. Brucie finally came out of the room, rubbing her sleepy eyes. "Oh, wow, it looks great. I don't know why, but I didn't think men cared about decorating."

"I love everything about the Christmas season and decorate every year. My dad made it a priority. Our house looked like a Christmas store. See all those Hallmark houses, snowmen and angels? They connect and when you push the button on one of them, the rest in that group chime in. Try the Santa band. The saxophone is my favorite," Riggins added.

She pushed the button and watched. It brought a huge smile to her face.

"Do you want to help decorate the tree?" Riggins asked.

"Yes, I think I would."

"Wait. Will you snap a picture of Riggins and me decorating the tree for my wife? She always worries that I'm missing out on special moments. Such a lovely woman, she is," Dan remarked with her face in his mind.

"I think that is a great idea, Dan." They posed holding ornaments up to the tree. He sent the picture right away to his wife.

Glancing out the window, it looked like a winter wonderland. Snowdrifts blew in the wind.

The snow looked like it was covered with glitter. Trees covered in clumps of snow. What a beautiful sight. Brucie sighed in awe.

While decorating the tree, cups of hot chocolate loaded with whipped cream and sprinkles sat on the coffee table and Christmas music blasted from the T.V. The Trans-Siberian Orchestra on the screen. The guitar players shook their heads down and back up, strands of long hair swishing like a gust of wind blowing by, hanging down their back and face. Dan and Riggins struck poses like the guitar players, swinging their heads as though they had long hair. Brucie busted up laughing.

"Plans are made for your mother to be here for Christmas

week. We will have extra security while *Rambo* here spends time with his family. I got gifts for Paula and the kids," he added, bending his head around the tree to make sure Dan heard him.

The doorbell rang. Both men grabbed their weapons and slowly approached the door, with Dan motioning to Riggins that he was ready. Brucie hid behind the tree. The door slowly creaked open and a UPS driver held packages, and some stacked on the ground. Not taking any chances, Riggins kept his eye on the driver while signing for them, making the driver uncomfortable. He backed away, looking back at Riggins with raised eyebrows. "Merry Christmas. Oh, here, I meant to give you a tip." Riggins handed him a twenty-dollar bill. The driver smiled and thanked him. When the driver pulled away, Dan came back out to help bring in the packages. Riggins was preoccupied and didn't realize Sam forgot to activate the yard alarm when he left. Good thing for Sam because it would be strike three.

"My sweet wife sent packages for you all." Dan smiled fondly.

"For me? She doesn't even know me," Brucie asked quizzically.

"That's just my wife. She knows what you've been through, and it blesses her soul to reach out."

"She sounds amazing." Dan nodded his head and smiled at Brucie.

"Where is Sam? He should be helping to decorate the tree," she asked.

"Decorating is not his thing. He went shopping," Riggins ended with a smirk to his face.

Dan noticed.

"You're missing the most important part of decorating," Brucie said to Riggins.

"Oh no I'm not. It's in that box over there," he said, pointing. She looked in the box.

"We add a piece each day to the nativity scene, and the baby Jesus is placed on the trough Christmas morning."

"That's really special. I hope I get to participate."

"Certainly. You can start by putting the manger on the table over here where it is front and center."

This really was lifting her spirit. "And thanks for arranging for my mother to be here during Christmas. I wish she could be here for the wedding, but that would be too dangerous."

"You're welcome and you're right. It's going to be hard to keep you safe, but I have several agents coming that day for extra security. Sam doesn't even know them."

"I hope these agents won't be missing Christmas with their families on my account. But, with all our fussing at each other and losing our tempers, you still go above and beyond keeping me safe. Thank you. I'll be honest, though, I need to be in my own home. When will that happen?"

"Unfortunately, that is the question we all have. We'll get them. When is the frustrating answer we're all looking for. And as far as the added security, they are all single and eager for the work."

"That makes me feel better. I understand how hard you're all working. You know what we need?"

The guys held their hands up.

"Christmas cookies." Her whole face lit up.

"That's exactly what we need," Dan answered. "I eat healthy year-round, except I do splurge at Christmas, and once in a while over the year."

Brucie looked through the cupboards and refrigerator and sighed. "Looks like you do as well," she said in Riggins' direction.

"Yeah, I do tend to eat on the healthy side. Make a list and I'll call Sam to pick up the ingredients."

"I have a better idea. Let's go to my cabin. Pretty sure I may have a lot of the ingredients I need."

"Sure. Grab your keys and I'll drive you."

Brucie and Riggins came back with bags and bags of baking products, cookie cutters, cookie sheets and everything she could think of. Then she wrote down what else she needed and gave the list to Riggins. His eyes popped wide open.

"You need all of this?"

"Yes, I do. I'll pay for it."

She heard Riggins on the phone with Sam. "Just get the stuff, and I'll reimburse you when you get here." His head swung in frustration.

"My list was a little intimidating, I guess?"

"Yeah, he asked what vanilla beans were."

"Once you guys taste my treats, you'll see. Just get your jogging pants ready for the day after Christmas. Trust me, you'll see why."

Later that day, it looked like a bakery. Peanut butter balls, cookies of all kinds, butterscotch scotcheroos krispie treats, fudge and cupcakes. The guys each took a turn at wiping flour, frosting and peanut butter off her face. She was a baking mess, but adorable. They helped clean up and put everything into containers. She filled a Christmas platter with some of everything that she made and scooted them out of the kitchen.

"Find a Christmas movie and I'll bring some snacks out." First, she brought out hot cocoa covered with whipped cream melting over the sides of the cups, and a speckle of sprinkles. Then she brought out the platter. Faces were bright with anticipation. By this time, Sam had returned.

"How about *Home Alone*?" Sam asked.

"Yes," she answered in an of-course tone.

"You weren't kidding. Everything is scrumptious," Riggins said, holding a hand on his stomach.

Sam kissed her cheek and thanked her. She smiled affectionately at him. Dan couldn't help but notice Riggins staring at her in an adoring manner. She was wearing a warm onesie.

Brucie and Riggins received a phone call at the same time and jumped up and into each other trying to depart from the living room. Riggins grabbed her arm to steady her from falling and mouthed the words "sorry," and she smiled and mouthed it back.

They came back into the living room. "Hey, did you get the same message?" she asked Riggins.

"Yeah, I guess we're meeting them at the Holiday Inn tomorrow to finalize plans before the wedding next week."

"Finally. I'm so excited. Those two have waited forever, it seems, and the wedding is going to be magical."

"Women," Sam said, jesting.

"Yeah, so what? Men don't care about the arrangements?" Riggins asked.

They all looked at each other, waiting to see who would be the bravest to speak up.

"Since I'm the only one who got married here," Dan explained, "I'll answer. I really didn't care about the arrangements. The justice of the peace would have been fine, but I wanted her to be happy. And she was. Although there were some intense moments beforehand. That's the part I could do without."

"I can understand your point of view, but it is important to women to have it just right. My wedding is going to be magical, too—one day! Don't look at me like I'm ready now because I'm so not ready."

Sam wiped imaginary sweat from his forehead. He was certainly enjoying the time they spent together, but they were not even close to being in a real relationship. At least he wasn't ready.

"Well, I hate to disappoint you all, but I want a say in my wedding preparations. I want us to both enjoy the day and compromise where needed and splurge where needed. I attended a wedding of a good friend and they had very few decorations. The outdoor location was breathtaking and didn't need all those fancy flower arrangements and things that couldn't add to the beauty. I don't remember what kind of trees they were, but white flowers hung down to the ground. It was incredible and kept the cost down. I do like the idea of soft, white fabric flowing in the breeze, though," Riggins commented with genuine interest.

"I never pictured you to be the kind to give one eensie weensie thought to it. Huh!" Brucie interjected.

"Sounds like a nightmare to me," Sam added. Everyone glared at him.

Twenty-Two

Speaking on the phone, Flagstone completed registration to rent a spot at a house across the pond from Brucie's cabin and under a fictitious name. It's no surprise he had several fake ID's. He wanted this to end once and for all. And NOTHING, nothing at all would stop him this time. It wasn't just the fact that Brucie saw him with the body, it was more. Much more. This became the most exciting hunt of his life.

"If it weren't for those stupid chimps, I would have killed the Java rhino, most sought after creature in the world. I almost got that sea creature, too, one day, the...the—Sheesh, what is that thing called?"

"I remember, it's the Vaquita. What a beautiful animal it is," Azar said in thought.

"Yeah, and then those stupid chimps jumped on us from the trees and smashed our weapons, but not before biting my hand. My fingers are still paralyzed. That scared the rhinos off. They'll pay. Among hunters all over the world, we would have exceeded our reputation. Now these agents have ruined our exotic hunting business. Nobody would have suspected these animals to be in this territory. It was a brilliant plan. Malarkie's stupid father paid with his life for it. Now, his son will pay, just as soon as we get that witch. Malarkie doesn't have any idea that I know who he is. And those chimps I want captured so I can kill them myself." He stared at the wall, face turning red, lips tight and lifeless fingers dangling.

"What'll we do after this is over?" Hafsa inquired sincerely.

"I haven't thought about it." His hands were squeezing each other so tight, they were turning white. "Here's the plan. It'll work this time. Now that we know where her home is located and that she is staying at Malarkie's place, it's as easy as pulling a trigger, except I will squeeze the life out of her.

"But wait! I just thought of a better idea. After I capture her, I'll hunt her down, just like all the other trophies hanging on my wall. I've never hunted a person like some dumb animal." His laugh was diabolical.

"You mean you are going to hang her head on the wall?" Azar asked with a deep gulp.

"Ooh, this is even better. Our next place will have a secret passageway and I'll display it proudly down there. It's in the works as we speak."

"But won't it…um, smell?" Hafsa interjected.

"Who cares right now? We'll deal with that when the time comes." He rubbed his hands together. "Here's the plan."

After an hour of preparation, Azar and Hafsa walked out of the room and quickly. "What'd ya think?" Azar asked.

"Deranged. He's freaking me out. After this is over, we'll split. We have enough money to go wherever we want. Our heads may be hanging on that wall one day, too, the way he's talkin'," Hafsa responded nervously.

———

Back at Riggins, Brucie and Sam hung out a lot more. She snuggled up to him easily and they talked and laughed the day away.

Riggins looked through the window from the back porch. "Is she really falling for that guy? How can she be so stupid?"

"More like vulnerable. Right now, her emotions are shooting in all directions, and she probably has no idea how to harness them. Not to mention Sam is quite the attractive guy. Don't go getting all huffy and yelling at her. If it hasn't changed her feelings for him, it won't make a difference now. Just maybe she has real true feelings for him and he for her," Dan said carefully.

Riggins sighed. "Do you really believe that?"

"I believe she is very emotional and is soaking in the attention because of her insecurities.

The rest of it is questionable.

"Look, as your friend I have observed all of you. From my expertise in profiling, I'd say you're in love with her."

"You've lost your mind. Have you not seen how angry we make each other? She is part of the assignment and nothing more."

"Okay buddy. You just keep repeating that," Dan replied, patting his shoulder before walking away.

Riggins placed his face between his hands and sat silently for a moment. Then he looked through the window. The sun shined on her, making her eyes sparkle and hair glisten. She was radiant, breathtaking, and looked so innocent. He shook his head and jumped up to go play with the chimps outside. Thankfully, their playground was insulated and covered. The frightful weather is no place for chimpanzees.

———

While coffee perked, Brucie jumped in the shower the next morning. She had arranged for Sam to drive her to work for a day of depositions at the office. Muffin and coffee in hand, they left for work. He hung out in the vehicle and kept his eyes on her building, except for the occasional walk to the restroom. He was bored to death. So, he called one of the Daisy Duke girls as he sat in the SUV.

Work took her mind off of troubles. She set up, not realizing what tragedy would be discovered during the depositions. As she typed, the testimony was excruciating to listen to. Now came time for exhibits. The pictures were entered into evidence. As hard as she tried not to look at them, there was no choice. The degree of abuse administered to these animals was heartbreaking. She coughed. Sputters kept coming from her mouth. She jumped up and threw her hands down. "I can't listen anymore." Hands grabbing her head, a monsoon of tears and sucking in of air wouldn't stop. The attorney pulled her into an embrace, holding her tight against him. He knew about the sorrow she was dealing with in her personal life. They agreed to stop the deposition and revisit it next week. She couldn't talk but thanked him.

An hour break worked wonders. Brucie didn't have the heart to tell her boss how she flubbed the deposition. Her boss had been so understanding and she acted unprofessional. But she couldn't help but wonder how anyone could sit through that testimony. You had to be a tin man in order to listen.

MR. HOWARD: "Could you tell me in your own words what happened to you?"

The child wouldn't look up. He struggled with words. Brucie looked at him in disbelief. The mother spoke out.

MRS. BROWN: "Sir, it is too hard for him to speak. Could I give my statement and then speak to him afterwards to see if he's able to talk?"

MR HOWARD: "I'm fine with that." He motioned out the door for his aunt to come and get him. A private room was set up just in case.

MR HOWARD: "Okay, Mrs. Brown. Please take your time.

MRS. BROWN: "Richard was born with several deformities. Kids were always making fun of him, and some of them were terrified of his features. I quit work and stayed home to home-school him. His father got sick and passed away a year ago. Richard is of sound mind, so being thirteen, I left him home alone so I could go to work. Income was badly needed, as you may suspect.

"To my stupidity, we lived in an unsafe neighborhood. One day while I was working, three teenagers broke in. After seeing Richard, they became scared. I'm relaying what Richard told me happened. They started calling him a freak and any horrible words you could think of. Richard has an excellent memory. I tend to wonder if it is a photographic memory. It amazes me.

"One of the boys pulled out a knife and proceeded to cut up his face. The other boys kept kicking his body. The leader of them, holding the knife, shouted, 'Now you look better.' They laughed hysterically and ran out. Richard was bleeding badly. Hurt badly." She stopped speaking, licking her lips over and over, and eyes holding back torrential tears. "He told me it would be better if he just died. His life would never be okay, nor mine. He somehow managed to call me when they left, because he didn't think he was going to make it and wanted to tell me—He wanted to tell me he loved me." She wiped the excess of tears away.

"As you can see, he did make it and helped the police sketch artist to draw their faces. He swears the three boys in custody are the ones who beat and cut him up."

By this time, Brucie was inhaling deep, intentional breaths. She tried to remain unattached to the case, but it was difficult. The boy was brought in again.

She smiled, picturing his sweet face in her mind. *He's so sweet, so lovable. There's good in him. Why God? Why did this happen to him? It's wrong.*

By the time her boss arrived, the deposition was over. Brucie's coworker and friend, Candace, had called their boss to report the disturbing depositions Brucie was assigned to, because she was worried Brucie wouldn't be mentally ready for such a tragic case.

Their boss saw Brucie talking with the boy while the mother listened. She was ready to take over the deposition for Brucie if she was having too difficult of a time with the case. She had no way of knowing if Brucie was on break or what, so she kept her distance. When she noticed Brucie had everything under control, she didn't interrupt her, and Brucie didn't even notice she was standing there.

"You were so brave in there. You know, you are the role model I hope my children will be like. My name is Brucie."

"You have a boy's name?" he said innocently.

She chuckled. If Riggins said that, she would have clobbered him. "No. The boy's name would be Bruce. If you ever want to talk with someone, just to talk, I would love you to call me. I could visit you, or you could visit me. Hey, I have an idea. I'm staying in a temporary home. We have two chimpanzees that are being cared for until a court case is complete. They are sweet and fun. If you would like to visit and play with them, here is my phone number." She handed the card to his mother and kissed his cheek goodbye.

Leaving for the day, Brucie threw her stuff in Sam's vehicle, jumped in and leaned against the door. "Sam, please just take me straight home. I'm exhausted."

"As you wish."

She entered Riggins' cabin and went straight to the bedroom, slammed the door and locked it. She fell on the bed. Angry tears, sad tears, caring tears spilled onto the blanket.

———

"What's going on?" Riggins asked about to lose his temper.

"I don't really know. She came out of the office and wouldn't say a word the whole drive. I sat in the SUV all day and didn't speak with anyone. I didn't do one thing wrong." He held up his hands in surrender.

Riggins called the office and spoke with her boss. He hung up. Dan and Sam watched his expression. He swung his head back and forth. "Who can blame her? I would lie in that bed for three days after the day she had. Oh, my goodness."

"What? What?" Dan asked.

"We'll discuss it later. Just know the cases were inhumane."

All the guys sat quietly. Conversation would be exhausting.

———

The next morning, Brucie ran out of her bedroom. "Riggins! Riggins! Where are you?"

He came running in from the back porch. Before he could speak, she spoke. "I need you to allow this abused boy to come over and play with the chimps. You and I can stay with him. It's really important to him, and to be honest, to me as well. I had informed them that they can't say anything to anyone. Sam can drive them here in his SUV since the windows are blacked out, so no one can see them. Trust me. Please."

Riggins scratched his face. Man, this could go very wrong. Brucie was desperate and telling her no would be bad for her and everyone else. He paced. She waited for his response, fidgeting.

He agreed, and they set it up where Sam drove the boy and his mother, and other agents would remain hidden up and down South Shore Drive.

Later that day, when they arrived, Riggins took one look at the boy and almost busted out in tears. He held it together for the boy's sake and introduced himself to Richard and his mother. He shook the boy's hand and escorted them inside. Brucie ran up, bent down, and hugged Richard. Next, she placed a kiss on his cheek. She embraced his mother with open arms.

Riggins watched Brucie with a warmness. She was genuine. *People in this world could benefit with a heart transplant from her heart.* He had never met someone with such passion. Not only that but caring for this boy was helpful to her as well. He could see how taking attention off of herself gave her purpose. He felt all warm and mushy inside, watching her with the boy and chimps. It was time to join her in the activities. Brucie and he fell in love with this child.

Sam laid on the couch all day seemingly uninterested in all of it.

When Richard and his mom left, Riggins asked her, "How could anyone hurt someone that special? That boy *is* special. If only children who think they're 'normal' could take notes from him. Thank you, Brucie. This has lifted my spirits."

She squeezed his hand. "No. Thank you. I'll never forget today. I pray Richard will be a part of my life even when things get back to normal."

"I was thinking the same thing. He doesn't have a man figure in his life. A busy life can be managed if the right circumstances arise, and this is the right circumstances."

Her eyes grew warm, and for a minute, she felt genuinely attracted to him. "You know, Malarkie, you make my head feel like a washing machine. It flips from warm to cold cycle, a rigorous swishing back and forth on the spin cycle, to the soft trickling of the rinse cycle. My head doesn't know when the next cycle begins."

He wiped his hands together and replied, "Well, then. Looks like my job here is done." He cracked a smile.

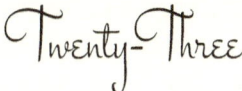

Twenty-Three

FLAGSTONE AND MEN threw their duffle bags once again on the floor of the cottage directly across the lake from Brucie's cabin. Too much heat, they left the state for a month. A tripod was set up and they took turns spying.

"I'm taking a nap. If you see any signs of agents or that witch, wake me up at once."

"Yes, sir."

"Azar, get over to her cabin and hide. She'll have to come home sooner or later."

"But it's really cold out."

Mr. Flagstone stared at him with eyes of ice. No words were needed.

"Yes, sir. I'll bundle up." He glanced at Hafsa and puckered his lips on the way out.

———

Brucie had taken a nap. Arms stretched behind her as she sat up. It was so quiet and getting dark outside. She stumbled to the door and peeked out. Nobody around. The Christmas lights were sparkling like stars. That brought a smile. Logs were sizzling in the fireplace. "I just love that smell. It makes everything feel cozy."

She walked out and checked the rooms to see if everyone was sleeping and spotted a note on the coffee table. "Sam, keep an eye on Brucie until we get back. Riggins."

Sam was sound asleep on the couch. Brucie went back to the bedroom and rummaged through her clothes. "I need more clothes. They'll never know I'm gone. It will take me a few minutes and I'll be back before they know it."

After quietly grabbing Sam's keys and disarming all alarms, she slipped out the back door.

A sense of calm came over her as she pulled into her driveway. "I miss you, home."

The door unlocked and she walked in slowly, looking in each direction before disarming the alarm. Convinced all was good, she walked around the cabin and inspected. She turned the faucet on in the kitchen and bathrooms to make sure the pipes didn't freeze up because of the record-breaking cold temperatures. Her body shivered, and she turned up the heat. She was unaware that Riggins or Sam came over daily to inspect the cabin. With a luggage bag packed, she started to leave, and then it hit her. "I need something really cute to wear to the dinner tomorrow. Riggins will get mad, but Sam and I are going to hang around and dance. I don't care. I've given up enough of my freedom. I need some fun.

"Am I being selfish? I mean, look at everything they have done for me, but I'm sure they're being paid for it. I'm an assignment, so yes, I deserve some fun, and you, Malarkie, will just have to get over it."

Luggage thrown in the back, she began to open the door, but stopped suddenly. The sky had darkened with a dreary feeling. The quietness was building a fear inside of her. It was as though she could feel eyes peering through her soul. She turned her head slowly to scan the area and heard a snap. Her body jumped and she let out a mild gasp. Not knowing if it was fear or being cold, her body trembled. Then she saw a squirrel jump to a tree.

Still scanning the area, she decided to check around her house to make sure there was no damage from the windy nights before. Her feet crunched through the snow. There was no living being around. Even that squirrel was smart enough to run into a hole in the tree. The sound of someone running through the snow and ice crackled in her ears. Fright froze her body immobile. She held her breath.

The truck seemed to be miles away. The bushes around her swished. Just as she started to scream, a hand went around her mouth and pulled her behind another bush. Fear crept in every inch of her body. Her heart was doing somersaults. Fear had reached new heights.

"Don't make a sound. It's me, Riggins. One of those men is running this way. They must have been casing your place out, just waiting for you. We'll discuss that later."

He removed his hands, and she closed her eyes and sighed. The snow crunching came to a halt. Riggins peeked out and took his stance. "When I say run, get out to the truck and drive back to my cabin." His breathing was heavy, but he was motionless. Her body shook like never before. They could hear the crunching and sloshing through snow and puddles start back up. The person came close and stopped.

Brucie and Riggins saw a man appear, panting under his breath. The sky was dark, and the moon was coming out, casting just enough light for Riggins to see him. Like a cheetah, Riggins jumped out and tackled the man, taking him by surprise. "Go! Run!" Riggins yelled.

Brucie took off while the men wrestled. She could hear punches being thrown, huffs of pain coming out of their mouths, but she didn't know whose mouth, rolling over snow, crackling and crunching beneath them. More punches. She covered her ears and squeezed her eyes shut. "I can't leave him," she murmured. "No, I'll go get Sam." Before she left it sounded like a gun went off and the sound of something solid hitting a body. The tires squealed in the slush, and she was at Riggins' house in no time.

With trembling fingers, she finally unlocked the door, and shoved it open. "Sam! Get up!"

Sam woke, squinting his eyes and wiping hands through his hair. He jumped up. "What? What's wrong?" he slurred.

"Hurry, Riggins is fighting with someone at my cabin, and it sounds bad. Really bad."

She started the truck's engine as he slid into the passenger's seat. She peeled out as slush sprayed around the driveway and over the truck.

Brucie almost forgot to put the truck in park before jumping out. Sam grabbed her arm.

"Slow down," he said calmly. "Put the truck in park and stay here. I'll go find Riggins."

"He's around the cabin, over there," she said pointing, voice elevated.

Sam pulled his weapon out and began to walk, but Gene pulled up in the police cruiser, lights flashing like a strobe light, the siren piercing their ears. Brucie jumped out of the truck and ran into Gene's arms. "Gene, I think Riggins has been shot. It's all my fault. I'm so selfish," she mumbled between a tear downpour and sniffles.

Gene placed his hands on both of her arms and moved her back to look in her frightened eyes. "He's okay. He and Dan have the man handcuffed and called me to haul him to jail."

Brucie wiped her eyes and kept holding her breath to keep from crying. By this time, Dan was walking up with the man known as Azar, who had black and blue marks on his face and swollen eyes. Brucie watched as Dan escorted him with arms the size of a branch from a huge oak tree, muscles defined and bulging. But then she heard yelling. She ran behind the corner to find Sam shoved up against the wall with Riggins' strong arm under Sam's chin pushing him against the wall, screaming, and spit flying.

"She could have been killed. Why can't you do your job?"

Brucie ran up and grabbed Riggins' arm. "Stop! It's not his

fault. I was sleeping and he fell asleep on the couch, which you very well know. This is all my fault. He is not to blame. Please, Riggins, please."

He removed his arm and Sam slunk down trying to get oxygen intake flowing through his veins once again. He coughed.

Riggins grabbed his left upper arm, and blood seeped through his fingers.

"Oh-my-gosh, you've been shot." The ambulance pulled up. She heard the siren and started pulling him around the cabin.

He pulled his arm out of her grip. "I'm fine. It's not serious."

She walked with him to the ambulance. Gene and Dan ran to him, patting his shoulder and congratulating his success in capturing one of the men named Azar. "Knock it off. I couldn't have done it without your help, Dan, so thank you. We've always made a good team."

Dan patted his other arm. "That we have, buddy." Sam straggled out and heard the conversation. His face turned red and he cussed under his breath. He would never fit in with these guys. Never.

While Riggins was being placed in the ambulance, Brucie strolled up. "Could I ride with you to the hospital?"

"That's not necessary. However, I would appreciate it if you take care of my little guys. Flagstone has a vendetta against them, too."

Her brows pushed together. "Why?"

"I'll explain it when I get back. She laid her hand on his and with warm eyes she said sincerely, "I'm really sorry for putting you in harm's way. I'm very grateful for the time and effort you have given to my safety. My promise to you is that I will never do something this stupid again. You're a brave man, Malarkie, and that's no malarkey."

His body shivered and he couldn't help but smile. To cover the sensation running through his body, exposing his physical tremors, he said, "It's getting cold out. You better get back, and, um, thanks."

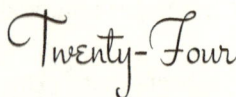

Twenty-Four

RIGGINS WAS RELEASED THAT EVENING. Dan quietly opened the door to his cabin so as to not wake up Sam and Brucie. They had both fallen asleep on the couch, television on low volume to some advertisement. Sam jumped at the quiet tap on the floor. His body jerk woke Brucie.

"They released you already?" she asked.

"Yes, like I told you, it wasn't serious."

She tilted her head and frowned. "Okay, tough guy. Being shot anywhere is a serious matter, but I'm glad you're okay."

"Thanks. Let's all get some sleep."

They stumbled to their beds.

The next morning, the chimps hollering and shaking the iron bars of their room-size cage woke everyone. Brucie didn't realize Riggins was in their room and stumbled right into him. He started to lose balance, and she grabbed his uninjured arm to support him.

"Sorry, but I thought you would be sleeping."

"We all slept in so late that these poor two are starving. I'll take care of them."

"Oh, no you won't. Either go back to bed or sit on the couch. I'll take care of them and fix coffee and breakfast. Go on, shoo," she said, waving him out.

While the chimps ate, she made chocolate oatmeal, toast and coffee. It was going on 11:30. She carried a tray of coffee and condiments out to the living room. Each man took a cup and thanked her. Next, she brought in bowls steaming with hot cereal, a pitcher of milk and some sugar, for those with a sweet tooth like her. Laying the tray on the table, she pulled the top of the coffee table up so Riggins could eat in comfort. She sweetened his bowl of hot cereal the way he liked and placed it in front of him.

His nose wrinkled. "Just what am I eating?" he asked staring at it like it was filled with bugs.

"Chocolate oatmeal, silly."

"Ah, yes, chocolate."

"It's good and nice and warm. The temps are below twenty today. I'm going to dress the chimps, so you guys eat up."

"Thank you for doing this," Riggins remarked.

"My pleasure. It may not be a Bobby Flay meal, but hey, it's perfect for this freezing day. And yummy, if I say so myself."

"It's chocolate, so of course it's yummy to you," Sam said, shaking his head.

"Just shut up and eat it," she said in jest.

"Mmmm, this is quite tasty, and she does make a good cup of coffee," Dan commented.

"I'll be darned. It is good," Riggins agreed.

Sam took a spoonful and spit it back into the bowl. "Yuck, is all I've got to say."

Dan and Riggins gave him the evil eye.

"What? Can't I have my own opinion? Don't worry, I won't hurt her feelings. I'll dispose of it before she gets back."

He grabbed the bowl and headed to the kitchen.

After lunch, Brucie heard yelling from the living room. "What now?"

She slowly opened the bedroom door and peeked around the corner. The guys were sitting up with rigid postures, their faces intense. More screaming. They were watching a football game.

"Good grief, Charlie Brown. These are grown men acting ridiculous."

The chimps were jumping up and down and hollering, too.

"I hate to say this, but you guys are a bad role model for these chimps. Very poor sportsmen-like attitudes."

"The refs are cheating," Riggins informed her, holding his uninjured arm toward the TV."

"Yeah, man, cheating," Dan added. Sam sat silent with his arms crossed, raising his eyebrows up and down towards her.

"Either you guys behave, or I'll take that remote from you," Brucie replied with hands on her hips.

"No-no-no-no. We'll behave," Riggins spouted with bulging eyes.

She watched another play. "Facemask! Oh yeah, facemask."

They all stared at her speechless. "I don't think so," Riggins said.

"I'm with him. I never saw it," Dan added.

After the replay review, the referee announced, "The ruling on the previous play is a facemask. A 15-yard penalty."

Brucie cheered, formed a fist, blew on it and rubbed it above her chest.

"All right then. I'm going to take a shower and get ready for our dinner with the wedding gang. You will need to get ready soon," she said, looking back and forth at Sam and Riggins.

"Why is he going? He's not part of the wedding party," Riggins said.

"To protect me. Besides, we're going to hang around and do some dancing afterwards. I assume Dan is coming along, so he could escort you home."

Dan shrugged his shoulders. "Yeah, I'm fine with that."

"I don't think it's a good idea," Riggins snapped.

"I have some buddies hanging out from the force to monitor any activity. She'll be protected," Sam assured him.

"If past events didn't prove otherwise, I would be okay with this, but—"

"But nothing. He even has a female agent to accompany me to the restroom. It will be fine. I promise," Brucie interjected.

"Very well, but you," he said, pointing with his index finger to Sam, "you better not mess up again. It will be strike three, and you know what that means."

"Yeah, yeah. Like I haven't heard that before," Sam snorted.

Riggins jumped up, mouth tightening. Dan grabbed his shoulder. "Just take er easy, man."

Sam stood with a defiant look. He'd had enough of Riggins always talking down to him.

Thankfully, the TV screen came alive with cheers. A touchdown. The distraction was perfect timing. The game was over, the men dressed for dinner and waited on Brucie. She walked out in a mini skirt, long-sleeved leotard shirt, boots and an early 70's cap, like she walked right off the set of *Mod Squad*.

Sam's eyebrows wrinkled. "Why are you dressed like that?"

Riggins looked her over. "You look absolutely fantastic. I loved that style back then."

"Yeah, back then, but not today's style," Sam interjected.

"You just have no taste, do you?" Riggins said, glaring at him.

"All right. All right. Dan, does this look stupid? You are the tie breaker and speak the truth. You know, do you solemnly swear to tell the truth, blah, blah, blah."

"Okay, you asked for it." He walked up to her, picked her up and twirled her. "I love it. It's fun and looks really great on you."

Sam rolled his eyes and Brucie caught him. "Are you going to be embarrassed to be seen with me? I can change clothes."

"No!" Riggins and Dan yelled in unison.

"Look, Brucie. We would never allow you to be seen in something that makes you a laughingstock. Wear it proudly. Not everyone could get away with it like you can," Riggins said with honesty.

"Okay, you've convinced me. 'Let's go girls'," she added, singing the words of Shania Twain's song.

At the restaurant, Britanica and Emmy ran up and moved

around with her in a circle, excited and loving her outfit. They ate and discussed final wedding plans.

"Britanica, this wedding sounds like something out of a fairy tale," Brucie said in disbelief.

"Well, the truth is that it is far cheaper than you would expect. Friends are donating what we need. It's so naturally beautiful that we don't have to add many flowers. We are going to have soft, flowing fabric and fairy lights all over the place. Riggins helped us with that part. He even bought the fabric."

"No kidding! He just doesn't seem like the type who could have come up with such an incredible, romantic design," Brucie said in wonder. She glanced over to Riggins' table, and he was watching her. When their eyes met, his face flushed, and he turned away. Brucie noticed and a chill trembled through her body.

"There's a lot you don't know about him. He may seem all *Rambo* and stuff on the outside, which you all know I adore, but there is so much more to him. I can't believe you haven't seen that," Britanica added.

"Brit, this isn't just about Brucie. He is out to avenge his father's murder. That's why he seems so intense," Emmy suggested.

"You're right. Your protection and avenging his father would make anyone tight as a drum," Britanica said, pondering as she looked over at him.

"Curious. Very curious," Brucie said in thought. She glanced over and saw Sam smiling and flirting with a waitress.

Emmy noticed and couldn't refrain herself. "So how are things with you and him?" she asked, motioning toward Sam with head tilting movements.

"We are getting along really well. Don't worry, he is not marriage material. He is just a good distraction from all the chaos. But truthfully," she said nodding, "I like being with him. He makes me laugh and keeps my mind off of such heavy thoughts." He looked over and winked at her. She smiled, even though the waitress was all goo-goo eyes at him.

"If I didn't know better, girl, I would swear Riggins is falling in love with you. The way he looks—"

"Stop right there, Brit. I annoy him to the living end. His face turns red with anger. I can see invisible smoke coming from his head and rarely does he talk to me other than business. Now, Sam and I are going to spend the rest of the evening dancing. And that concerned look wondering if I'm physically up for dancing, take comfort that I'm totally fine, ankle and all. See you next Friday for rehearsal." They joined hands and jumped up and down like school children.

"Finally, I get to be Gene's wife. It seems we have waited an eternity to get here. I love him so much." Brit's eyes teared.

"And look at his loving eyes gazing through your soul." Emmy quivered. "I can feel how much he loves you and it just gives me goosebumps."

"Em, you ready? You need your rest," Webster said and kissed her cheek. His warm eyes shot out a deep love for her as well.

"Why does she need her rest, Web?" Britanica said with a questionable look. Emmy sneered at him.

Slowly, giving it thought, he replied, "She's been under the weather. That's all."

"Em, why didn't you say anything?" Brit's concerned face asked.

"Because. He is making much more out of it than it needs to be. I'm fine and I'll be fine for the wedding. See you then."

They scooted out so quickly that Britanica and Brucie looked at each other for a minute but didn't add their two cents to the mystery.

Brucie kissed Britanica's cheek and grabbed Sam's hand. "Come on big boy. It's time to dance."

Dan watched Riggins' face turn red and his hands form into fists. He leaned over and whispered, "Yeah, buddy. There's no feelings for her. Come on. Time to get you home."

Sam and Brucie danced the night away. They laughed and had a great time together, to the point Brucie couldn't help but think how much she liked being with him but kept that piece of information to herself.

Twenty-Five

THE NEXT DAY, they all sat around the living room watching everything and anything. Brucie, bored to death, legs in constant motion, began to talk, and talk, and talk. All three guys trying their best not to be agitated would nod their heads and make short conversation. Finally, Riggins could take it no more.

"Are you on speed or something? I mean, talk about loquacious. You have no idea what this program is about. Do you?"

"Well, excuse me, Brit. I can tell you've been hanging around her. She used that word last week. Then a few days later she said something like 'my, you're in a garrulous mood'. Which means the same thing."

"So that's where I heard that word from, Britanica," Riggins said trying to remember.

"Well, who doesn't know the meaning of it?" she asked. Sam slowly raised a finger. "It sort of brings back sad memories. The days Brit felt as though she was the stupidest person in the world. The low self-esteem days were heartbreaking to hear about. But now she just uses big words out of habit. She's an incredible person," Brucie commented.

All three guys held up their coffee mugs and toasted Britanica.

"I have a great idea. Let's play poker. Anyone game?" She smiled brightly looking back and forth at each of them.

"Sure, I'll play," Dan replied.

Riggins held up his one hand to emphasize he wouldn't be able to with the other arm in a sling.

"No thanks," Sam said. "My eyes won't stay open. I can't fight sleep anymore. You wore me out last night, young lady."

Riggins glared at Sam, not liking his choice of words.

"Head to the table, Dan. I'll get the cards," she said.

They were playing for an hour when Riggins strolled into the kitchen, just in time to hear poker talk.

"I'll raise you three chocolate truffles and," she thought for a moment and slowly pushed a plate with a piece of cake into the middle of the table, "my piece of…dream chocolate cake. Can't believe I'm doing this. It tastes like a dream, true to its name." She gulped.

"I have been eyeing that cake this whole time." Dan licked his lips. "Okay, I'll be back in a jiffy. Watch her," he said in Riggins' direction.

Riggins shrugged his shoulders.

Dan came back to the table and dropped a handful of candy into the middle of the table. "I'll raise you my stash of mallo cups. I keep them hidden for occasions where healthy eating can take a hike. Chocolate, marshmallow and refined sugar at its best."

Her mouth dropped and it looked like the sun shined in the brightness of her eyes. In two minutes, they laid their cards face up on the table. Brucie let out a shriek and jumped up from the table. She pulled the heap of candy and cake to her side. Her head pushed up and when she looked into Dan's saddened eyes, she broke.

"All right. You can have a bite of my cake and I'll give you a couple mallo cups back. One bite. I mean it, buster."

He shook her hand, grabbed a fork and cut off a huge piece of cake.

"Hey! That's more than a bite and you know it. Put some back or I'll coldcock you," she protested, lips scrunched together.

"Hey, buddy, I'd believe her if I were you," Riggins said, with a raised eyebrow.

Dan brought the fork up to his mouth, took a look at her face and stopped. "Is he right? Are you going to hurt me?"

"I'm true to my word. So, you can be a coward and put some back or take it like a man."

His mouth opened. Riggins sighed quietly, and Dan put the fork back on the plate. "Call me chicken."

"You made the right call, buddy. You made the right call," Riggins remarked.

"I'll have to agree with him," she said confidently. She got another fork and cut off one bite's worth and handed it to Dan. He carefully ate it while watching every move she made to be sure it wasn't a trick.

He stood still, licking his lips like he was in a trance. His head moved slowly in her direction.

Riggins watched curiously.

"I can't do it. Never have I tasted anything so sinfully delicious in my life. I'll fight you for it. Not kidding."

She grabbed the cake and ran for the bedroom, barely able to close and lock it. Dan pounded on the door. "Brucie, I'm not kidding. Give me that cake before I break this door down."

"Never!"

"Then, this is war." He walked backward and prepared to knock the door down. A hand rested on his shoulder.

In a very serious tone, Riggins remarked, "It's not worth it, buddy. By now, she's eaten the whole thing and all you'll get is a bad shoulder."

The door creaked open. Brucie held the empty plate up, licking her lips. Chocolate rested on the corners of her mouth.

"Tell me where to get that cake and I won't hurt you."

"Next week at the wedding. It will be there," she informed him.

"You better not be lying to me."

She made a cross over her heart.

"Riggs, I'm heading outside for some fresh air." Dan walked outside with his head drooping.

"He almost acted serious," Brucie said.

"I believe he was. When Dan goes off his healthy eating diet, you don't want to cross him. We wrestled for pie one time, and let's just say, he was in it to win it," Riggins explained.

"Oh! I'm glad you told me. I'll be more careful next time."

She sat down by Sam, who remained quiet all this time. He wrapped his arms around her and pulled her over to him. He kissed her passionately and she loosened in his arms, kissing him back. The last thing they heard was the door slamming shut.

"Why does it bother Riggins so much that I enjoy being with you?" she asked Sam.

"Truthfully, he's a jerk. He never wanted me assigned to your case. I think he knew you and I would hit it off and it would destroy his macho, macho image. He has never treated me as an equal, and I'm getting sick and tired of it. So, you being with me is poetic justice."

"But what I'm getting at is that he actually seems jealous. We argue so much, and he is so arrogant and condescending at times. Why would he be jealous because we spend time together? It's not like he even likes me. And it's not like anything will turn into a relationship between you and me. You're not marriage material, and I'm not in the right frame of mind to be in a relationship. Not for a while. It would take an act of God to get me interested in a serious relationship with any guy," she explained.

"Who knows? Don't give him another thought. Just keep your thoughts on me." He pulled her over and kissed her warmly, passionately and steaming hot.

She pushed him back. "Slow down there, would ya?"

He let out a huge huff and pushed himself up from the couch. "I'm going to get some fresh air." He was gone before she could reply.

———

"Your majesty, do you mind if I go to the bar for a while, or will that be strike three?" Sam asked Riggins. His voice had a sound of being on edge.

"I'm your commanding officer, and you better remember that. Get out of here."

Riggins couldn't make out what Sam was saying under his breath, but he had an idea.

Sam hung out at the bar until closing. Mostly in the back seat of his truck with Daisy Dukes girl. Riggins watched him stumble into the house and, of course, not resetting the alarm. Sam fell over on the couch before he could give him a piece of his mind.

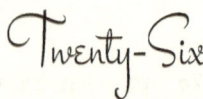

Twenty-Six

Finally. The day of Britanica's wedding arrived. It was a magical, sparkling, snow-covered day. Riggins provided very tasteful, soft, white linen that flowed in the breeze, creating an eloquent and more magical setting. The twinkling lights gave a diamond sparkle over the snow.

"Stoney, nobody is here. The chairs are empty. Oh, my goodness," Karyn, Britanica's mother said, worried.

Her sweet husband put an arm around her shoulder and replied, "They'll be here. Probably waiting until the last minute so they don't freeze. Britanica and her natural winter wonderland wedding. That girl," Stoney, Britanica's father, said to offer Karyn encouragement.

Just as he ended his statement, cars started driving in a line all the way past the top of the hill. It seemed the whole town showed up to Riverside Park, dressed warmly.

"Now, feel better?" Stoney asked Karyn.

"Yes, and because Britanica is marrying a man as wonderful as her father. I'm warming up already."

Becky from The Mane Attraction hair salon did her magic. The women attendants looked gorgeous. Feeling the nerves of the time approaching to walk down the aisle, they all looked at each other. Emotions ran high. They teared up and mascara smudged their faces.

"Now look what you've done. Back in the chair, girls," Becky said in jesting. After a laughing bout, the wedding march began. Emmy and Brucie walked down the aisle, Emmy dressed in a red, low-back glistering gown trimmed around the scoop of the dress and wrists in fluffy, white, fake fur. Brucie wore the identical gown but in a color green. Their hair had been curled and twisted loosely on one side.

Gene wore a white tuxedo with a red satin vest and candy cane striped bow tie. Webster and Riggins dressed in black tuxedos with green, satin vests and candy cane striped bow ties.

The flower girl walked down in an adorable candy cane striped dress, and with white gloves tossed snowflakes onto the red carpet.

The wedding march elevated as Britanica sat on a reindeer-driven sleigh, decorated with flowing linen and white flowers cascading from the garlands. Stoney helped her out of the sleigh, and they walked down the aisle. Oohs and awes were loud. Britanica's gown had custom-made snowflakes delicately sewn into the lace of the gown. Her veil sparkled with more snowflakes, and entwined in the bouquet were edible wafer paper snowflakes with edible glitter. She was a sight to behold.

After Stoney kissed her cheek, Gene grabbed her hand and stared with a galaxy of love, and Britanica's gaze reciprocated his thoughts. Emmy, Brucie and everyone else had such an emotional experience witnessing such a powerful love story.

Instead of vows, they both prepared a Shakespeare quote. Gene went first.

"I love you with so much of my heart that none is left to protest." *Much Ado About Nothing* (Act IV, scene i).

It was Britanica's turn. "I do love nothing in the world so well as you—is not that strange?" *Much Ado About Nothing* (Act IV, scene i).

Just as Britanica hoped, soft, beautiful snowflakes dropped from the sky. Even though it was really cold outside, their love warmed everyone's hearts. Soon the ceremony ended and as Gene and Britanica walked down the aisle, that trail of glittering lights wove between them. They watched, but this time, Britanica invisibly scooped them up in her hand and blew them at Brucie. She winked at Gene, and he laughed.

"That's just plain dirty. Brucie doesn't even know what hit her. She is under the Christmas magic spell."

Britanica rubbed her hands together and watched Brucie tremble as if a cold chill traveled up and down her body, just as she intertwined her hand in Riggins' arm as they walked down the carpet. Britanica and Gene gave each other a high five.

It was too cold outside so the reception was held at Holiday Inn at Kelly Lake, same as Webster and Emmy's wedding. The food was great, but Brucie noticed Dan standing and acting mighty suspicious by the wedding cake.

"That dirty dog. Look Riggins." Dan had cut a piece of cake from the back and ate with his back toward the crowd.

Riggins busted out in hysteria, and Brucie couldn't help but laugh.

People danced, but then Webster strolled up to Gene and Britanica and asked if he could dance with his sister. Webster looked in Britanica's rainy eyes and a tear dropped down his cheek. "You know you'll always be my kid sister, even though we're twins. Let's face it, I act a lot older than you. Emmy or Gene can never separate our bond, not that they would want to, but I'm happy for you, Brit. Really happy."

She hugged him tight, and her rainy tears turned into a downpour.

"Hey, I noticed you have candy canes sticking out of your bouquet. I'm proud of you, Brit."

"Me, too, and they don't even burn my hands. No longer my kryptonite. They taste mighty good, you know."

Webster grabbed one from a table and showed his agreement by the loud crunching.

"Hey Web, who invited Daisy Dukes girl?" Britanica asked.

"I don't really know. Sure hope that Sam fella didn't bring her along," Web replied. "Isn't he supposed to be dating Brucie?"

"Something like that but look at the attention he is giving that Daisy Dukes girl. I wouldn't put up with it," Britanica pointed out.

"Of course you wouldn't have noticed, being all in love and all that mushy stuff on your wedding day, but I already pointed out to Riggins how Daisy Duke's girl looks at her texts all the time and runs out the door very strange like. As if she is carrying on a secret conversation. I don't know, with all the intensity and fear going on, maybe I'm just paranoid, so I'll leave it up to the agents," Webster commented.

"Why does she have to dress so sleazy like? Obviously, she is in great shape, but does she have to flaunt it all the time? I mean, shouldn't I be the center of attention? That sounded arrogant. I didn't mean it that way," Britanica ended saying with a drawn-out sigh.

"Have you not noticed Sam can't take his eyes off of her and her him?" Webster added.

"I've noticed," Britanica replied in a scornful tone.

The rest of the evening was magical. Everyone was having a great time. Even Riggins.

Brucie danced with everyone who asked. But Riggins noticed her looking around, suspecting she was looking for Sam. He knew Sam and Daisy Dukes girl were out in the hallway in some corner. He didn't want her to find Daisy in his arms, because this was a day of celebration and memories. He didn't want her to look back at it someday and remember anything bad. But he had to do something, because it was obvious she was on a mission to find him now.

He gently grabbed her hand. "Hey, do I get a chance to dance with you?"

"Of course. I haven't seen Sam in a while, so let me find him first and then we'll dance."

As she started to head down the hallway, he stopped her.

"Couldn't we dance right now?"

"What are you hiding, Malarkie? What don't you want me to see?"

He thought about what to say. He was impressed with her skill in analyzing someone's words or expression. Maybe from observing in the courtroom. He wasn't worried for her safety, because he had brought in five other agents that she didn't know about. He had one of the agents follow Daisy Duke's girl ever since Webster brought her suspicious activity to Riggins' attention.

"Don't look for him. Please. I don't want that jerk to ruin your memories."

She looked at him warmly. "Thanks, really. But I have to know what's going on."

"Then, I'm coming with you," he said adamantly.

She looked at him curiously. As they walked past a room with the door shut, she spotted the back of Sam's head in the room. Her eyes stared knowingly into Riggins' eyes. With a shrug of the shoulder, she twisted open the door handle.

Sam and the Daisy Duke girl were kissing passionately, sweltering heat, even moaning. They didn't hear them walk in or notice Riggins motioning for the other agents to come.

"Wow! You are nothing but slime, Sam." Brucie made the remark without a bit of anger.

She already knew in her mind what she would find.

Sam jumped to attention, trying to regain composure. At the same time, two men walked in the room and grabbed the Daisy Duke girl's cellphone. Sam looked confused, holding his hands up. "What's...what's going on?"

"I do not like you, Sam I am. I don't want to date you here or there. I don't want to date you anywhere. I wouldn't ride with you in a car or go on a date with you to a bar. I don't like cheaters, Samuel Peters. I would not, could not see you anymore. I could not, would not date someone who is such a bore. I do not like you, Sam I am. But I do like green eggs and ham," Brucie said with a smirk.

Riggins gave her a high five and they laughed heartily at her wit. Sam stood with a crinkled face not understanding any of what she said.

"To take it a step further, strike three, Sam I am. You're fired, and with this agency you shall never again be hired. Not only are you incapable to trust, but you are too stupid to realize this is a bust. Your girlfriend here works for the foe. If you did any type of research, that, you would know. I have never liked you, Sam I am. I would rather eat green eggs and ham. So, Sam I am. It's time for you to scram!"

Sam looked over at the undercover agents. "What the heck are they talking about? Green eggs and ham?"

"Doctor Seuss!" a woman agent said with a "duh" expression.

Sam squinted his eyes, shook his head confused, and left.

"I'm pretty sure his parents never read to him," Brucie remarked.

"Obviously. That was my very favorite child's book," Riggins exclaimed.

"Mine, too," Brucie replied with enthusiasm.

"May I now escort you to the dance floor, Bruce?"

"Absolutely, Full-of-Malarkie."

They laughed and laughed.

While dancing, Brucie asked, "What was going on with Daisy Dukes' girl?"

"She has been talking to Sam and relaying what he says back to Flagstone. Webster brought her to my attention, and we have been listening to her calls and monitoring her texts. We can't prove it yet, but pretty sure it's between her and Flagstone. We are close, Brucie. Really close."

"Honest Riggins? You're not just saying that?"

"One hundred percent truthful."

As they slow danced, tingles went up and down their bodies. They both trembled mildly.

They danced the rest of the dances together. Britanica nudged Gene and said excitedly, "Look, Gene, look."

Her and Gene's mouth dropped as they watched the twirling lights sparkle between Brucie and Riggins.

It was time for the bouquet toss. Brucie was talking a mile a minute and didn't even notice that the bouquet landed in her hands. Everything went silent. Brucie looked down and gasped. When she looked up, her eyes met Riggins' eyes. Just like Britanica's experience, ostrich bumps, instead of goosebumps, traveled through her and Riggins' veins. The shocked look on their faces and rubbing their arms up and down confirmed Britanica and Gene's suspicion.

Britanica glanced over at Emmy, Webster and Dan and gave a thumbs up. They gave it back. Just before leaving for their room that evening, Britanica and Emmy pulled Brucie aside. "Brucie, I don't think it's a good idea for you to stay at Riggins' place now." Emmy nodded in agreement.

"Give me a break, you cuckoos. Nothing is going on. A few innocent dances and you have to go looney tunes on me."

"Oh yeah, nothing's going on. Codswallop!" Britanica exclaimed as she shook her index finger.

Brucie looked at Emmy for support, but Emmy just shook her head and index finger in agreement with Britanica.

"Okay you *Wizard of Ozes*, just where should I stay, pray tell? Whose lives should I endanger by staying with them instead of a trained agent?"

Britanica and Emmy squirmed knowing she was right. "You're right, but you better behave, young lady or else."

"Since when have I become a concern? This is the first time Riggins and I have been congenial to each other and you already have us sleeping together."

———

"It's Christmas magic, Brucie. You're under its spell. You have to learn how to handle the magic, is all I'm saying," Britanica said talking from experience.

"Brit is sort of an expert on Christmas magic, Brucie," Emmy added.

"Okay, so you two can sleep peacefully tonight, consider me warned."

"Sleep? Who sleeps on their honeymoon? I have no such—" Britanica exclaimed humorously.

"Forget you, Brucie. I think it's Britanica we have to be concerned about," Emmy said in jest.

They laughed so hard.

A little more dancing went on. Then Emmy ran up to Britanica and shook her shoulder.

"What's wrong, Em?"

"Look!" Emmy said with excitement and pointing.

Riggins and Brucie were dancing in a corner, embraced in a sweet but passionate kiss. In her mind Britanica pictured sparks flying like they were being welded together. Dan ran up with Webster and got Gene's attention. They high fived.

At the car, dangling with cans and soap writing on the windows, Webster, Emmy, Riggins and Brucie waited for Britanica and Gene as they hugged and kissed all the guests goodbye. The guests lined up on each side of the hallway as the newlyweds walked out, throwing wafer paper designed like snowflakes as they passed by. They were smart enough to stay within the confines of a heated building than their crazy wedding party standing outside.

After hugs and kisses, Emmy grabbed Britanica's hand before she entered the car. "We wanted to wait until you returned from the honeymoon, but we just couldn't wait. We didn't want to take away any attention from you guys."

"Em, I can't take it. Just tell me," Britanica insisted.

Emmy and Webster wrapped their arms around each other and announced together. "We're having a baby."

Britanica was too sentimental to hold back happy tears. Between sobs, she managed to say, "We were right, Brucie."

The car pulled away and Emmy, Webster, Brucie and Riggins stood frozen as they saw what looked like a strand of twinkling lights swirl around the car and up into the sky. They looked into each other's eyes, hoping one of them had the guts to explain what they just saw. Then the chill in the air hit them all, so they ran back into the heated building.

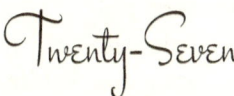

Twenty-Seven

RIGGINS AND BRUCIE changed into warm, comfy bed clothes and sat on the couch.

"I'm too hyped up to sleep. That wedding was honestly magical, like fairy-tale magical.

"What is your interpretation?" Brucie was thinking about the magical, swirling lights, but didn't want to look stupid, so she refrained from asking him about it.

"I can't believe I'm saying this, but yeah, it was fairy-tale magical. There were times I couldn't explain if I tried what I was feeling or imagining," he replied.

"Care to elaborate?" she asked with a curious tilt of the head.

"Not on your life. Tough guy image to uphold, ya know?"

She nodded her head. "Yup, I know."

"Soooo, caught the bouquet, huh? Do you believe in those superstitions?"

"After the crazy things that happened tonight, I'm sort of beginning to believe," she said staring ahead.

"Care to elaborate?" he asked, copying her attempt previously.

She tilted her head, formed a sly smile, and answered. "Not on your life." They chuckled.

"I don't want to ruin the evening, so if you're not up to answering my question, I won't be offended," he said cautiously.

Her cautious eyes stared nervously. "Continue with caution," she replied.

"Now that we don't hate each other's guts—Right? We don't hate each other's guts anymore; right?"

She shook her head and giggled. "Right."

"Well, I was just wondering how you're doing after the horrific loss you went through. If you prefer not to answer, it's okay." He waved his hands, emphasizing his point.

"Truthfully, I don't know if I'll ever recover from losing my dad. He played a special part in my life. We were close, like always together close. Either hanging out or on the phone. Sometimes he would call and just offer a joke to lighten my mood because of a horrible day I had. You know he was a judge before retiring. He had the nickname of Constitution Carl. Now, judgeships are politicized instead of following the rule of law. He's the reason why I became a court reporter.

"I actually started out in law school, but decided I wanted to listen to all the testimony without having to be active in a case. It's just so interesting to watch how these attorneys use or abuse the court system. And I was told I'm a natural at my skill. I completed school before two years was up."

"Impressive. Could you type something for me and interpret it?"

"I'd love to. I'm going to grab my stenograph and be right back."

After setting it up, she typed his name. She tore off a piece of steno paper and handed it to him.

```
R        EU  G
TKPW     EU    PB    S|
TP       U     L
                  F
    PHA
     HRA             R
 K       AO  E
                          FPLT
```

He stared at it, forehead wrinkling. How is this shorthand? What does it say?"

"It says 'Riggins full of Malarkie, and the FPLT is a period."

"All of that says that?"

"Yes. We write in syllables or abbreviations. We type by sound and syllables and it all just works out."

"If it is supposed to be shorthand, how come it seems longer?"

"It is way too hard to explain. Let's try this.

```
R        EU   G
TKPW     EU    PB    S
S
              A
 SKWR    E  RBG
                          FPLT
```

He stared at it. Okay, so it says Rig gins is a—the old Brucie would have called me a jerk period, but the new one?"

"Very good. Sorry, but you're right. The new Brucie would say Riggins is a wonderful, incredible and courageous man."

"Not handsome?"

Her head shook. "Unbelievably handsome, especially since you took my advice and grew your hair out."

"Maybe it was my idea. Did you ever think of that?"

She walked around the room and looked at the few pictures of him and his family. In the pictures his hair was always short. She held up the picture of him with his parents. "Your pictures are proof that it was because of me you grew your hair out. I say just a little longer where it hangs down about an inch from your very manly jawbone."

He rubbed his jaw while staring at the ceiling. "You don't say."

"My turn to ask you a question that may make you uncomfortable. So, please, if you can't answer, I won't be offended."

He nodded.

"You've talked about your father, but what about your mother? Is she still alive?" Brucie asked.

His face grew somber. "Yes, she lives in Florida. I have a sister named RyAnna. She wanted both of our names to begin with the letter "R". I can hear her now: 'Riggins. RyAnna, come here.' My mother lives in a cottage at the back of my sister's property. Mom helps with my niece and nephew. She likes living there, and having her own place gives them all privacy."

"When was the last time you saw her?"

He lowered his head and rubbed it. His eyes became blurry. "It's been a while."

Brucie could see his emotional pain. "I'm sorry. We don't need to discuss it."

"No! It's okay. I think I need to talk about it. You're the first person who has ever asked me about her. Dan and Gene know how sensitive the matter is and are hesitant to bring it up, because it is so painful for me to talk about."

All of a sudden, he couldn't find a comfortable position, squirming until he took a deep breath. "My sister is angry at me. She has been for years. And she has every right to be angry. When Dad was murdered, I hung around and helped Mom. Losing her husband, my dad, just tore her heart in two. I swear I heard the physical tearing of her heart, because it was so painful for her. As months went on, she put up a very good front. She didn't want to be a bother or upset us. My sister was really close to Dad, too.

Even though Mom hid her feelings, I could feel the sadness. The loneliness."

He lowered his head as a few tears dropped. Wiping his nose with the back of his hand, he sat back up. "I couldn't look into her empty eyes any longer." He took a deep breath. "There was such a sadness, even in her laughter. I don't know how many times I put a pillow over my head at night to block out the quiet sobs coming from her room."

He looked up at Brucie as a trail of tears flowed from his eyes. "I couldn't bear it anymore, Brucie. It hurt too much. I was of no use to her. There were no words or comfort that could take the pain away. That's when I started accepting missions in other countries. I was always gone, and it was a good excuse not to have to go home.

"I abandoned my mother and sister in their most vulnerable times. My sister wrote and called me a lot, mostly telling me off. I just listened and didn't defend myself because she was right. I send a good amount of money every month. Mom has Dad's pension and life insurance, but I had to do something to help, even though she doesn't need the money."

The back of his hand wiped his nose area. "I just can't handle looking into the eyes of lonely, unbearable pain. I just can't."

His hand rubbed his face upward over the forehead and through his hair, rubbing his head back and forth, not even realizing he was doing that. Tears dribbling down his cheeks, he looked up at Brucie. "It killed me!" He dropped his head and used a hand to support his heavy head. "It...It just killed me," he said as his tormented words dwindled to a whisper.

He coughed from choking on his tears, trying to stop the flood of tears from breaking through the dam. Brucie sat down next to him and began to bawl like a baby. They embraced and cried together.

When they finally settled down, a thought came to Brucie. "Riggins, don't answer me right now, because I want you to think about your answer before you reply. I'm having the same feelings with my mother. It's a twin story. I was thinking that my mother and I could go with you to visit your mother and sister for Christmas. This way, you and I can deal with these emotions together. Help each other through them. We could go shopping for gifts, I could make more Christmas cookies and candy and just go."

He started to answer, and she held up a hand. "Think about it and answer me after you've really put some thought into it."

His eyes were warm, bloodshot, sniffling like he had a serious cold. "Thank you. You have no idea how much better I feel. That was the first time I have been able to actually explain my emotions. Even I could never figure out how to explain my thoughts until this evening. And, to the woman who used to make my face feel like fire."

She laughed. Her hand went to his face, and she held it softly. "I feel better, too. Thank you. But now being emotionally drained, I need to sleep, so goodnight."

Her lips pressed against his just barely. When she pulled away, he gently grabbed her shoulders, looked genuinely into her eyes, and kissed her. Slowly. Building. Shivers running up and down their arms.

He pulled back and said, "You have no idea how long I've wanted to do that."

"Secretly, denying my feelings, I'm pretty sure I wanted you to do that, too," she admitted.

He held her hand and pulled her up. She went to her room, and he pulled out his cellphone and spoke with the agents staged outside and around her place. Dan had flown home to his family after the wedding.

Across the lake from Brucie's cabin, a pair of binoculars searched for movement.

Flagstone threw a sharp, pointy dagger into a cutting board and growled. Wanting to make her and Riggins, and those mangy chimps, pay for ruining his multi-million-dollar business ate away at his insides. He couldn't relax. Wouldn't relax until they were all dead.

Twenty-Eight

BRUCIE'S EYES SLOWLY OPENED, her nose wiggling up and down. *What is that heavenly smell?*

Bacon? Yes. Coffee? Yes, yes. Blueberry muffins? No. She sat up. "Yes. Yes. Yes."

Hair a tousled mess, and breath begging for mouthwash, she stumbled out of the room, nose in the air following the aroma. Standing over the stove, Riggins closed the oven door as he laid a pan of muffins on a rack to cool. "Good morning."

She yawned and mumbled out, "Good morning to you. The scent of all of this," she said, waving her arms around, "drew me out like I was floating."

He walked up to her. Put his hands around her waist and kissed her lips. Then he backed up and curled his upper lip. "Whooie," he said, waving his hand back and forth in front of his face.

"Okay. All right. I'll brush my teeth."

"Please," he said, laughing.

She folded her lips and snarled at him. In minutes she was back, hair bushed, breath minty fresh and a sunshine smile. Just looking at her bright, cheerful face brought a smile to his face. He grabbed her and kissed her, slowly, faster, and melting. When he let her go, her body drooped like jello.

"If I had known your kisses would do this to me, well, it would have happened a long time ago."

His smile showed all his teeth. Before they could be seated, commotion from the other room was loud and louder. The hooting and hollering was so loud, they both covered their ears.

"Quiet!" Riggins yelled. The chimps moved their mouths in silly formations and looked at Riggins.

"Well, come on. Get in your seats."

They walked in their chimpanzee way and Brucie grabbed each of their hands. "Nope. I need a kiss first." They both kissed her cheek and climbed up the chairs and sat down. "Talk about mouth-wash, you two could sure use some." Her face crinkled.

They ate their food, and Riggins surprised them with a blue-berry muffin. Their hooting and hollering was confirmation of their enjoyment.

"Hey Riggins. If you rescued these guys, how did you know their names?"

"I didn't. I made up their names and they learned to adapt to them."

"Oh! Well, are you worried this freezing weather isn't good for them? They're used to hot weather."

"Yeah, I have been. This assignment is taking longer than we anticipated. If it doesn't get straightened out pretty soon, we'll have to make new arrangements. It will be like losing my own children. I just love these guys, but I'm not ready to move to a hot climate. Dan is building them an addition to his house and an inescapable backyard playground. In the playground sits two big trees. He will try it out before releasing them to make sure they can't escape. His children are really excited. And, when they go on vacation, we can chimp sit."

"We?" she asked, pointing to him and herself.

"Yes, we." He smiled. "I'm not letting you go, Bruce."

Her eyes warmed. "I don't want you to let me go, full-of-your-last-name."

They held hands as they ate. "Riggins, how did you learn to cook so well and make such great coffee?"

"When I first started out in the agency, I had a lot of free time on my hands, so I took some cooking classes. I actually had an assignment with that Bobby guy from one of those cooking channels. He was being stalked. He taught me to make coffee, and a few more tricks."

"If you're talking about who I think you are, I love him. I mean, I love him. Could you introduce me to him?"

"I don't know if that's such a good idea. I mean, you love him."

She slapped his shoulder. "You know what I mean."

"All right. When this is all done, we'll go visit him."

"On a different note, we never talked about the news from Emmy," she excitedly mentioned.

"That's right. How awesome is that?"

"A little Emmy or little Webster. How cute. Wonder how long it will take Britanica and Gene to have a baby?"

Her phone chimed. Riggins' phone chimed. They read their group text from Britanica and Gene. "Guys, is it possible for me to be pregnant already? I feel something kicking and I got morning sickness. You know, like Bella on her honeymoon with Edward. Just like that. Hey, maybe Gene's a vampire!" She ended her statement with a smiley face.

Brucie's fingers typed at fast speed. "Is this a joke, Brit?"

A quick response. "No!"

"Huh!" Brucie released from her breath. "Riggins, she's not kidding."

"Oh, my! I'm at a loss for words," he replied.

The phone chimed again. "Our kids will grow up together, have sleepovers. Brucie, hurry up so all our children can grow up together. Hurry up," Emmy ended.

Britanica responded. "She's right. Hurry up, Brucie."

Brucie and Riggins looked at each other. Eyes wide, mouth dropped until Brucie gulped. "I don't know how to react to that.

We need to get to know each other for a little while. Don't you think? What am I saying?"

"You're saying exactly what I'm thinking. I won't push you, but I'm pretty sure you're the one for me. I won't have to wait long to ask for your hand in marriage, but we'll get to know each other better, even though we've been living in the same house for a month or more. What else do I need to know about you? I feel like I know all I have to know about you."

"Riggins, I saw something strange at the wedding. Something magical. I was too embarrassed to say anything. I—"

"—saw it, too," Riggins interjected without any body movement.

"The twinkly lights that—"

"—swirled around us?"

"Yeah, those. What—how—where did it come from?" Britanica only spoke to Emmy and Pastor Beard—Mustache, Britanica's nickname for the pastor, about the magical lights. Brucie was unaware that this happened to Britanica and Gene in the past.

He held his hands up. "I have nothing. Back to my summation, just how do you feel about what I said?" He walked up to her slowly, gently holding her hands, a face serious with a pleading look.

She scratched her head. "I feel like I'm going crazy."

It was obvious her remark disappointed him. He let go of her hands. "Is that it?"

"Look Riggins, this is happening at warp speed. We need to land the Starship Enterprise for repair and maintenance before it takes off on its next voyage. What if we're not meant to be together? We haven't discussed anything to do with marriage, our jobs, children, all of that."

"'Beam me up, Scotty.' I'm ready for this adventure. I don't think most couples think about all of that. It sort of works itself out. If I hated children or you did, or if you hate blueberry muffins, now, that, may be a complication."

She slapped his arm. "Very funny. Are you coming to church with me today?"

"Well, now, since Sam isn't here to take you, I suppose I better. Hey, did you really like him?"

"Not as someone in a relationship, but he was funny, good looking, and filled a void in my life when I needed it filled. I knew it wouldn't amount to anything. He certainly isn't the kind of guy I want to settle down with.

"What happened with him?"

"Beats me. Look, even before you showed an interest in him, I never liked the guy. He wasn't dependable, as you well know. Our assignments are too dangerous for somebody that clumsy. He has to want to do a good job before anything ever comes available for him. Maybe he should try Hollywood. His shallowness would be perfect as an actor."

"Ouch!"

"What? Him or Hollywood?"

"Both."

"Then both. Now, go get ready for church."

"It's way too early."

His phone chimed.

"Good. My phone just alerted me that *Magnum P.I.* is on. It's the episode called 'Did You See the Sunrise?'"

"I love Magnum. We all meet at Gene's and watch it all the time," she informed him.

"Come to mention it, way back when, he, Dan and I used to watch it all the time. Now, no talking."

"Well, I never. Okay. I'll zip it." She emphasized her remark by pretending to zip her mouth and made the zipping sound.

As they snuggled up on the couch, Ivan came on the screen. Brucie's face wrinkled and her eyes squinted. After a few moments, she jumped up. "Hhhh!" she gasped, both hands covering her shocked mouth.

Riggins paused it and leaned over to look at her face. Her eyes were wide. "Brucie, what's wrong?"

"That's that sweet man who plays on the old television show *Here Come the Brides*. I think his name was Olaf, the big Swede. Emmy, Webster and I used to go over to Britanica's parent's home to watch reruns. He was so sweet in the show, but now look at him. He's a monster. The horrible thing is that he plays the part so well, like he's not even acting. I can never watch him be sweet again. Not now. I will never be able to erase this horrible image of him."

"Brucie, it's an act. Watch me."

Riggins started acting the part of Ivan. Brucie's eyes widened more. Then he switched it up and played the part of Ivan on *Here Come the Brides*.

"I watched the show myself a few times over there. Did you know Karyn was madly in love with Robert Brown, her friend, Dorothy was in love with David Soul and Britanica was in love with Bobby Sherman?"

"Of course I knew that. Britanica still has the pillow she used to pretend she was kissing Bobby Sherman. Who could blame her?"

"Hey! Don't tell me you have a pillow with Bobby Sherman kisses?"

"Nooo. I have one with Tom Selleck kisses."

"Say it isn't so."

"I'll take you to my cabin and show you my lip gloss smudges, if you want."

His mouth dropped. She kissed it and jumped up to take a shower, constantly looking back at his shocked face, giggling with delight.

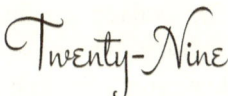

Twenty-Nine

HEAVY FOOTSTEPS PACED THE FLOOR. Back and forth. Back and forth. Flagstone grabbed the binoculars from Hafsa's hands and scanned Brucie's property. He threw it down on the couch and cursed up a storm.

"I've had enough. Tonight's the night. Listen to my plan and get prepared. It's foolproof. It is the perfect plan, unless you flub it up. That *Rambo* agent is gone. I haven't seen any other agents, so I'm guessing they think we've left the state because Azar has been captured. Now, listen up and listen good." Slobber drooled down his angry mouth, wiping it with the back of his hand. Particles spreading in the air.

Hafsa wiped them off his face, mouth forming downward. "Yes, sir."

———

Snow coming down fast, the truck skidded at a halt. Riggins and Brucie arrived at his cabin after church just before it got too dangerous to drive through. They changed clothes and made lunch for the chimps and themselves. As they all ate lunch, thoughts popped up in Brucie's mind.

"Riggins, you never told me why," she leaned over and whispered, "Flagstone wants these chimps. They're not exotic."

"In an African preserve, these guys stopped them from killing some exotic animals. They jumped on the men, broke their weapons and paralyzed three of Flagstone's fingers. Some workers heard the commotion and walked up during it. They said the chimps were enraged like they'd never seen before. They can be very dangerous if provoked. That's the first time Flagstone escaped prison. He lied and told authorities that he was out for a drive and tried to stop these poachers. The authorities bought it.

"In a year, he was at it again. That is when he started his exotic hunting business. The beautiful animals that were killed as trophies makes me sick to my stomach. What sport do hunters get in killing animals, well, for sport? I don't get it. They are such beautiful creatures.

"Then he took his sickness further and began capturing exotic albino animals. That's where my father came on the scene and, as you know, murdered. They moved around to other countries. I have to give him credit. Bringing these exotic animals to Wisconsin was a plan we never expected. Most of them belong in hot climates. Thankfully, through all our devices and our agents' steadfastness in searching, they found out he came here. It wasn't easy and took about six months, but we found him. He was about to become a multi-millionaire."

"Wow! I see your point. Who would have thunk to bring exotic animals to Wisconsin? That man is sick."

"Brucie, don't let your guard down. He is sick. You are nothing more than a challenging hunt to him. His mind is not right."

"I'll remember that, I promise."

"Since Dan went home, I brought in five other agents. You haven't noticed them here, have you? Well, except for the one in the room with the chimps, that is."

"No, I haven't. Where are the other agents?"

"They are hiding around your cabin and my property. Don't worry. They have portable heaters and the best clothing for this

Artic climate. I mean, really. Are we becoming part of the Artic?"

"I know; right? Global warming my foot. It's more like the ice age."

"I'm going to get the agent out of the chimp's room and give some of the other agents a break. They won't bother you. Do you mind?"

"Not at all."

Riggins and the other agent changed places with two of the agents outside. Brucie fixed them hot chocolate and some soup and sandwiches. They plopped down on the couch and recliner and bundled up with some blankets. Brucie spent time in the bedroom to give them privacy.

It was late afternoon, and Brucie relieved the agent from the chimps' room and played with them for a while. She took them out to the kitchen for a snack. A smack sound was made as they high-fived the agent who was watching over them on their merry way to the kitchen.

Brucie made a big pot of beef stew, salad, and cornbread muffins with lots of butter. The agents ate with much gusto. Their phone chimed. They read the text and prepared to relieve the other two agents who had been outside.

The other two came in, warmed their hands and feet by the fire, cheeks turning to normal, and sat down for the meal. It was their turn to bundle up in the living room and relax. It was already dark out. Around this time each year, the sky begins to darken around 4:30 p.m.

Boredom setting in, she texted Britanica. "How's the honeymoon? Any more symptoms, vampire girl?"

Brucie read the response. "Wonderful, magical, incredible and no more symptoms. How's everything there? And by that, I mean with you and Riggins, too."

"Still nerve-wracking, but also wonderful and magical. We did it, Brit!"

"Did what?"

"We made it through these past couple days without an argument. What did you think I meant?"

"Oh! Never mind. I'm glad."

"Brit! How could you?!"

"Sorry, Charlie. Honest."

"Go back to paradise while we freeze like ice cubes."

"That's a plan. Love you, girl."

"Yeah, yeah. Love you, too."

First, Brucie watched some music videos. For King and Country played. For some odd reason, her body felt a chill. She turned down the volume, sat silent, and rubbed her prickling arms up and down. Was she cold? Scared? The caution in her mind was concerning. She jumped off the bed and slowly opened the door. The agents were still watching T.V., bundled up in many blankets and one of them was snoring. The smell of beef stew still lingered. It was a comforting smell. The Christmas lights twinkled, and the decorations and nativity relaxed her. She felt calm, so she crawled back in bed and covered up, enjoying some comedies on television.

———

Hafsa threw the binoculars down. "What about Azar? How we gonna get him out?"

"I don't know. The stupid idiot should have been more careful. I don't have time to think about it." He looked at his watch. "It'll be really dark in an hour. There's some burritos in the freezer. Heat some up and eat before we begin. This is it." He formed a really evil, maniacal smile. His eyes glazed over and the can in his hand crushed.

"So, we're just going to let Azar sit in jail?" Hafsa said it softly. He was a big man, but Flagstone was just insane, scary. And he carried the money.

"Why don't you do what you're told, unless you want to end up like that witch?" He snarled and spit sprayed in Hafsa's face,

Flagstone came in so close to him. He jumped up, and the next sound heard was the buzzing of the microwave.

———

Riggins and the rest of the agents looked like the abominable snowman on *Rudolph the Red-nosed Reindeer*, except they had silk leaves and branches attached for camouflage. It was remarkably effective. They couldn't even see each other with the amount of snow on the ground and in the trees. Infrared goggles searched the area. All they found were heat sources of small rodents.

Brucie got the chimps ready for bed while the agent monitoring them stepped out for some coffee and snacks and small talk with the other agent. Once the chimps were locked in their cages, in bed, the agent could relax in the living room. Brucie joined them.

Her eyes were drifting just as the door opened. In walked Riggins and the other agent named Joe something or other. She ran to him.

"You have got to be a popsicle."

"Believe it or not, these suits and our portable heaters keep us nice and toasty. This isn't windburn on my face. It's from the heater."

"No kidding. That's awesome."

"Hey, Joe, would you mind grabbing some coffee and a snack, then stay with the chimps?

They'll rebel if they see you eat or drink anything, so keep it out of their room. There's a bed, so you can get comfortable. Oh, and a T.V," Riggins asked.

"Now, that's a cozy stakeout, if you ask me. Thanks, man," Joe replied.

Riggins bundled up and sat on the couch with Brucie. He kissed her lips. Then they stared into each other's eyes for just a moment, and it was all over. He kissed her passionately. She accepted. They kissed for minutes. A throat clearing startled them. They both looked over.

"Sorry, but this is the only route to my destination."

"Get out of here, G.I. Joe," Riggins said.

Brucie laughed at his nickname.

Joe smiled whimsically and gave a salute as he walked off. Brucie and Riggins laughed.

"Oh! I almost forgot. I made a big pot of beef stew and corn-bread. Could I fix you a bowl?"

"You bet. I heard it was scrumptious from the other agents. Hey, would you mind fixing Joe some, too? He has to be starving."

"My pleasure."

Riggins laid his head back on the couch and sniffed the air. His nose made the inhaling sound. Brucie brought in a tray for him and went and brought Joe out of the chimp's room. The men were in beef stew heaven.

"How did you learn to cook so well? Are you sure you don't know Bobby?" Riggins asked.

She smiled widely. "Actually, it is his recipe."

"That makes sense. So, you going to try and beat Bobby with his own recipe?"

"Yeah, no. I'm good where I'm at," she answered.

"Yes, you are." They started making Joe uncomfortable.

"I've seen enough. I'm out of here you two lovebirds. Oh, and thanks for the meal. It was excellent."

"You're very welcome," she replied with a warm smile.

They watched T.V. for a while, but Riggins noticed she was exceptionally quiet, for her anyway. He turned his head and glanced at her. She was staring at the T.V. but not watching it.

"Hey, you okay?"

No answer.

"Brucie," he said louder.

She turned her head in a daze.

"What's going on?"

"Huh? What?"

"What's up, Brucie. You're kind of pale."

"Well, truthfully, I had an uneasy feeling today. I was trying to figure out if I was scared or just cold. My body filled with goose-bumps, but I still have a caution in my spirit. I don't know what to make of it."

"I do. Maybe God is trying to warn you. Sort of like a gut feel-ing. Take it seriously. I'm going to check with the agents to be certain they're okay."

"Good idea."

While Riggins was on his phone, Brucie checked on the agent and chimps. Joe had fallen asleep and was snoring. The chimps turned over in their bed. That was a relief. She sat back down and he joined her.

"The days seem to drag on and on. Not that I don't appreciate all you've done for me and in enjoying your company, but I miss my home. The comforts of home."

Riggins sympathized but was a little disappointed that she wanted to go home. He was enjoying being with her and never wanted her to leave. Once the mission ended, would they end as well? He couldn't help but wonder.

"Did I ever tell you about the time Britanica and I had a fight?" she asked.

"Not that I recall."

"We were in college. I was sort of a wild child, drinking, cussing, just a wild child. I had temporary, untamed colors in my hair, a rhinestone on the side of my nose and a bellybutton ring."

His thoughts went to—wish-I-could-have-seen-that mode. His eyebrows raised up and down subconsciously.

"She wouldn't budge that goodie-two-shoes. She didn't say anything to me, but yet I felt in my mind that she was judging me. To make a long story short, I got fed up with it. Of course she never liked my boyfriends and hated when I joined political protests. Like I understood what I was protesting. To me it was just part of the college experience. So, I told her off."

"Was she making comments to you?"

"No. It was like I could read her mind. Anyhow, we got into a big argument. I even pushed her down on the bed, gathered my stuff, and left. We didn't speak for months. She sent texts that said she missed me and was sorry for making me feel bad about myself.

"Truth is, I was feeling bad about myself. I quit going to church, got drunk all the time, and pretended I was having a blast. One day it hit me. She was so happy, going to church and all that stuff. Being one with the college didn't faze or influence her. She stayed true to herself. I missed our talks. Britanica had a way of convincing you like she was the Holy Spirit. She still does to this day. But you know what? I have learned to appreciate our friendship. She is a good influence and a truly good friend. I don't know where I'd be today without her."

"I'm glad. What's funny is that I have been evaluating my past as well. My dad was so mad at me. I rebelled also. You won't believe this. I was planning on becoming a geologist, or archeologist. I was an avid spelunker," Riggins admitted.

"Say what?"

"I constantly explored and studied caves all over the world. It was quite exciting, but also quite dangerous. I can't count the times I ran into poisonous snakes, insects, even criminals. One time I got very sick. Deathly sick. I was in the hospital for three weeks with an unstable diagnosis. Must have caught some disease. Probably from a bat. My dad told me it was time to settle down and figure out what it is I want to do with my life. I was running out of money. That is when I trained to be an agent. And thankfully, I really love my job."

"Wow! Mr. Adventure, huh? I dig it."

"You dig it, Britanica."

"I warned you that girl has influence over me" she laughed.

He shook his head. "I think we better both turn in for the night. I'll sleep out here on the couch since you had an uneasy feeling today."

"That actually makes me feel safer. Thanks." She kissed his cheek and went to bed. He laid down on the couch and pondered on the things she said. It bothered him that she felt a warning and was eager to get home. Being exhausted, though, he passed out.

Thirty

An alarm went off on Riggins' phone. He blinked his eyes for clarity and sat up. Joe's door hurled open.

"Did you get the warning that someone entered Brucie's home?"

"Yes. Dress the chimps and yourself and get them out of here. I'll contact the other agents and head over there." They all responded to Riggins.

"Schnooper, get back here and keep Brucie safe."

"Yes, sir."

Riggins ended his call and pounded on Brucie's door before opening it. It flew open so fast that hair blew in her face. She jumped up with a crazed look. "What's going on?"

"Brucie, get up and throw on your coat and gloves. Dress warmly. Someone broke into your cabin. You need to be ready to leave in an instant. I'm going to your place. Come activate the alarm when I leave. Hurry!" His adrenaline was pumping at a super speed.

Brucie's hands literally shook. She had a hard time putting a robe on. Riggins stood at the door, waiting for her. He kissed her cheek and left. A gust of freezing wind blew in as he opened the door.

"Be careful, Riggins. Please." She held her hand up next to her eyes to try and see him, but the snow, rain and wind mixture kept blowing in her face. She immediately closed the door and shivered from the cold.

It was too windy for him to hear her, and he ran down his driveway. She ran back to the chimp's room. "Joe, you almost ready?"

"Yes," he answered. "In a…in a…in a minute."

She stopped and wondered why he was stuttering. "Are you sure you're okay?"

Something else was concerning. A familiar scent. A hand went to her dropped mouth. *I recognize that cigar smell. No! How would he get in or past me and Riggins?"*

The chimps started hooting and hollering, the bars on the cage clanging. "They sound upset."

"Go! Brucie, get out of here."

The next thing she heard was him sighing and hitting the floor, something solid smashing to the floor after he fell, and the chimps hollering. Joe had managed to unlock their cage but not able to pull the door open. Brucie froze in fear. She knew in her soul that something was wrong. "I'll be back in a second," she yelled.

She ran to the room, threw on an Oompa Loompa style coat, grabbed gloves, but before she turned around, a huge hand went to her throat. She could smell cigar smoke up close. Flagstone squeezed as he turned her around to face him, moving her backwards, Brucie gasping for air. She stared into his evil eyes and her heart pounded in fear. Her hands grabbing his, trying to release it so she could breathe.

He released it just enough for her to catch a breath, the reddening of her face returning slowly to normal.

Her eyes were wide, body frozen like ice. "Don't worry. I'm not going to kill you here. After I take you some place they won't look, I will set you free and hunt you down like an animal. I'm really excited about that." His face showed no remorse, just insanity.

"How did you get in here without setting off the alarm?"

He tapped his head. "I used my brain. Hafsa set off your alarm while I ran up here. I saw the agents run to your house. As soon as Riggins opened the door, I broke in."

She looked around at the doorway, expecting Joe to jump him. Without looking, he said, "He's not coming. I hit him so hard, he'll be out for quite a while, if not dead." He broke out in a boisterous laugh.

His evilness was making her mad.

"Now, I'm going to take you and those mangy chimps out of here. Don't make me knock you out." He gritted his teeth.

As his hands slipped off her neck, she kicked him in the groin, took her elbow and swung it at his nose. He fell over, moaning in pain, holding his groin area. Her self-defense classes with Britanica and Emmy sure paid off. Just as she lifted a lamp to knock him in the head, the chimps ran in and jumped on him, biting, tearing at his body. They were loud; freaky loud. He yelled in pain. Brucie noticed on his one hand, three fingers just dangled lifeless like.

"Bogie, Bacall, come on. Let's go." They climbed in her arms. She stopped just long enough to see if Joe was breathing. She exhaled a deep breath. He was alive, but blood trickled down his face. No time to hunt down her keys, they ran out the door and the alarm blasted. She looked at the chimps and said the word, "safety." They had practiced this drill over and over. They climbed up trees, jumping from one to the other until they found their warm, insulated safe spot. They curled inside of it and held their arms around each other. They didn't make a sound. The drill was carried out to perfection.

The howling wind swirled ice cold slush in her face. Some splashed down the front of her neck. The shock of the cold caused body spasms. The snow and ice crunched under her feet. It was physically draining to try and run through it. She knew he would follow her tracks, so she ran into the woods, stumbling over dead trees, branches, sharp rocks cutting through the feet of her onesie. There was no time to put on boots.

She shrieked in pain, but quietly. She listened for his footsteps. Nothing. Her gloved hands rubbed the strangulation marks on her neck, swallowing as she remembered the fear, she felt that she was going to die. All of a sudden, the stinging in her feet was sharp, excruciating, but she couldn't stop running.

Listening before takeoff, all she could hear was the pounding of her heart. Was it coming out of her chest? It literally hurt and felt extra heavy. Her face looked like a Shar Pei. She was freezing, but perspiration beaded on her forehead. Cellphone in hand, she called Riggins.

"Riggins, he's after me." She said it so fast, and because she was freezing, her words were a jumble of mumbled words.

"Listen to me Brucie. Listen! I can tell you are freezing and scared. Take a deep breath and tell me slowly what you were saying. You can do it."

She did what he said, but the freezing air burned her lungs. She coughed and regained composure. If she were to survive these frigid conditions, she had to stop panicking.

"Flagstone knocked Joe out. He's pretty hurt. The chimps are in their safe space. At least I used the safe space word, and they took off that way. I managed to escape Flagstone, but he'll be after me. I am down the road running toward Rose Lane in the woods. Now that my tracks are off the road, I'll get back on it. He's insane." She was walking to the road as she spoke.

"Keep your phone on until I find you. Keep telling me of your location. Keep running and find a good hiding spot."

"I'm so…cold…so tired."

"Don't give up Brucie. We have a life together to live. You can do it."

She stopped and listened for the ice crunching. In the far distance, she heard something but couldn't identify what it was. She took off running again. She fell. Her hand landed on something on the ground behind her as she tried to push up. She shined her cellphone flashlight on it.

All she could do was scream. "Aw, aw, aw," covering her mouth. She cried hard, gulping in air, coughing.

"Brucie, what's wrong?"

Her hand covered her mouth to control the sound of tormented crying. "I just...I just found Mr. Kinnard's dog. It's dead. He's been shot." She couldn't quit crying. Tears were freezing solid on her face and tears dripped from her nose.

"I'm so sorry, Brucie. I really am. What about Mr. Kinnard?"

Brucie hesitated. Her body trembled uncontrollably. "I don't know if I can do it. I don't want to find him dead, Riggins." She hiccupped and cried more.

"You don't have to, Brucie. You shouldn't have to see it. Any of it. I have the coordinates written down of your location."

She readjusted her other hand to push up. As she did, the light flashed behind the dog. There lay Mr. Kinnard. Dead. Eyes staring into the blank darkness. She gasped. Forcing herself to talk, she inhaled a deep breath. "He's dead, too. Riggins, he's dead." Tears plummeted down her face. She couldn't see because everything was a blur. She tried catching her breath. But the sound of debris crackling, snow crunching not too far away, drew her attention.

"Feeling her despair, he fell to his knees in the frigid snow and slush, tears trickling down Riggins' face. His heart broke for all she had seen and been through.

"I'm taking off," she said, sniffling. "Someone is close behind me."

"Where are you?"

"I just passed that really nice house and garage that have a barn shape. There are two woodsheds neatly stacked with wood."

"I'm coming. Keep telling me where you are at." He had to keep her talking for survival's sake. They had installed a tracking device on her phone, and he was following the coordinates.

Her breath was heavy, lungs burning, lips quivering. "I just passed Rose Lane."

"Start looking for a hiding spot."

She kept running. Looking behind her, she saw a light shining on the ground. Someone was following her tracks.

"Is that you following me on the road, shining your flashlight?"

"No! I'm running on the other side of the road in the woods, heading your way. I'm crossing over to the road. It will take me a moment. Ow!"

"Are you okay?"

"I just twisted my ankle. Don't worry. That won't stop me from finding you."

"Oh, Riggins. I'm so scared and I'm so tired. My lungs feel like I swallowed fire. I have to stop."

"No! You have to keep going. My GPS is directing me to your phone. Find a marker and head into the woods to hide. Do it now, Brucie!"

She could barely say the words. "O-k-a-y."

Riggins hobbled through the pain. He looked around for the light she mentioned before getting on the road. He didn't see it, but he did hear heavy stomping, snow and ice crunching loudly and then ungodly cursing.

"Riggins, I'm walking back behind that stump with the smiley face. It's barely visible because of the snow. There are some boulders I can hide behind in the wooded area."

"Good. Make several tracks in all directions so he can't find you, even going across the road, then turn back and go hide. My GPS will guide me right to you." He was whispering.

"I can't feel my feet. Even the pain of frostbite is gone. I'm scared, Riggins. I'm going to lose my feet. I didn't have time to put boots on."

He thought about what she said, and concern chilled his bones. She was right. You can't be exposed too long to the freezing elements before disaster strikes. "I have another idea. There is a home right in that area. Make a few more distracting footprints and carefully walk to the home. Go to the back door. If nobody is there, break in. I'll deal with it. No lights. Lock the door. If someone is there, ask them if you could come in and get warmed. They should know you. I'm close. Now, go. Hurry!"

"I kind a like that plan. Hurry Riggins but be careful."

Riggins hid behind a large tree listening. The crunching snow was louder, closer. He could see images of a man as the moonlight filtered through the clouds. He crouched like a lion. It could be one of the agents, but he doubted it. Flagstone wanted Brucie and wanted her badly. He wasn't going to let anything stop him this time. That much he knew.

The sound stopped. Dead silence. He poked his head out. A light was shining around the wooded area and then back on the road. It had to be Flagstone, and he was getting close to where Brucie was hiding.

Brucie softly pounded on the back door. Nobody was home. *Smart people. Probably in Florida.* S*unshine, warm weather.* She found a brick right below the steps and broke the small window above the door handle. Then she slipped her hand in and unlocked the door. She walked in very slowly, saying "Hello. Anyone here. It's Brucie Clark from down the road." No answer.

The heat was barely on. She found the thermostat and turned it up high. With fingers numb, then in pain, and numb and back to pain, she finally got the onesie off. She laid the onesie on a radiator and found blankets. Searching, she made up a hiding place behind some boxes in the bedroom, stacking them high enough so she could scrunch down without being seen. Then she covered up, pulled some boxes over on her lap and tried to hide her body shape. Finally, her breathing returned to normal, pulse slowing down.

Even her feet stung like a hive of Wisconsin's murder hornets were stinging her. Her face wrinkled in pain. She held her breath and released it, still in excruciating pain. Then her thoughts floated to Flagstone, and she pictured his insane expressions. He was an empty shell. No emotion. Nothing human about him. "What makes a person like that?" she whispered in disbelief. "Poor Joe. I hope he's all right. The chimps! I hope the heat is warm enough for them in their safe house."

Either she was paranoid or imagining it, but she could swear the sound she just heard was of someone walking around in the snow. Her body began to shake. She was too cold, too worn out to fight anyone, especially that Satan man.

Enough was enough. She bowed her head and prayed. Then she recited scripture. "Fear thou not, for I am with thee." She kept saying the name of Jesus. "Whosoever shall call upon the name of the Lord shall be saved." She kept repeating the verses over and over.

The next sound she heard was the door handle being turned. She hugged herself, body unable to stop trembling. She took several breaths to steady the hyperventilating style of breathing. All of a sudden someone let out a huge heaving sound. "Umpf! Ppfft."

Loud voices. Louder voices. The sound of fists connecting. Gasps. More punching, rolling over the snow and ice. Crackling and crunching.

She was too scared and too cold to move. But what if it was Riggins? What if he needed help? She struggled, shoved the boxes off of her, which made a loud noise, wrapped up in the blankets and walked to a window, peaking through the curtain. She couldn't make out who was fighting, just images of two people fighting in the dark.

Brucie shined her flashlight around the room, looking for a gun case. Drawers pulled open and slammed shut. In the closet she felt around and something metal stopped her search. She pulled out a vacuum cleaner attachment. That would have to do. She turned on the outside light.

The door creaked open slowly. Snow was slushing around, spraying in the air. The men were covered in it, fighting to the death. Everything was happening too fast and she couldn't decipher who was who, but she knew it had to be Riggins and Flagstone.

A thought came to her. She raised the vacuum detachment up and ran down the stairs. Slam!

Oh no, she couldn't figure out who she hit.

Riggins grabbed his head and looked at her quizzically. "Why did you hit me?"

"I'm sorry. You were moving so fast that I had to take the chance." Flagstone produced his evil, killer smile. Why did his eyes always glaze over?

Riggins noticed and yelled, "Go! Run!"

She looked at her bare feet. The fight had distracted the freezing pain that radiated in her feet.

Just as she took off, a depleting "huff" sound resonated through the air. Flagstone pulled himself up, stumbling and trying to get his wits about him. She ran like a deer. Survival skills set in. *Please don't be dead, Riggins. It's all my fault. What an idiot I am.*

Just then a small black car passed Rose Lane and saw her running. The brake lights came on and they reversed the car. A window automatically rolled down. "Brucie, is that you?"

"Yes! Please, help me."

A woman jumped out of the car and helped Brucie get into the front seat. Another woman looked at her confused and concerned. "Where should we take you?"

"I don't know. I don't know." She scratched her head. "Let me think. A crazy killer is after me. Please just drive."

They both looked cautiously into each other's eyes. The look asked, "Has she lost her mind?"

"I can see by your expressions, you think I'm out of my mind, but my situation has been kept secret. I'm Brucie Clark, the person who saw the murderer with the agent's body, she said to the ladies, Linda and Jenny, whom she hadn't seen in quite a while. "The story has been all over the news. The killer is out to kill me. I have been hiding at an agent's cabin, but this crazy man found out. He knocked Riggins out. I pray he's not dead."

"Okay. I'm Linda and this is Jenny, in case you don't remember us. It's been a while since we have seen you. We met Riggins at Kitty's Bar and Grill and some Sam fellow. How can we help you?"

"We'll take you to our house, Brucie. Jenny and I live next door to each other," Linda affirmed.

"No! If he saw your car, he'll kill you. And I won't be in either of your houses and place you in danger."

"How about this idea? I'll run in the house and get you some clothes and boots and blankets and you can hide out in my garage slash chicken coop. No chickens. There's a hole in the ceiling with a floorboard. You can stand on the car, and I'll help push you up. It's a very flimsy ceiling, but you can hide in it. Can you call the agents and police, or would you prefer I do it?" Linda added.

"That sounds like a plan. Jenny, can you hide your car?" Brucie asked.

"I'll pull it right in the garage. Brucie, you need medical help ASAP."

I know, but we have to stop him now. He's murdered Mr. Kinnard and his dog."

Jenny's hand went to her mouth. She gasped but couldn't talk.

"We need to do this quickly," Brucie said. "I guarantee Flagstone is hunting us down right now."

Jenny sped up now that she was on the highway.

"What is the address so I can pass it on to the agents?"

First, she dialed Riggins' phone number, praying in her mind for him to be alive.

"Brucie, are you okay?" His voice was tired.

A choking sound escaped her lips. "Thank God you're alive. Yes, I have an address for you where I'll be hiding. A couple women picked me up."

"Can they be trusted? Do you know them?" he asked.

"We haven't seen each other in quite a while, but, yes," Brucie said, looking over the women, "they can be trusted."

"Good. I'm almost to my truck and heading your way. I'm

pretty sure Flagstone is hunting you down. He doesn't even care about getting caught. He only cares about killing you. You know, the biggest hunt of his life. The man's really nuts. I just heard on the police radio that a truck right down the road here has been stolen."

"Oh, boy. We're almost to my hiding spot. The address is off of County Road W, Mountain, WI. I'll be in the ceiling of one of the women—her name is Linda—her garage. Call me when you're close and I'll guide you to the right house. The road continues across the street the other way, so it will be difficult for you to find without my help."

"Good. Make sure they provide you warm clothes and blankets."

"Be careful, Full-of-Malarkie."

"I will, Bruce."

They both ended the phone call with a smile on their faces.

Jenny pulled her car into her garage. Linda lived right next door. They hopped out of the car fast. "We need to do this quickly for your safety," Brucie stated.

"Go to the side door of my garage and I'll be there shortly. Run," Linda said, her voice trembling.

"I'm going to grab Reese, my dog, and come help. Leave your front door opened for me," Jenny said.

Jenny let Reese out and ran next door to Linda's house. Linda already had clothes, coats, socks and boots and blankets. She handed some to Jenny. I have one more thing for her. She grabbed a loaded handgun. They kept Reese in the house while they very carefully ran to the garage, slipping in the side door. In the house, the cats, Sprinkle Dinkle and Skittle Wittle hissed and ran to a hideout. They could hear Reese bark from outside.

They helped Brucie dress, handed her a flashlight and helped her crawl up the hole. The blankets and gun were handed to her, Linda explaining quickly how to use it. Brucie scooted back so Flagstone couldn't see her if he looked for her in the garage. Then Jenny and Linda wiped their footprints off the car and went into

Linda's house. They turned the television on immediately to make it seem like they had been there all along.

———

Flagstone stopped at a bar next to County Road W. He sat down and drank a beer, then casually slipped into conversation with the bartender about how he was looking for the owner of a small, black car because he accidentally hit their fender with his truck.

"Well, there is more than one small, black car around here, you know, but two ladies around here drive one and they live just across the road," the bartender said.

Flagstone gulped down the beer, wiped his mouth and slammed the mug down hard. With his freaky smile he said, "You've been most helpful. Thank you."

He carefully drove down the street and parked along the side of the road, grabbed the rifle and began his hunt. He didn't know at the time if he knocked Riggins out or killed him. He had heard a car door slam and needed to see it before Brucie got away, so he ran as fast as he could to catch sight of it. In his mind, he had to be on the lookout for any suspicious vehicles knowing Riggins would be right behind him if he regained consciousness by some chance, or other officers looking for a stolen truck. His only chance to get away at the time was the fact he had been driving a stolen vehicle.

———

Brucie sat extra quiet, body trembling from the cold and fear. Her head perked up. It sounded like someone walking in the snow, that crunching sound. Maybe it was Riggins, but at this point, she had no way of knowing.

The lights were on in Linda's house, but Jenny's house remained dark. A squeak of the side door opening into the garage caught Brucie's attention. She held her breath and didn't move. Brucie sent Jenny a fast text.

. . .

Brucie: Someone just opened the side door of the garage. I can't see but be cautious. Don't let anyone you don't know in your house. Act casual and use a different name in case it is Flagstone and he saw your car. I don't know how he would know it was you in this short time, but let's just be safe.

Jenny clutched her phone and looked at her neighbor. "Linda, Brucie thinks Flagstone is outside. She told me to use a different name. Um...um, how about Marlane Howard? I've always liked the name, Marlane."

"Okay, that sounds fine," Linda said. "I'm scared, Jenny—I mean Marlane. I'll remember to call you Marlane. This guy's a killer."

"Truthfully, I'm scared, too. Look, in order to keep him off track, we have to remain calm and act normal," Jenny said. "Just don't unlock the screen door if he comes up." She took a deep breath. Linda copied her.

A knock on the door caused them both to jump. "Stay calm," Jenny recited.

Linda, with shaking hands, slowly opened the door, leaving the screen door locked. "Yes?"

"Hello. I'm looking for the driver of a small, black car. I didn't get the opportunity to find out the make and model. I accidentally hit her fender with my truck and had an urgent meeting to attend, so I left. I want to give her my information to set things right. Do you know anyone around who drives a car like that?" The man's eyes were intimidating. His head was moving around to try and see inside Linda's house.

"Let me see," Linda said patting her lips with an index finger. "Can't say that I do, but that's because I'm new here. Only been here for a couple of months. That's my sister, Marlane. She's visiting and helping me unpack." At least her words were mostly the truth.

"Who is your neighbor?"

"I haven't met my neighbor yet."

"What type of vehicle does your neighbor drive?"

"I've only seen a man and woman drive off in some type of SUV. Pretty sure they don't drive a small, black car. Oh!"

The man jumped.

"I saw a sedan of some kind and a van in the driveway."

Jenny thought to herself, *Emmy nomination performance. Good job, Linda.*

All of a sudden Flagstone bent down as a truck drove slowly by. Linda saw a hidden rifle. She turned her head with eyes the size of a golf ball. The audible sound of his boots as he ran away scared Linda. She slammed the door so fast that Flagstone looked back at her as it closed. He could see the truck slow down as it passed the stolen truck. He wasn't certain if it was Riggins or a cop, but at this point, he couldn't take any chances. Agents and police were after him, and he knew it.

Back into the garage he ran. Inside, he breathed in and out loudly to catch his breath, followed by horrendous curse words. Flagstone shined his cellphone flashlight around the garage, looking for a place to hide. It shined up at the ceiling, right where the hole was.

———

Brucie slapped a hand to her mouth after hearing Flagstone's voice. She very quietly typed Riggins a text that Flagstone was in the garage, and she heard him breathing nearby, praying he doesn't crawl up the hole in the ceiling where she sat.

Riggins texted back for her to hold tight as he skidded in the snow-and ice-covered driveway.

Quietly, Brucie scooted to the hole opening of the roof in order to see where Flagstone was hiding. She had to inform Riggins before he busted into the doorway. The side door swishing open caused her to look and she could see Riggins standing in the doorway shining his flashlight around the area.

Flagstone jumped up from the side of the car and moved toward him, a *shk shuck* sound loud and clear.

Brucie feared for Riggins' life, and now able to see Flagstone clearly, she managed to jump down from the hole, and she fell on top of Flagstone, causing him to fall to the garage's cement floor.

"Uhhh," Brucie muffled.

Flagstone lost the rifle in the fall, but his hands went to her neck. The puffy coat made it too hard for him to wrap them around her neck, though.

Riggins could hear the commotion, which led him to shine his flashlight in that direction. He tore into the garage and jumped on Flagstone. "Brucie get out of here!" he frantically yelled. They began to wrestle, Riggins on top of him. His fist connected with Flagstone's face and the pop was loud.

Brucie saw Linda's gun and grabbed it. She shot a bullet in the ceiling. Both men stopped and sat up.

"I'll shoot right through your head, you murderous demon. Get up. I said, get up!" she shouted at Flagstone.

Flagstone snarled and bared his teeth. "I should have strangled the life out of you when I had the chance." He spit on the ground.

By this time Riggins was standing next to Brucie. He took the gun from her.

"No, Riggins. He needs to die," she spat. "He's killed so many people, so many animals. He doesn't deserve to sit in prison for the rest of his life while we pay for him to live. He needs to die. Rid the world of his evilness."

Riggins put his hand on hers. "I would so love to kill him, right here and right now, but we can't." His mind wandered for a split second to his dad. This evil man took his father's life from him. He shook the thoughts off. "We just can't. We would be no better than him."

Just as Riggins took the gun from her, he heard a rifle cock. He turned fast, aimed the gun at Flagstone and both weapons fired at the same time. Riggins and Flagstone dropped.

"Riggins! Riggins!" she yelled in panic as she bent down.

He was still conscious, moaning and resting his hand just above his heart on the left shoulder area, blood seeping through his gloved fingers. She moved the flashlight around him, then heard another sound.

She looked beyond Flagstone and saw him searching around on the ground for his weapon. She lifted the gun and aimed it at him.

"Don't do it, Flagstone. Don't do it."

He glared at her as though his spirit had already left his body, as though his spirit belonged to Satan himself. The look terrified her. Riggins whispered a warning, "He's going to kill you. Stop him."

As soon as she heard the trigger click, she fired. Flagstone dropped the gun and stared blankly into the night. She shined the flashlight on him to be certain. Her breathing became erratic. She'd just killed a human being. Too much! Too fast. She couldn't think clearly.

Very softly and quietly Riggins said before passing out, "Call the ambulance."

She dialed 911 and yelled into the phone, "Officer down." Adrenaline pumping, she blurted out the address and urged them to hurry. Far away she could hear sirens. She connected to one of the agents while running to the house, banging on the door, and screaming at the top of her lungs for more blankets. "Blankets!" she kept screaming.

Linda ran and got some. Brucie grabbed them from her, ran back inside the garage and covered Riggins.

Brucie listened to his heart. His breathing was raspy.

Jenny and Linda tore into the garage. "Brucie, are you okay? Brucie?"

"Yes, Flagstone is dead, and Riggins has been shot. Please bring me some towels to stop the bleeding," needing medical emergency care for both her and Riggins. They returned in a second. Tears plummeted down Brucie's face as she pulled a blanket over both her and Riggins as she laid beside him, pressing towels on his wound. In tears, she spouted, "I love you, Riggins. I love you. Stay with me. Don't leave me." She didn't even know what she was saying.

Was she going into shock? She didn't know.

Jenny and Linda stood at a loss of how to help. They grabbed one of the blankets lying on the ground and covered them both for extra warmth. Then Linda pulled the garage door up at the sound of several sirens coming nearer.

Snow and ice sprayed across the air as a truck squealed to a halt. One of the agents jumped out and ran up to Brucie, looking at Flagstone on the ground. Just as he reached the garage, the ambulance and police cars drove in. The sirens were making her feel dizzy. Mentally and physically, she had been through too much.

Brucie tried desperately to keep it all together, but her consciousness was fading away fast. Before going into unconsciousness, she heard the sirens of the ambulance and police cars pulling up. Tears dribbled down her cheeks as an ear-piercing hooting and hollering echoed through one of the police cars. She glanced over to see an officer trying to calm the chimps down. As the EMT's placed her and Riggins on gurneys, the chimps whimpered. Just barely she could hear them.

But as soon as they lifted Flagstone's body onto a gurney and began pulling a sheet over him, anger and fear resonated in the chimps' voices. She reached a hand towards them, wishing she could comfort them. But, once inside the ambulance, she glanced at Riggins and her mind and body couldn't handle anything else, and she passed out.

Jenny and Linda watched the ambulance pull away. Their eyes a blurry mess. One of the agents gave Jenny and Linda the hospital location and explained to them that they needed to stay home until their statements were taken. They both remained silent until the agents took down their statements.

———

One of the agents drove the chimps back to Riggins' place. They were still going berserk and somehow, he fastened an arm leash around each of them in order to guide them safely into the house. Finally inside, because they were so agitated, he was scared they would tear him to bits, but Joe stumbled out of a bedroom, rubbing his head. They ran to him, almost causing him to fall. Joe felt unstable, and he placed his hands on the railing to steady himself.

Joe made it to the couch and collapsed, trying to stop the dizziness. With both hands holding his head, he asked, "Are Brucie and Riggins okay?"

"I don't know, Joe. By the time I got there, the medics had pulled in. Riggins was shot, Brucie fell unconscious in the ambulance and Flagstone is dead. I'm going to call Dan. He'll want to know."

Joe could hear the frantic conversation but was too unstable to get up. The agent came back into the room. "Dan's catching the next flight here. I couldn't calm him down, because I have no way of knowing if they're all right or not."

"Don't beat yourself up, man. I think I need an ambulance myself. We need to get these guys in their beds and calmed down first. Help me up."

True to his word, soon the chimps were snug as a bug and sleeping. The agent called for the ambulance and in about half an hour or longer, Joe was being treated and escorted to the hospital.

Chute Pond looked like Las Vegas with all the lights and sirens. Anyone close by stuck their heads out the window to try and figure out what was going on. Officers and agents nearby ordered them to stay in the houses. Chris from Kitty's Bar and Grill walked out to his car and looked down the road as two bodies were being carried out of the woods. They were covered in a tarp of some sort.

By the end of the night all the agents and police were offered a warm fire, coffee and food inside the bar. Nothing else could be done until morning. Tires sliding in the slush, brake lights flashing, and tires squealing out of the parking lot ended the evening.

Thirty-One

BRUCIE LAY in her hospital bed, hooked up to IVs, monitors, with constant beeping. She was out cold, covered in many heavy blankets. She had been given sedatives and pain killers, but her mind still whirled in her unconsciousness.

In her dream, she was surrounded by dark, eerie dark, cold and freezing temperatures.

Silence. Complete silence. A blurred face in the background came close, closer, until completely visible. His evil eyes, that deranged smile, a face that produced hate, no conscience, no human emotion stared into her eyes.

Her body flew up to a sitting position. She screamed, bloodcurdling screams. Her eyes opened but she was still lost in unconsciousness. Screams kept coming. Hands on both sides grabbed her arms, trying to calm her down, but caught off guard by the sudden explosion of fear and anger.

"Brucie, it's okay. We're here. We're here for you," Britanica managed to mumble out between sobbing. Emmy on the other side of her was too upset to speak. She rubbed Brucie's arms, crying, sniffling.

Britanica managed to get control and gently shook Brucie. "Brucie, you're okay. It's us, Britanica and Emmy. Open your eyes."

Now perfectly still, eyes opening very slowly, Brucie looked around not knowing where she was, or what was going on. Nothing. Her head turned and looked at Britanica and then slowly turned to face Emmy. Finally, she was coherent. Hands to her chest, she broke out in gut-wrenching sobs.

Emmy and Britanica embraced her, cried with her until she felt safe and alert. The crying slowed. They sat back on the chairs and with tearstained faces, watched her.

Then Brucie's eyes widened, and she yelled, "Riggins! Where is Riggins? No! No! He can't be dead. Tell me he's not dead."

With a firm grasp on Brucie, Britanica replied, "He's not dead. Brucie, he's alive in another room."

"So, he's going to be okay?"

"The doctors can't say for sure, but they think he's going to be fine. He lost a lot of blood."

"That's not good enough. He saved my life. Look at all the people who lost their lives because of me. Mr. Kinnard and his dog were killed. Huh! Joe! Is he dead?"

That was news to them, and they resumed crying. They didn't know Mr. Kinnard and Wylie like Brucie did, but they had run into him many times and chatted. Joe's name didn't register with them.

"You're supposed to be on your honeymoon, Britanica! You shouldn't be here," Brucie said with a groan.

"Are you kidding? You think I could enjoy myself knowing two of my best friends are in critical condition?"

"Hhhh!" My feet! Do I still have feet?" Hands covered her mouth as tears fell some more.

Britanica and Emmy looked at each other with raised brows.

"I don't understand what you mean," Emmy said.

"Look and see if I still have my feet. Please." She said each word slowly, all with the same timbre. She squeezed her eyes shut as Britanica and Emmy, with frightened faces, lifted the blankets from her feet.

Letting out a relieved exhale, Britanica answered. "Yes, both feet are still there."

Brucie was holding her breath, almost blue in the face and exhaled deeply.

"What's this all about, Brucie?" Emmy asked.

"Running, falling through the snow and slush, I didn't have time to put on boots. I had severe frostbite. My lungs hurt like fire burned in them."

Both women rubbed her legs. "You poor thing," Britanica remarked trying to hold back the tears.

"Your mom's on a flight right now. She'll be here in a couple of hours," Emmy said.

"Guys, I have to visit Riggins."

Britanica tilted her head, her mouth spread in a weird shape, and she spoke hesitantly.

"There's no…way they will—"

"Make a way! I mean it. I have to see him with or without your help." Brucie started to swing her legs out and they both stopped her.

"Okay. You're right. I would insist if it were Gene. Emmy, grab that wheelchair."

They slowly helped her in it. When Brucie tried to step down, she moaned in pain. Her bandaged feet hurt something terrible. They grabbed her arms to keep her from falling, slowly lowering her in the chair. Checking first to be certain she wouldn't fall out, Emmy pulling the IV hookup behind her, they pushed her to Riggins' room. Gene and Webster stood over him. Brucie's hands covered her face and she wept silently, tears bursting through her fingers. Everyone surrounded her.

"We've been taking turns staying with you and Riggins," Gene said feeling unsure of what to say.

She stared at Riggins without responding. Bleep, bleep, bleep was the only sound in the room. Everyone in the room had sullen faces. Webster put his hand on her shoulder. She looked up at him still in a daze.

"He's going to make it. I know it," Webster commented.

Gene stared at Britanica with a scornful face. There was no way they could promise such a thing, make false promises. Britanica's mouth puckered up and she waved her hand back and forth to keep him quiet. If Brucie knew the truth, would she go into shock? She was way too unstable at the moment.

"Can someone—" Brucie started to ask.

"Could—"

Before Britanica could correct Brucie's grammar, Emmy's mouth dropped, and she held her hands up with a universal meaning: "Really!"

This was going on behind Brucie's back. Britanica squeezed her eyes closed and hand formed a fist as she pounded her head silently.

"Now, what is it you were trying to ask," Emmy said glaring at Britanica.

"Can somebody pull me up next to him?"

Gene and Webster reacted quickly, and with gentleness lifted her up. Her eyes closed shut and she breathed like she was in a Lamaze class. Her body shook from the pain soaring through it. Behind her, both women covered their mouths and lowered their heads as tears quietly fell. It just hurt too much to see their friend in such pain, emotionally and physically.

Brucie opened her eyes. Silent tears dropped over Riggins' arm. Her head bent over, and she kissed his cheek. He stirred. She gasped. They all gasped. His eyes opened for a very brief second. It was like the reverse role of *Sleeping Beauty* and the prince.

Brucie was too weak to stay standing and started to slip. The men grabbed her arms to help lower her in the chair. A nurse came running into the room.

"What's going on?" His heart monitor was at a faster pace. Her face was scornful.

"She needed to see him," Britanica offered.

"She needs to be in bed," the nurse huffed.

Brucie held Riggins' hand. "I'm not leaving him."

The nurse huffed louder.

"Do you have any idea what these two have been through?" Britanica asked confrontationally.

"Do you want them to get better?" the nurse responded sarcastically.

Gene waved his hands. "Hold on, before I arrest both of you. Brit, she does need to get back into her bed. Look how pale she is."

Britanica gave him the evil eye, looked down at Brucie and changed her expression. "You're right. Let's go, Em."

Very softly Brucie tried saying, "No, no," but was too weak to protest.

"We'll bring you back when you're a little stronger. We promise," Emmy said.

The wheelchair squeaked all the way back to the room. Riggins' heart rate was back to normal by this time.

———

Like a bull in a china cabinet, a fast and loud clomping of a person running echoed in through the hallway. There was yelling. A struggle. All of a sudden, metal racks went flying, clinging and skidding into a wall. Crash! Utensils clanged to a stop. Huffing and grumbling. "Stop him!" was yelled over and over.

"I'll break your bones in half!" Even if you weren't in the same room, you could hear spit coming out with each enraged word.

"Sir, only family is permitted," a nurse yelled running toward him.

Gene and Webster ran down the hall. There was Dan. Veins bulging from his head, heavy breaths, fists the size of a cannonball. "That is my best friend in there," he said through gritted, teeth, slobber spraying.

Before the guards stupidly tried to hold him down, Gene yelled, "Wait! Leave him alone."

The next thing that happened looked like *Hercules* threw the guards into the wall. They groaned.

"Dan, stop!" Gene yelled.

He looked over at Gene. His chest heaved in and out, face bright red, body tense. His breathing lowered to normal. Gene walked up and held his badge out for the distraught guards to see. Patients and staff stood in the background like some superhuman lunatic was about to destroy them, like watching a superhero film.

"Everything's okay folks. Go back to your duties," he said waving his badge around. "This is one of the good guys—a federal agent."

"A real live *Rambo,*" a patient yelled.

Webster gently grabbed Dan's arm and got him to walk with him.

Gene walked over to him and patted his arm in a manly fashion. "Hey, you need to calm down before we enter Rigg's room."

Dan took a deep breath. "Is he... is he okay? Brucie? Is she okay?"

"Both in critical condition but alive. They're going to make it. I feel it in here," Gene responded with a fist on his heart.

Tears came to Dan's eyes. "Something told me not to leave. This is all my fault."

Gene stopped. "Are you kidding me? Because right now you would offend Riggins. Don't you dare say anything like that to him. Do you hear me," he yelled. Face tensed.

"Yeah, but—"

"Riggins felt so guilty that you were away from your family at Christmas. He relaxed the minute you got on the plane."

"Okay, good buddy. I hear you loud and clear."

They entered Riggins' room slowly. The monitors played a hospital melody. Smells of antiseptics and cleaning agents exploded with the realization of being in a hospital. Dan lowered his head. Droplets began slowly and then flooded his face. Webster laid his hand on Dan's shoulder. "We'll give you some alone time with him. We'll be down the hall by Brucie."

After they walked out, Dan wiped his eyes for a few seconds and walked back over to the bed. He squeezed Riggin's hand.

"Hey buddy. It's Dan. I came the second I found out. My wife wanted to come but there was only one seat available on the plane. She told me to give you a kiss, but, well, let's just pretend I did." He giggled. Riggins stirred and a moan escaped his lips. His eyes blinked but he couldn't keep them open.

"Hey buddy. Take it easy. Don't push it. We're all here for you."

A nurse walked in. He explained how Riggins blinked his eyes. She said it could have been an involuntary twitch. Dan's expression saddened. Not what he wanted to hear.

He rested in the chair. Emotionally, he was drained. His eyes fought closure, but soon enough his head slouched down. Gene walked in and looked at Dan wondering how air could move through and not be blocked by the way his head rested almost on his chest. Just as his hand moved to touch his shoulder, Dan jumped. He looked around fast.

"Can't believe I dozed off. That's not like me."

"You needed it, but that could not have been a very relaxing sleep the way your head was hanging."

A huge, wide-mouthed yawn lasted for seconds. "Uhhh. Yeah, you're right. Hey, I need to visit Brucie."

"Not possible. They gave her some strong sedative. She's out like a light. Britanica and I are going to hang out tonight. Come back tomorrow. Then we'll go home and sleep, and Webster and Emmy will stay tomorrow night. The other agents are staying at Riggins' house. I'll give them a heads up that you're coming. You need to get some sleep."

"You know what, you're right." He patted Gene's shoulder and left. Some of the hospital staff moved out of his way, remembering his outrageous behavior. A patient yelled from his room, "Night *Rambo*."

He looked around wondering why they all acted so strangely, and the *Rambo* remark threw him for a loop. He held his hands up to say, "no trouble" and drove to Riggins' house. Could he make it? His eyes were heavy. Just ahead, a deer jumped out in the road and froze. His tires screeched just inches from the deer. Now he was awake. It turned and leapt through the forest.

At Riggins' place, without conversation to anyone, he crawled into bed.

Britanica fell asleep in a recliner in Brucie's room and staff brought a recliner in Riggin's room. Gene's eyes automatically closed as he reclined.

Thirty-Two

HORRIFIED SCREAMING WOKE BRITANICA UP. She jumped up and ran to Brucie. A nurse ran into the room. Gently shaking her, Britanica called her name. "Brucie, Brucie. Wake up. It's okay."

Her eyes opened and she scanned the room with a fear-stricken face.

"Hey there. I'm right here. Look at me, Brucie."

Finally, reality won over. She ran fingers over and over her forehead.

"Did you have a nightmare?"

"I keep seeing his evil face."

"Whose?"

"Satan! Who do you think?"

Immobile, Britanica's eyes widened, and her mouth dropped slightly open. "Do you want to talk about it?"

Brucie rubbed her neck remembering how she gasped for air as he choked her. "It's too scary."

"Well, it's up to you. If you want, I could say a prayer."

"Okay."

Britanica held her hand and prayed. Brucie lay back against the pillow. Britanica walked to the doorway and spoke quietly to the nurse. "This is the second time she woke up screaming. I think it would be a good idea to have our pastor visit her tomorrow."

"I've seen this before. All that medication can cause nightmares, but your idea is worth the try."

She walked back to her bedside. "One of us will always be here for you. Your mom should be here any minute."

Her mother walked in that very second. She ran to the bed and bent over to embrace Brucie.

They cried softly together. She stroked Brucie's hair looking at her with warm, loving eyes. Britanica gave them some privacy and went to Riggins' room. There was no change. She and Gene conversed over Brucie's nightmares and prayed together.

———

Later that day, Gene woke up feeling crushed. Britanica shared the chair and was lying almost on top of him. He shook her. "Brit, Brit, wake up."

"What? What?"

"I can't breathe," he strained to say.

"Oh!" She pushed her hand down hard on his stomach and pushed her body up. "Ufff," he spouted. "I think you ruptured my spleen."

"Sissy." She laughed. "Besides, your spleen isn't down there."

"Bru…cie," they heard come from the bed. It was said in a whisper.

They both ran to Riggins' side.

"Riggins? Can you talk to me?" Gene asked.

He took a few breaths. Without opening his eyes, he slowly and quietly said her name again.

"Bru…cie?"

Britanica's hand slapped her mouth. Tears dropped.

"She's okay. She's in a room down the hall. Her mom's sitting with her. Are you able to hear me?" Gene asked him.

Silence.

Gene grabbed his hand. "Squeeze my hand if you understood what I said."

Very mildly he felt a squeeze. He removed his hand and embraced Britanica. A nurse came in and checked his vitals. They stared at her waiting and waiting and waiting.

Very sympathetically the nurse said, "His vitals are stronger today, but nowhere close to being out of the woods." She smiled and walked out.

Every florist in Wisconsin had to be flowerless. Both rooms were filled. A few visitors sneezed endlessly. Balloons floated, stuffed animals everywhere.

The next day, Brucie's room was filled with visitors. Only one or two people at a time were able to visit Riggins.

The scream coming from his room was terrifying. The gang looked out of Brucie's doorway as hospital staff ran to Riggins' room, pushing Dan outside. One nurse was carrying a defibrillator. The squeaking of shoes was nerve-wracking. Brucie's trembling hands covered her mouth as the gang ran to his room. The cardiac monitor was flatlining. They paced across from his room, some heads downward while hands lie in a praying form to their mouths.

All was calm now. They stared into his room and could see the cardiac monitor lines moving up and down. His heart was beating again. The most precious picture and music to a loved one's eyes and ears. Everyone had been so startled that they ran from Brucie's room, forgetting about what she must be going through. Britanica ran back just as Brucie slipped to the floor.

"Help! Help me!" she shouted.

Brucie's mom and several of the gang ran to Britanica's call for help. In seconds, Brucie was back in the bed, nurse staff checking her vitals. "I'm sorry, Brucie. I was so worried about Riggins that I forgot you couldn't get out of bed by yourself."

"Is he—"

"He's fine. I promise."

Brucie closed her eyes, and within minutes she was back to sleep.

———

It's been a week. Riggins regained consciousness and was able to sit up and talk a little. The pain was still severe. Brucie had to go through therapy and that, too, was very painful. The good thing was that the natural coloration was coming back into her feet. Blood was circulating normally.

Before they helped her back in bed, she insisted on seeing Riggins. The nurse wouldn't budge, but Emmy and Britanica convinced her that this would help with the healing process. For both of them. She hesitantly allowed it.

Gene talked while Riggins listened. A squeak, squeak, squeak stopped him from talking. He stared at the doorway. The women pushed Brucie inside. Her eyes were on Riggins. Gene shook Riggins' shoulder.

"Hey, you have a visitor," he said joyfully.

Riggins weakly turned his head toward the doorway. When he saw her, a smile spread across his face. "Bru...cie," he said quietly. This was the first time he was conscious, and she was allowed in his room. His hand barely moved, but it was enough for her to take notice. She grabbed it and, of course, teared up. His hand tried to touch her cheek but fell back down. He closed his eyes.

"Hey, it's okay. We're going to be seeing a lot of each other. Take it slowly. I'm in the same boat."

So many questions and so many answers, but they both knew it would happen eventually.

Out in the hallway there was a commotion. "Dan! Hey, Dan! *Rambo!*" Dan had become a hospital celebrity. A real live federal agent, just like in the movies. He strolled into Riggins' room with a wide smile, two bouquets of gorgeous flowers. He saw Brucie and bent down and kissed her cheek for an extra-long time and handed her a bouquet.

Hearing all the commotion Riggins watched the scene. He actually laughed for a second.

Dan came up to him, bent down and kissed his forehead with a big, puckered explosion. That brought a well-needed laugh-a-thon.

"Hey, buddy. Man, you look awful."

Riggins rolled his eyes. Another explosion of laughter.

"Not that it matters now, but hey, the police found Flagstone's weapon that killed the two agents. It was hidden in a pile of branches near that stump with the smiley face. It wasn't easy to see because we had to almost dig the branches up to find it."

"Well, the other two are in custody, so this will seal the deal," Riggins commented with a slight squinting of his eyes. He refused to take pain killers unless absolutely necessary.

"All right. All right. Enough excitement for a while. Everyone out while I check his vitals," a nurse said considerately.

Brucie smiled and whispered goodbye. He nodded. Exhaustion claimed him. They all went back to her room. Once in bed, she asked in a very somber manner, "Will he recover fully, or will there always be complications? Tell me the truth."

Nobody had the answer and the thought of it brought down their mood.

Thirty-Three

At the hospital, Christmas music blasted through the speakers. Decorated trees and garland had been set up at every station.

Britanica and Emmy walked down the corridor carrying boxes of decorations. A piece of garland hung down to the floor and Britanica tripped from it, resulting in a huge Christmas tangled mess. Ornaments clanked down the hallway.

Emmy held a box and all she could do was laugh. "Well, at least you're in the right place if you twisted your ankle."

Shaking her head, Britanica stuck her tongue out. "Nah, nah, nah yourself. Help me up, would ya?" From somewhere in her box, they heard the Santa figurine they had purchased say, "Ho, ho, ho."

"Ahhh," Emmy gasped, mouth almost dragging the floor because of Britanica's bad grammar. Since she had overcome her learning disability, Britanica would only speak in proper English.

Britanica wrinkled her nose exposing a few upper teeth. "What?!"

"Your grammar. I don't think I have ever heard you use such poor grammar," Emmy replied. "You are human after all."

Britanica pushed herself up and picked up the decorations, smirking at Emmy. Then her face brightened. "Bet you can't tell me which sign is an apteral design," she said pointing to some signs on the corridor wall. One day Webster came over to her parent's house and was studying the signs. He explained what they were to her.

Emmy's shoulders shook and she wore a whimsical expression. She walked up to a particular sign, and with her chin, pointed to it. "Who's the *Wizard of Oz* now?"

Britanica's mouth dropped. "You cheater. No way could you know that."

"Your brother was studying architecture, and it was in a book." She stuck her tongue out and walked to Brucie's room.

Walking into Brucie's hospital room with a pleased expression, Emmy looked over and knew Brucie would want to know what her satisfied expression was about. She didn't want to waste their time knowing Britanica would find a way to challenge her if Brucie knew about it, so she thought it best to end it before Brucie questioned her, "Don't ask," Emmy said quickly.

"We wish you a merry Christmas," Britanica sang as she entered Brucie's room.

"Well, what do we have here?" Brucie's face turned bright.

"Em, do you still have that thermos with hot chocolate?" She stuck her nose up at Emmy, still trying to get over their goofy episode.

Brucie watched curiously.

"It's the *Wizard of Oz*, if you please," Emmy corrected her in fun.

Britanica snorted at her. All three of them laughed.

"Good news, guys. I'm out of here in a couple of days," Brucie said.

They both turned to her. "That's fantastic," Emmy squealed.

Britanica blew out a sigh of relief. "Don't worry. We'll come back and take down all these decorations. My, but the Christmas tree sparkles beautifully. We haven't been to see Riggins yet, so how does he like the decorations? He's a man. He could care less, I suppose," Brit said.

"You're wrong, Brit. He loves Christmas. You perked up his day by decorating his room. He did say that Las Vegas would be jealous of all the lights."

"Hah, just as we predicted," Emmy said with a laugh. She and Britanica high-fived each other.

"Hey guys, now that my mental state is back to normal, I have to talk to you about something," Brucie said.

They both looked nervously at each other not knowing if she was going to reveal something spooky. Emmy sat at the foot of her bed and Britanica pulled a chair over.

"Let's hear it, girl. We're all ears, excluding those teeny, tiny things Emmy calls ears."

"Hey," Emmy responded offended.

"They're absolutely adorable, Em. Now shut up and let Brucie speak." She kissed Emmy's cheek in fun.

"Look, this is serious."

They sat up straight. "Sorry, please go on, Brucie," Britanica replied sympathetically.

Brucie twiddled her fingers, looking down. "I saw something strange at your wedding."

"Mmm-hmmm. The twinkling, twirling lights that went between you and Riggins?" Brit asked.

Brucie stared at Britanica flabbergasted, not able to reply.

"Look Brucie," Brit added, "this all started when I was a little girl. You weren't around and I had some very depressing moments. You already know all about that. One day I wrote a Christmas wish to Santa." She held her hands out. "Before you say anything, I know Santa's real, but I know it was the Lord behind all of it. He knows my big imagination, and as far as I can tell, made it fun for me. Let's just get that part settled first. I asked Santa to give me true love one day."

Emmy and Brucie looked at each other and shook their heads.

"What? You don't believe in Santa?" Britanica looked at them, disappointed. Brucie held her hands up and made a very goofy face. Britanica waved them both off.

"Let me just continue. As soon as I wrote it, it began snowing, like a blizzard. I ran to the window and saw the lights swirl around Gene as he tried escaping to his house. Then when I came home from college and we all got together, the lights swirled around us again. Emmy listened to my story and told me it was Christmas magic, and that Gene was my true love, which, as you know, is true. She never saw the lights except at the Candy Cane dance and she also heard Santa as he left. You heard it too, Brucie.

"Emmy was always beautiful and could have had any guy she wanted. She never had to resort to making a Christmas wish."

Emmy slumped over out of guilt.

"Gene and I saw it happen at my wedding. But first it swirled around us, and I pretended to scoop the lights into my hands and blew them your way. Then they circled you and Riggins, your true love. End of story."

"Yup! It's Christmas magic Brucie. Don't try to fight it." Emmy's face was bright with excitement.

"What if this is just a fluke? Maybe you dreamed it up in your imagination, Brit. I mean, what if I feel obligated to Riggins for saving my life? If that's it that will wear off."

"No. It's because you felt something for him at my wedding, before he saved your life," Brit responded.

"Still, maybe I felt indebted to him for keeping me safe."

"What are you afraid of? An incredible love story with a hunk of a man; not to mention, one that is madly in love with you. Brucie, women are attracted to him like bears to honey. Don't blow it. Stop trying to analyze it to death. What are you waiting for? True love comes once in a lifetime. Think it through and quickly."

"I'm with Brit. True love is real, and you should keep in mind that if God is guiding your relationship and if you choose to deny it," Emmy said as she swiped her hands together, "it's all over for you."

"How do I know it is God pushing us together?"

A long, soft pbbbbbt sound blew out of Britanica's mouth. "Did you think you were hallucinating the lights? It's God's fun way of getting your attention. Look, I tried to deny it, too. It's scary to believe it's not a hallucination. Emmy, who didn't experience any of it, believed right away. She doesn't even have an imagination."

Emmy's shoulders dropped and her mouth fell looking at Britanica.

Brucie covered her giggle. "Okay. You win. I'll honestly start to believe without questioning everything."

A squee resonated in the corridor. Donny walked into Brucie's hospital room holding a big bouquet of flowers, Maria hanging on his arm. Britanica yelped as she ran up and hugged him.

"Hey, girl. You just crushed my bouquet," he said.

"I'm sorry. I'm so excited to see you. And you, Maria," she added squeezing her hand.

"I know we saw each other at the funeral, but it certainly wasn't the right demographic to catch up on what's happening in our lives. It's been far too long," Donny commented and kissed her cheek. He walked over to Brucie and kissed her forehead. "You always were the troublemaker." He winked at Brucie.

"There's truth to that statement," she replied squeezing his hand.

They spoke for a while and got caught up on anything new in each of their lives. Before Donny left, Britanica pulled him outside into the hall. "You two have been dating for a while. Anything permanent?"

"You nosey little cutie pie, I'll tell you when it happens."

She held her breath and clapped.

After Donny and Maria left, the girls talked for a few more minutes. Emmy choked on her own saliva looking through the doorway.

"You okay, Em?" Britanica asked.

Emmy, trying to stop coughing, pointed to the doorway, waving her hand toward it.

Britanica jumped up and ran. She just caught sight of Sam walking into Riggins' hospital room.

"Oh my, oh my!"

"What's going on?" Brucie asked.

"Sam I am just went into Riggins' room. What should we do?"

Brucie thought for a moment. "Nothing. Riggins can't physically fight with him. Go listen at the doorway. Hurry up, you two."

They were out the doorway before she finished speaking. Britanica held up a finger mouthing "Shhh." Emmy gritted her teeth and formed fists. Britanica made a "really" expression. They peeked into the room and heard Sam speak.

"I'm here in good faith," Sam said holding his hands up. Riggins stared at him cautiously.

"First off, I want you to know that I'm really happy you're getting better. I also want to tell you how sorry I am that I let you down."

Riggins' face was blank.

"I also want you to know that I have really learned a lesson."

Riggins frowned.

"You have every right not to believe me and I deserve that. After everything that happened, all I could do was be ashamed of myself. Watching you put yourself in danger, always on top of things, brave and insightful reasoning, well, let's just say made me a new man. Your anger and disappointment in me were justified.

"Look, I don't blame you for not believing me, but I want you to know I have spoken with several directors from other agencies. I confessed all my irresponsible actions and told them after watching you, I would like a chance to train more and prove myself one more time. They agreed and are giving me a chance. I'll make you proud this time. I just wanted to apologize and ask your forgiveness."

Whispering in the hallway, Britanica said to Emmy, "Maybe he accepted Jesus."

Emmy shrugged her shoulders.

Sam continued. "These balloons are a gesture of my sincerity, plus they add color to the room, not that you need anymore, but hey, why not?"

He extended his hand. Riggins looked into his eyes and slowly accepted his handshake. A smile formed.

"If you need anything, anything at all, I would be more than happy to help you out. Just say the word."

Riggins nodded his head.

"Well, then, I'm going to visit Brucie for a minute and give her this basket of chocolates. I heard you two are seeing each other. It was so obvious you had a thing for each other. Being with Brucie, although I really care for her, was my devious way of making you angry. Sorry about that and happy it worked out for you two."

Riggins just nodded he understood.

"Take care, Riggins."

Brucie and Emmy hightailed it out of there, skidding on the floor almost into Brucie's bed.

They sat down quickly.

Sam walked in. "Ladies." He walked over to Brucie and handed her the chocolate. They took the hint and walked out of the room and waited just outside her door.

"I'm really glad you're feeling better. I'm also really sorry I let you down. Can you ever forgive me?"

Thinking, she replied, "Yes, I do forgive you."

They talked for a few minutes, and something came to his mind. "I almost forgot." He pulled a book out of his jacket and handed it to her. "You're right. This is a great book." It was *Green Eggs and Ham*. "Take care of yourself." He bent down and kissed her lips. She smiled as he left.

After a few minutes, Britanica and Emmy went back inside Brucie's room. They all noticed two women walk past the door. Confused faces. Not needing a nudge, Britanica jumped up and peeked out the door. The two women went into Riggins' room.

"I wonder who it is?" Brucie thought out loud.

Inside his room, Riggins had closed his eyes. A gentle hand touched his hand. His eyes opened. His mouth dropped. "Mom? RyAnna?"

With a compassionate face, his mom said, "Yes, son. It is us." Tears blurred in her eyes.

RyAnna walked to the other side of his bed and grabbed his hand, tears streaming down her face. "Dan called us."

"You're not going to believe this, but my girlfriend in another room—At least I think she's my girlfriend. I don't really know, come to think of it." He gave a quick shake to his head. "We planned on visiting you at Christmas, but as you can see, that's not going to happen. You can ask her yourself, so you don't think I'm lying. Her name is Brucie."

"Son—"

With tears dribbling down his face he tried to talk. "Mom. RyAnna. I have to explain. I can explain it now. I'll never abandon you again. Never."

Before he could continue, his mom said, "Not now. I already know what you're going to say, and I understand. We'll talk later."

"I may not be released for another week or two."

"That's okay. We'll hang around."

"You can stay in my cabin. I think the only agent there now is taking care of my chimps."

"Chimps?" RyAnna asked.

"Long story."

"We were told we could only stay for a few minutes. Dan told us about Brucie and gave us her room number. We'll visit Brucie and head over to your cabin if you're sure," RyAnna asked.

"Absolutely, I'm sure. Thank you. Thank you for coming. Oh! My friends will help you return the rental. I'm sure you're driving one, and you can use my truck. That way you won't have to worry about it." He called Gene before they left and set it up.

They both kissed his cheeks and introduced themselves to Brucie and friends. Then they waited for Gene and returned the rental.

Thirty-Four

Brucie was released and back in her home. She visited Riggins and his mom every day.

RyAnna had to get back to her family and job. Riggins was on the road to recovery. Sick of being in the hospital and working hard at physical therapy, he endured the pain and worked extra hard so he could get back home. Dan had taken the chimps to Florida, and all were quite happy at their new home.

Gene stopped by to see Riggins. They watched a college football game together. Running through Gene's mind was a conversation he had with Dan as they sat in the hospital cafeteria while Riggins slept. Dan told Gene the story of Riggins and another female agent named Ziva working an undercover case a while ago. Being undercover, they pretended to be married, and it worked brilliantly in helping to capture the perpetrator in question. The story fascinated Gene and the story popped back to memory.

"Have you heard from Ziva?" Gene asked.

"I've been wondering when her name would pop up. How did you know about her? Hold on, big-mouth Dan told you. I know it was him because he always talks about this case. The answer is no, I haven't heard from Mrs. Malarkie.

"I'm pretty sure Brucie would dump you if she knew about her. I'd keep that quiet," Gene remarked.

"That doesn't sound honest. She'll find out about her soon enough the way this story seems to stay alive. You know how these guys are. They always kid me about her. Everyone is in love with Ziva. I'm surprised it took this long for the story to come out," Riggins answered.

"Gee, Riggs. I'm not sure, but I don't think it's a good idea to tell her yet."

"What's the big deal? It could be potentially damaging to our relationship if it is dropped on her. I mean, what would I think if it were a reverse situation? I just think it's smart to bring it out in the open before some idiot blurts it out," he added.

"The only time I have ever heard the name 'Ziva" is on *NCIS*," Gene said.

"If memory serves me correct, I believe that's exactly who she was named after. Both parents are Jewish and both loved *NCIS*."

"How about that," Gene remarked.

The doctor walked in. "Good news. Looks like you'll be released tomorrow, but physical therapy will continue for at least another month. No assignments."

"But Doc, I'm going stir crazy. I have to get back to work," Riggins pleaded.

"Absolutely not. I will make certain your director has full understanding of the consequences and formalities of this release. You're not ready, and another injury could put you in a wheelchair for life. Keep that in mind."

"Okay, you scared me. I'll listen."

"Great. Your recovery is exceptional. All the staff comment on how hard you're working at it.

In truth, it should be another two months of recovery after a near-death experience. You lost a lot of blood. A lot."

"If you ask me, angels were watching over him," Gene insisted.

"You know what? I tend to agree with you," the doctor replied.

———

Arrangements were made. His mother had cleaned up his house after all the agents left and made his room nice and cozy. Flowers and balloons galore were sitting in every spot available.

Gene and Brucie drove him home. She and Riggins had really hit it off. So well that she was a believer in Christmas magic. They carefully helped him up the steps. His mom opened the door, excited for his return. She hugged him gently. Being Riggins, he scolded everyone to let him walk alone. After all, he was doing a lot of that in therapy. Macho man was rising from the dead.

He walked around checking everything out. He strolled to the chimp's room. It was still set up for them. His eyes blurred. Brucie walked up and held his hand. Embarrassed, he turned his head.

"Hey, it's okay to miss them. I do, too," she said.

He gently squeezed her hand.

The gang had a surprise return party planned for him the next day. They wanted to see how he adapted to being out of the hospital for the first day before confirming it was a go.

That evening he and Brucie sat in the living room talking. His mom had gone for groceries.

"You look completely normal. How do you really feel?" he asked her.

"Feelin' good. Really good. I've been back to work for a week, and everyone has been so supportive and helpful."

He patted her hand. "I'm glad to hear it. I was worried about you. And I heard that boy you deposed in a deposition who came to play with the chimps, I believe Richard was his name, and his mom stopped in to see you."

"Yes. It was an absolute delight to spend time with Richard and his mother."

"I bet it was. Hey, you seem distracted. I don't want you to worry about me. I will recover totally. I mean, like it never happened," he said facing her with a serious look.

"Of course you will, but that wouldn't make any difference to me."

"Well, you never know, but I'm glad to hear it," he responded.

She was quiet for a minute, looking down at her nervous hands.

"Something's wrong. What?" he asked.

"Do you...do you ever think about that night?"

"Yes, I do. I don't like to, but it was so intense, so scary thinking I may lose you, that I can't help but think about it," he admitted.

"Me, too. Riggins, Flagstone's evil face, that deranged smile, those Satan eyes, keep coming to me in my sleep. It's terrifying. I know he's dead, but could Satan use him even supernaturally to make me go insane? Why can't I stop seeing his face?" Her head lowered and she held both sides of her face tightly.

Riggins touched her shoulder. "He can't hurt you anymore. I think it's time to talk with the pastor to confirm that."

"Britanica's been bugging me forever, but I refused. It is just too scary to talk about. I guess knowing you saw that face, I could discuss it with you. I don't know, maybe I am going crazy. His face comes to me whether I'm awake or asleep. He was an empty shell. It was disturbing to see," she confessed.

"It would be so easy to brush those feelings off for me, because trust me, he's not the first monster I've dealt with and probably not the last. You know, I've dealt with so many bad people, all that anger from the hurt they caused has kept me from going to church. It's hard to hear the pastor preach how good God is after seeing all the pain and suffering. Maybe it's time for me to get this out in the open. I think it may do me a world of good, as well as you, to speak with the pastor. Together. If you're okay with it, I'll make arrangements," he said.

She sat there thinking, staring at the wall. She turned to face him. "Okay, go ahead. It's probably a good idea. Having someone with me who knows how evil this man was will help me get through it. And I think you need some closure as well. Thank you."

"You bet. Besides, look how much you have been there for me through all of this. I don't think I would have survived this one without you. Thinking about you gave me strength to keep going." He shook his head and laughed.

"What's so funny?"

"I remember how much we hated each other at times. You could get my blood pressure climbing higher than anyone in my whole life. I guess I never pictured us getting along."

"You and me both." Memories flashed in her mind. Then she couldn't keep it in any longer and in a soft voice asked him, "Hey, I was wondering how you're doing with Flagstone's death."

"I haven't had much time to think about it, but there is a form of relief, not just because he murdered my father, but because he won't be able to kill anyone or any animal ever again. I guess, I do feel better about it."

That evening Brucie walked around the cottage looking for her mother.

"There you are. Aren't you freezing out here?" Even with a warm coat and gloves, Brucie kept rubbing her arms. Exhaled breaths looked like steam.

"No, but I guess the starry night captured my thoughts. Look how beautiful."

"Golly. Sometimes it feels like a dream to see such beauty as this. Creation declares God's glory.

"Mom, if you don't feel like talking about this, I totally understand. It's just...it's just that I want to ask how you're doing. I mean, I can't imagine. For me, I miss Dad so much that a day doesn't go by that I don't bawl like a baby."

She held an arm around Brucie's shoulders rubbing them up and down, tears solidifying on her face from the icy temperatures.

"I will always miss him. Always. But you see those stars up there?" she said pointing to the sky. "Those scientists have no clue what they're talking about. Those stars are our dearly departed loved ones twinkling up there to remind us that they will always be in our hearts. If we miss them, just look up at the stars. He's up there and it gives me warmth and love. Don't you feel it?"

"That's a beautiful thought, Mom. I always knew there was something extra special about the stars. I do feel the warmth. Thank you for pointing that out."

Her mother squeezed her, and they walked back inside feeling much better.

———

The next day, Brucie took Riggins to therapy. While away, his mom, the gang and agents from far and wide pulled in, hiding their cars at Brucie's and the tavern across the street.

Riggins was worn out. He worked hard, and harder than most patients. It was excruciatingly painful at times. Determination. Just plain determination. The therapist assisted him in weightlifting. Seeing that he could handle it and was building up his strength, they continued daily.

Dehydrated from the workout, in the car he gulped down a huge mug of water, wiping the excess off his mouth with his hand. It was hard, but Brucie kept the surprise gathering quiet. Even Dan flew in for the event. She pulled into the driveway after texting Britanica at the stop sign of South Shore Drive. He didn't pay any attention.

When he opened the door, at full blast "surprise" was yelled. He fell back from the surprise, and Brucie standing behind him, held onto him so he could catch his balance. His mouth dropped so low, and his eyes almost popped out of his head. The excessive talk and cheering was almost unbearable. Everyone ran up and hugged him. But then, he heard it. He shushed everyone. The hooting and hollering was resounding. He ran to the back and Brucie right behind him.

"Bogie! Bacall!" He opened the cage door, and they climbed up his arms. Then they climbed over to Brucie making the funniest and most endearing sounds. Dan walked up and he and Riggins embraced hard, arms heartily patting each other's backs. They pulled apart and Riggins said, "Man, it's good to see you, to see these guys," he turned towards the living room, "to see all of you." There wasn't a dry eye.

As they mingled in the living room, people began to separate in the room, leaving an empty section. Riggins jumped, then grabbed and hugged a woman Brucie didn't recognize with such compassion. They kissed each other on the lips, and he held her tight. A little too tight for Brucie's taste.

The crowd grew excited. "It's about time she got here," Agent Schnooper said, nicknamed Schnooper the Snooper. And man, how he lived up to his name. A real asset to the department.

"Who is she?" Brucie asked curiously.

"Mrs. Malarkie. Who else," Joe replied joyfully.

"Mrs. Malarkie?"

"His wife. You know…" Joe remarked quizzically.

She stared at this beautiful woman. It was obvious they meant something to each other by their greeting. Her face grew mildly red, tears burning the back of her eyes. Riggins hadn't taken his eyes off the woman named Ziva since the reunion.

Britanica looked over and realized Brucie was losing it. Before she could push through the crowd to get to her, Brucie had shoved everyone out of her way so she could exit the door. Riggins was still unaware. Until a very disturbing silence caught his attention. Riggins looked at everybody's face.

Britanica ran after Brucie, but she was long gone.

Riggins' face asked questions. Gene, feeling guilty, trying to avoid eye contact with Riggins, just said one word, "Brucie."

He dropped his hands off of Ziva, shook a finger at Gene. "I told you; didn't I?"

Gene's shameful face just nodded.

Before Riggins could run out the door, Joe and Dan stopped him. "We'll drive you," Dan said.

———

Lungs burning, still not in the best of shape, Brucie ran full speed down the road, away from her cabin. She was in no mood to talk to Riggins or anyone. Like Deja vu, her friend, Jenny, drove by, came to a screeching halt and braked immediately, window dropping. "Hey, need a ride?"

Heavy breaths in and out, Brucie replied, "Yes," Then jumped into the car.

"Where to?" Jenny asked.

"Where are you heading?"

"Home."

"Do you mind if I come with you?"

"Of course not. Want to talk about it?" Jenny asked softly.

Choking on her words, Brucie said, "Nope. Not even a little. I just need to get out of here." She could barely finish her sentence.

Jenny patted her knee. "Jenny to the rescue it is."

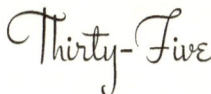

Thirty-Five

"RIGGINS, I'm so sorry for talking you out of telling Brucie about Ziva. Can you ever forgive me?" Gene asked with a solemn face.

"There's nothing to tell, unfortunately, Brucie doesn't know that. The kidding remarks from these guys were just something I'm used to and even expect. I need to explain to her mother. Please just take me there."

Brucie's mom had seen the whole episode and left right after she did. Riggins arrived on her doorstep, and she opened the door, her face full of intimidation. "Could I please come in for a minute…please?" Riggins' pleading softened her attitude and she moved away from the door. He explained it all in record time. Gene ended the conversation, taking full responsibility.

"She won't answer my calls. What if someone grabbed her when she took off running?

What if she's—dead?"

Riggins held both her arms. "I'll find her. Don't worry. If you hear from her, you have to notify me right away."

"What else could it be? She knows I'm panicking. What daughter would leave her mother succumb to such terror?"

"Maybe her phone died or maybe she's just too upset."

"Or maybe Flagstone has other goons working for him, hiding, waiting for the perfect opportunity to catch her."

"I don't believe that for a minute. He's dead and no one is going to care about carrying out a dead man's wish and risk dying or going to prison. That just doesn't make sense."

"Okay. I'll keep trying."

"Thanks," Riggins said relieved.

———

Brucie looked down out of habit as her phone chimed again.

"Brucie, please just let me know you're all right. That's all I ask," were her mother's pleading words.

"I better let my mom know I'm okay. It totally slipped my mind how scared she is, thinking I've been abducted, or worse, murdered."

"Good girl. You're doing the right thing," Jenny responded.

Her mom read the text and sat very still for a moment. Relief. Anger. Happiness. Then she sent Riggins a text that Brucie was okay and staying with a friend. No more information was provided. "And she needs her space."

"Turn around and take me home, Gene. She's with a friend, but no other information was provided. She wants to be left alone." He sent out a group text so that all the agents could stop looking for her.

In about an hour, Brucie's phone chimed. She read Britanica's text. "I just found out what made you so upset. It's not what you think. If you want to talk, I'm here. Actually, Gene is to blame for this whole thing, but I still love him."

At first, her text made Brucie laugh. Britanica could never stay mad at Gene, but what the heck did she mean? Her brows wrinkled as she stared at it.

"What's so funny?" Jenny asked.

"Britanica, that's all."

"That girl is a hoot. I just love her."

"Jenny, I have an idea. Would you want to stay at my house tonight? You can certainly bring Reese."

"I don't know."

"You have been such a help to me. It would be fun for my mother and us to sit around in our onesies, eat popcorn and chocolate and watch a comedy. I have a spare room and Mom and I would share my room for the night. Please. I know my mom is a mess, and you are so easy to talk to that I think she would enjoy your company."

"How can I say no to that? Sure. Let me get my onesie, some dog food, Reese, and we'll go."

"You're the best, Jenny."

While she got her stuff together, the phone chimed again. One text was from Joe. "I'm so sorry. I didn't know that you didn't know about Ziva. I gave you the wrong impression. I'm sorry, Brucie. Don't be mad at Riggins."

Mumbling under her breath she said, "Don't be mad at that jerk for being married and not telling me. Where's she been all this time anyway, full of your last name, Malarkie?"

"Did you say something, dear?"

She waved her hand down. "No, just mumbling."

Another text. "Brucie, I love you. You're the only girl for me."

Her phone chimed again as she finished reading Riggins' text. "He's telling you the truth. He's not in love with me. It's you he loves. This is a huge misunderstanding. You have to listen to him, from Ziva."

She stared into outer space. "They were pretty affectionate with each other, whether I misunderstood or not."

"Ready to go?" Jenny asked strolling into the room with a dog leash.

"Yes, I am."

Brucie informed her mother that they were on the way and that she didn't want to talk about anything or have any company, but please make some popcorn, prepare tons of chocolate snacks and jump into your onesie. Girls' night. A comedy and laughter.

That brought a huge smile to her mother's face.

The next morning Brucie stumbled out of bed, followed the coffee aroma and found her mother and Jenny sitting at the table. They were laughing like old friends. Reese stood at the back door, barking. Everything still fuzzy, hair like a rat's nest, she squinted her eyes to adjust to the bright sunlight shining in from the door window. The door felt like an ice cube, and she backed up. Then her eyes doubled in size.

"What is he doing out there?"

"Who, dear?"

"Riggins." She said his name with the "duh" tone in her voice.

Her mother jumped up. "I didn't know he was there," she said looking out the window.

"So that's what Reese is barking at," Jenny commented strolling to the back door.

Riggins sat on the pier, bundled up for the cold, feet slightly swinging.

"Brucie, call him in before he gets frostbite. You know what that feels like."

"Mom! It's not my fault he was stupid enough to hang around and in freezing temperatures. No. I don't want to talk to him. Can't I at least have my morning coffee before I go to war?" she spouted.

Jenny snickered.

"As you wish," her mom replied disappointed.

She fixed a cup of coffee, sat down, checked her texts and threw the phone down. She glanced at her mother and jumped up. "Okay. Will it make you happy?"

"What? What are you talking about?"

"Pppplease," her lips rolled. She went to the door and opened it. They all wrapped their arms around their bodies.

Reese ran behind Jenny shivering. "Riggins, get in here," Brucie yelled with contempt. He didn't hear her from being so bundled up.

She held both freezing hands up to her mouth and yelled louder. "Riggins."

He turned, looking around and then glanced at the back door. She waved him in, frown and all.

He got up slowly, walking like an astronaut in space wearing such a bulky mess. He moved inside the door and shut it, cheeks a bright red. Sheepishly, he looked at Brucie with unsure eyes.

"Well, let's hear it," she said tapping her foot.

"Brucie, let him take off all those layers first and you both go sit by the toasty fire," her mother said.

"Okay, Mom." Brucie looked at Riggins. "You heard her, strip." The look from her mom was priceless.

"Well, I think it is time to get Reese home. Friday, then?" Jenny said to Brucie's mother.

"I'm looking forward to it."

"Riggins, Brucie, have a good day." Jenny winked at Brucie.

Her mother brought in two cups of coffee and set them on the coffee table. "Well, guess I'll take my shower."

Riggins nodded to her. He put his hands together and blew, then rubbed them together. "Man, it's cold out there."

At first, he just held the hot cup of coffee between his hands.

"You don't say, Einstein," sarcasm at Brucie's best.

"Okay, I'll get to it. All I ask is that you listen before saying anything. Please."

Her eyes rolled. "Anything to get this over with."

He rolled his eyes.

"The team have always referred to Ziva as Mrs. Malarkie. It's been a joke for years. We were assigned to a case overseas where we had to pretend to be husband and wife. We did a good job and fooled everyone."

"No kidding," she huffed.

His shoulders slumped and his lips puckered. "Let me finish, please."

She crossed her arms and stared straight ahead.

"This was a high-risk case. Murder, espionage, sex trafficking, distributing weaponry, and on and on. It was so dangerous that we couldn't take a chance of blowing our cover. To make a long story short, we achieved our goals and stopped these terrorists. Even after, the team made fun of us and started calling her Mrs. Malarkie. That's the whole truth and nothing but the truth."

"Did you sleep together?"

"Yes, we slept together, as in sleeping and nothing else."

"How long did this go on?"

"Four months."

"Four months! You slept together for four months, and nothing went on? Do I have stupid written on my forehead?"

"I can't tell. Your hair's kind of everywhere."

She reached up with her hand and felt the mess. "You might remember this phrase I used at the beginning of our acquaintance. "You're full of your last name, Malarkie!"

"Oh, yeah, Bruce! I'm telling you the truth. It's you who are too insecure to trust me or even trust yourself."

Fists tightening on her hips, face turning shades of red, she extended her arm and pointed to the doorway. The doorbell rang, bringing her out of a crazed trance. She opened it.

Not good.

Her breaths were now heavy, teeth grinding.

"Please, I just came to clear my name. Please."

Brucie's head jolted toward the living room and Ziva walked past her and scooted close to the wall.

"Go ahead. Speak!" Brucie almost demanded.

"Riggins and I are close, but brother and sister close, not lovers. You are the first woman he has ever spoken about, ever cared about. I can't let you believe a lie. Those guys," her fingers moved around to emphasize beyond these walls, "are friends and just kidding. Yeah, I wish Riggins would have told you before they started making fun. I'd be angry, too. This team endured very dangerous situations, losing someone dear to all of us: his father, for instance. Besides, I'm engaged," Ziva said holding her hand out.

"Huh? Why didn't you tell me?" Riggins said as he picked her up in his arms and twirled her around.

"Everything happened so quickly, there wasn't time."

He put her down and walked back a little, staring at Brucie.

"Brucie, we are a close-knit team and will always be. At least once a year we come together, and we plan to keep the tradition going. I need you to trust him, because I don't want to lose one of my best friends. You are the only one for him. What else can I say to make you believe me?" Ziva asked.

"That's a lot to think about. Thank you for having the courage to speak to me. And you," she said sarcastically to Riggins, "I can be pretty difficult."

"You don't say," Riggins blurted, then formed his lips into "oops."

Brucie disintegrated him with her eyes.

"Well, I have a plane to catch. I hope this clears everything up." Ziva kissed Riggins' cheek and they hugged warmly. She hugged Brucie and whispered, "If we didn't commit to keeping things professional, I would have fallen for him hook, line and sinker. He's a catch. Don't let him go."

Brucie smiled sincerely.

"Hey, you better call and tell me about this fiancé of yours. Will I approve?" Riggins asked.

"Pretty sure you will." She made a clicking sound and left.

"Brucie, everything she said is true."

"I feel so foolish. Your friends must think I'm so childish. It's just...it's just that you two looked like you were deeply in love."

"We are...as a friend, a brother and sister. There are no romantic feelings for either of us. If that were the case, something would have happened between us years ago. I need you to believe me. It's you, Brucie, I want to spend the rest of my life with. There is some Christmas sparkle between us. You can't deny it."

That string of lights swirled around them and out the window. They stared in disbelief.

"Okay. Explanation accepted." A loud shout came from around the corner. They both shook their heads knowing her mother was listening. He pulled her close, stared into her eyes for just a moment and the kiss melted all their troubles away. They kissed for minutes. The kiss ended and Brucie, wobbling, made her way to the couch.

Riggins looked into her eyes, deep in thought, then pulled her softly, slowly towards him. He kissed her in a way that tingled right into her bones. It was different. It was a forever-after kiss. She sat in thought for a moment, not wanting the feeling to leave, but that darn stomach.

"You hungry?"

"Starving," she answered.

"I got it," her mother said, heading for the kitchen.

"Mother, you have to stop listening to my private conversations."

"I will, Dear."

The doorbell rang. "I got it, Mom."

Brucie opened the door to find Britanica, Gene, Webster, Emmy and the team of agents there. They didn't speak.

"Get in here! All of you." Brucie backed up and they entered, loud and boisterous. Britanica and Emmy talked a mile a minute, Gene moving straight for Riggins.

Hesitantly he asked, "Everything okay?"

Riggins stood up with a stern expression on his face, his hand extended. "Yes, it's all good." They embraced.

The chatter was noisy. But hooting and hollering quieted everyone down as Dan strolled in with the chimps. More embracing. The chimps climbed up on Brucie. She kissed them and moved to Riggins' side. He grabbed Bogie and kissed Bacall. Brucie's mom walked into the living room. "Oh my."

Brucie handed Bacall to Riggins. "Come on, girls, we have a huge breakfast to fix." They, the kitchen and appliances, were covered in flour and whatnot. The guests ate, taking turns. At the end, Riggins, Brucie, both mothers, Britanica, Gene, Emmy and Webster sat down to a much-deserved breakfast, scavenging what was left.

———

The next morning Brucie drove her mother to the airport. Since her father's death, there were still matters to attend to: house and yard upkeep. Weeks went by.

Back at home, not able to get to the phone before it went to voicemail, Brucie walked back to the utility room to check on her clothes drying. Just as she stepped back into the room, the buzzer went off. She jumped a mile high. It never failed to scare the pants off of her, and this time for real.

Being in a hurry, before entering the laundry room she threw on the first pair of lounge pants she found, and they had stretched out from being worn so much. She meant to throw them away, but always being in a hurry, she would throw them in with the rest of the clothes. Her head bent down, and she stared at the lounge pants hanging at her ankles. Realizing they were coming off as soon as she found a pair that fitted, she wiggled closer to the dryer.

How did that bottle of fabric softener get in that spot? Her lounge pants got twisted and on to the floor she went. As she attempted to pull herself up, the doorbell rang. She dropped her head in frustration. Throwing her head back, she yelled, "Coming."

Next thing she knew, Britanica and Emmy stood in the doorway laughing at the scene. "Couldn't you wait until I opened the door?"

"You said come in," Britanica replied holding back her laugh as Brucie pulled herself up with the pants still lingering around her ankles.

"I said 'coming'."

"My bad." Britanica looked over at Emmy and they busted up.

Brucie's cellphone rang again.

"Since you are in sort of a situation, want me to get it?" Britanica asked.

"No. Let it go to voicemail. How about you two go make coffee and I'll be right out. Sound good?" she added sarcastically.

They took the hint.

Just as she stepped out of the laundry room the phone rang again. "For goodness sakes." She ran for the phone and checked the phone number on the display screen and quickly answered.

"Ms. Smith. Is everything okay?"

"I don't know, Brucie. Your mother is acting strangely."

"Explain, please."

"She has been outside every day cutting palmetto bushes down. When one sprouts, she clips it off. She walks around the grounds pulling any new ones out of the ground. It's just very strange."

"You know she is a neat freak."

"Yes, but this isn't normal. What do you think is going on? When I try to talk to her, she brushes it off and says she is just trying to keep up with the yard work, that it keeps her occupied. In the evenings I catch her sitting in front of the TV, but she never wants company because she developed an allergy from the palmettos. I believe her about that because her face swells up like a grapefruit and she is in a lot of pain from the allergy pressure."

Something clicked in Brucie's head. "Ms. Smith, thank you for calling me. I will give her a call and get to the bottom of this." They spoke for a few more minutes and she clicked the phone off, staring at it. Britanica and Emmy stood in the doorway with their arms crossed, faces worried.

Brucie looked over at them. "I think my mom is going crazy since she lost Dad. Ms. Smith told me what was going on. At first, I didn't think anything of it. Just Mom and her OCD at work. But then it occurred to me that a palmetto bush is the reason for my dad's death. She is trying to kill all those palmetto bushes in her yard. Ms. Smith said she does this every day. And now, Mom has developed an allergy to them.

"Is it possible she is doing this not even realizing why?"

The girls walked over and placed a hand on each of Brucie's shoulders. "From what I have read, it could very well be a possibility. Subconsciously, she is getting even with the palmetto bushes for the cause of her husband's death. I really don't believe she has any idea what she's doing. In her mind, she's just keeping the yard clean and tidy. This will pass, but it may be a good idea to bring her back here and stay with you. At least for a while," Britanica answered.

"Mom would never. She would be uncomfortable imposing on my life. But, too bad. I'm going to call her and bring her back. Look at these pictures. There must be over one hundred large lawn bags waiting to be picked up." Mrs. Smith had just sent her the photographs.

Brucie's head fell downward, and her hand held back the sobs, but the tears poured down her face.

Britanica and Emmy sat her down and consoled her. Later that day, Brucie called her mother and made arrangements to fly there and bring her back, refusing to take no for an answer.

Thirty-Six

EVERYTHING WENT BACK TO NORMAL. Riggins accepted a local position and became a permanent resident at Chute Pond. The gang still hung out together and life went on as normal. Emmy had a small baby bump beginning to show and Britanica's wasn't visible yet.

Riggins' mother spent time over at Jenny's one evening, and Brucie spent the evening at Riggins' home to help babysit Bogie and Bacall while Dan and his family went on vacation. After getting the chimps in bed, they both sat down on the couch as dinner cooked. The aroma teased Brucie's stomach, causing her to press hard against it to quiet the bear growling inside.

"I didn't realize I was this hungry. Work was hectic and I skipped lunch."

"Well, that's a good thing. When you taste my ribs, the growling will turn to oink, oink," Riggins said with a chuckle.

She laughed at his remark.

"I had depositions for an ongoing case that I had worked on months ago. This poor woman innocently stumbled upon a crime scene, but she didn't know it at the time. The man thought she saw him commit murder and started stalking her with intentions to add her to his murder list. Sound familiar?"

"Quite familiar."

"Her words haunted me for months. It's been about four or five months now and I still can hear her telling me, 'You think your life is stable, really good. In an instant, it becomes bad.' She said this to me right as my life turned bad with Flagstone. You know, she's right. We never know how our life can change in an instant. We think everything is so great, the sky is the bluest we had ever seen, butterflies flitting from flower to flower, and then, wham, we step next to that pile of leaves and a rattlesnake jumps out of it and bites us. It can happen so fast. Kind of a scary realization."

"I truly see your point," he replied. "But the one good thing is there are no rattlesnakes around this part of Wisconsin."

"You know, that actually does make me feel better. Except, Flagstone was my rattlesnake.

"Oh, yeah, she also said something like 'We pray for love and then we curse love.' When I found out about Mrs. Malarkie, love was nothing but a curse in my opinion."

He giggled at the remark.

Riggins planned a romantic dinner. Candles, soft music, flowers and a sumptuous chocolate cake.

"This dinner was so sinfully delicious. That cake, oh my goodness, it should be outlawed. I would steal for it."

"You and Dan. He was off his healthy eating diet, and I bought him a piece. An hour later I went looking for him. I called him and he said he went for a drive. Two and a half hours later he strolled in with two full-sized cakes. I was warned that if I told you about this cake, we would no longer be friends. 'It's mine and all mine,' he said with the boxes wrapped in his arms. He deprives himself of sweets way too long and it turns into an emergency. I'll never figure that out about him." Riggins laughed at the memory.

"Trust me, I understand him completely," Brucie mentioned as she took another bite of the cake.

They cuddled up in front of the fireplace. It was just so romantic. A soft fragrance from candles filled the air. The fireplace crackled and blew warmth their way. Riggins got up and went to his bedroom. He came back and stared comically into her eyes.

"What's up?" she asked in wonder.

He held up a pair of handcuffs. "I forgot to tell you that there is a warrant out for your arrest."

Her mouth took on a weird form. "Huh?"

"You have the right to remain silent"—

"Hold on there. Could I at least know what crime I have committed?" Her hands were flinging out in front of her face.

"Theft."

"Theft?"

"You have stolen my heart, Brucie Clark."

She relaxed and leaned against the couch. Flames in the fireplace reflected a warmness in her eyes. "Is that so? Do you want it back? What is my punishment?"

He got down on one knee, pulled open a decorative box with a shiny, chocolate diamond engagement ring. She gulped and remained speechless.

His face was soft, serious, eyes sparkling. "You have to marry me. It's that or a lifetime in prison. Take your pick." He cracked a genuine smile. "Oh, and my heart is yours to keep."

"I may need to consult my attorney."

His face grew very serious. He dropped his head, swallowed a few times while rubbing his eyes with the thumb and index finger. He looked up with loving tears clouding his eyes. "I will love you forever. Until I take my last breath. And even after that. Please marry me, Brucie Clark."

She sniffled and covered her mouth. One tear dropped. Then she slapped his arm. "What took you so long? I've been waiting for months. You know how I love romance novels?"

He nodded his head.

"When I read remarks like you just said, it makes me roll my eyes, like, yeah, sure. Some guy is really going to say something that romantic, and then you do just that. And you know what?"

His shoulders shrugged again.

"It's not just what you said, it's how you said it. There was such a warmth in your voice and in your face. My arms feel like a pillow opened up and the feathers jumped on my arms, tickling me softly." She folded her hands and held them to her mouth. Fighting sentimental tears, she said, "That was the most romantic thing I have ever heard. I will write that in my journal because I never want to forget those words.

"And, to your question, yes, I would love to marry you, and I will love you until I take my last breath, too."

Seriously choking up, her thoughts blurted out, "Riggins, I feel like my heart is floating up in the sky, going through soft, fluffy clouds and the sun shining warm beams on it. I am so happy right now."

The kiss was tingly, romantic, warm and toasty.

"I wanted this evening to be special and just knew chocolate had to fit in the proposal somehow," he added.

She held her hand out and admired the chocolate ring.

"I have another chocolate ring in case this one gets messed up or melts because of the heat between us." He wiggled his eyebrows. She laughed.

"This gives me a great idea. We'll have chocolate rings at every place setting on our wedding day. The chimps could be our flower girl and ring bearer. What do you think and what day should we choose for the wedding?"

"You told me you didn't want me to push you, and here you have been waiting for my proposal. You pick the day and I'll be there, but this groom wants a say in the wedding preparations."

Her expression changed and a sadness engulfed her face. Riggins sat quietly in order to give her the opportunity to figure out how to say what was on her mind. He gently squeezed her hand.

"My dad won't be able to walk me down the aisle." She slapped a hand to her mouth. Then she held her breath for as long as possible while tears stung her eyes. "Riggins, don't say anything. This is a very happy occasion and I want to set aside anything sad. The thought hit me out of nowhere, but just tonight, just for tonight I want to savor this happy moment."

He held her tightly to let the sadness depart. A tender kiss to the forehead. She pulled back and smiled with pure happiness. As time passed that evening, calls were made, and the word was out.

They cuddled up in each other's arms.

He chuckled.

"What's so funny, Mr. Malarkie? Oh no, Brucie Malarkie. I don't know if I can do it."

"I get it, not that it wouldn't disappoint me, Bruce, if you don't take my last name, but I understand."

"You know what, who cares? I want to become Bruce Malarkie and that's not malarkey."

They both laughed.

Watching him giggle, she asked, "Hey, what you were laughing about?"

"Oh. I was just remembering our first encounter, where the chimps threw acorns at you and how much we detested each other at the time. My thoughts remain true to this day: 'Chocolate, chimpanzees and a court reporter at Chute Pond, who knew.' Seriously, who would have guessed?

"You know what's even funnier?" he asked.

"What could be funnier than that?"

"I loved you when I hated you."

"Mmmm," she responded.

"At least I thought I hated you."

Flashbacks filled her mind of the first day they met. Then she stared at her stenograph sitting in the corner of his living room, remembering that one deposition.

She remarked, "It's a funny thing."

Don't miss out on your next favorite book!
Join the Melange Books mailing list at
www.melange-books.com/mail.html

———

THANK YOU FOR READING

———

Did you enjoy this book?

We invite you to leave a review at your favorite book site, such as
Goodreads, Amazon, Barnes & Noble, etc.

DID YOU KNOW THAT LEAVING A REVIEW...

- Helps other readers find books they may enjoy.
- Gives you a chance to let your voice be heard.
- Gives authors recognition for their hard work.
- Doesn't have to be long. A sentence or two about why
  you liked the book will do.

About the Author

Linda Phillips moved back to a winter wonderland in Wisconsin until a sneaky sunray snuck through the overcast clouds and beamed down on her, pulling her right back to sunny Florida. When she's not daydreaming about a sweet romance story, she tends to Monster I and Monster II, affectionately known as Sprinkle Dinkle and Skittle Wittle, her two cats.

lindalouphillips.com

 facebook.com/LindaLPhillipsAuthor

 linkedin.com/in/linda-phillips-61347270

Also by Linda Phillips
WITH SATIN ROMANCE

Novels

Marry Christmas

Chocolate, Chimpanzees & a Court Reporter at Chute Pond

Follow Your Heart

(A Stand Alone Fantasy Romance Series)

Moon Water

Dew of Heaven